MW01488978

REVIEWS

"An archeologist finds ancient evidence of a shocking truth, and powerful forces including the Vatican and the CIA unite to stop him from revealing the secret. Hartman's wickedly good plot twists and clever language lead to surprising revelations. The time has come for *The Kairos*.

> ~Kittredge Cherry, author
> *Jesus in Love: A Novel*

"After carrying *The Kairos* around the country/world in my suitcase for more than a month, I finally read it on flights and in concourse lobbies. AND I LOVED IT."

> ~Rev. Dr. Mel White
> Author: *Stranger At The Gate*
> Founder: *SoulForce*

"Lute is as earnest and inept as a biblical scholar would be if he were dodging shadowy killers, and his flight is realistic and suspenseful. [The author] sets him amid three-dimensional characters whose crises of conscience are nuanced and well-drawn.... Lute's odyssey makes for an intriguing balance of action and reflection."

> ~Kirkus Reviews

The Kairos' intriguing, highly controversial premise takes readers on a fast-paced ride from the Holy Land to California to Alaska. Lute Johnson is an engaging protagonist worth rooting for. A deftly- executed thriller in a crowded genre. We will be hearing more from this talented newcomer. Highly recommended.

> ~Sheldon Siegel
> *New York Times* Best Selling Author
> *Perfect Alibi* [The Mike Daley Mysteries]

For my
Buffalo Bible
Study Brothers
Bill & Fred!
Paul Hartman
8-12-19

THE KAIROS

" Fear Not! "

Paul E. Hartman

Copyright © 2014 Authored By Paul E. Hartman
All rights reserved.

ISBN: 1499661487
ISBN-13: 9781499661484

CHAPTERS: THE *KAIROS*

Prologue: God on the Yukon River. 1
1   Truth or Consequences 3
2   A Purloin of Great Price. 9
3   Blessed Are the Thieves 13
4   The Ben Gurion Gate. 18
5   Mission San Diego 23
6   Qumran Ruins, Israel 29
7   Manuscript 1Q-Cether-1: Boy Yeshua. 32
8   A *Kairos* Declined. .34
9   The Warrant. 40
10   Daymares 45
11   Manuscript 1Q-Cether-2: Yeshua 51
12   A Father's Fury. 54
13   Pacific Outpost. 60
14   Communion Begins .68
15   *Kairos* Interruptus. .77
16   Naomi 83
17   Wins and Losses 89
18   Finally, Harald's *Kairos* 94
19   Manuscript 1Q-Cether-3: Yeshua & Johanan . . .102
20   *Kairos* Declined, Redux. 105
21   A Midnight Decision 116
22   Tell Your Troubles to the Dock. 120
23   "Rome, We Have a Problem" 132
24   Full-Court Press-Contacts. 139

25	The Inquisition	145
26	Manuscript 1Q-Cether-4: Commitment	152
27	The New Centurions	154
28	Closing In	158
29	Flee, Fly, Flew	167
30	A Rolling Flame Gathers No Moth	173
31	Shame in Shadows	177
32	An Unscheduled Fright	182
33	Set My People Free	187
34	At Sixes and Sevens, and Zero	195
35	To Know Which Way to Go	196
36	Holy See, Holy Do	201
37	Morning Has Broken	203
38	Manuscript 1Q-Cether-5: Body and Soul	207
39	Messages	209
40	Moses, Meet Luther	211
41	Holy See, Holy Do (2)	217
42	Reformation on Deck	222
43	Toilet-Stalling for Time	228
44	Flaps Up	232
45	Peaks and Valleys: The Olympics and the Shadow of Death	237
46	Luther in the Sky with Diamonds	240
47	Newsroom	243
48	Manuscript 1Q-Cether-6: Love Not Fear	245
49	Vistas at the End of the World	246
50	The Parsonage	251
51	The Second Birth of Moses	258
52	The Gatekeeper	267
53	Cherokee's Afire	271
54	Stonewalled	277
55	Toward Circle	281
56	Operation Disinfect	291

57	Penult and Penumbra....................294
58	Newsroom (2).........................298
59	God on the Yukon River................301
60	Manuscript 1Q-Cether-7: Getting Home Safely....304
61	Going Home 306
	Acknowledgements 314

GOD ON THE YUKON RIVER

Friday, June 21, 1991
11:58 p.m. Alaska Daylight Time
On the Yukon River 50 miles south of the Arctic Circle

Even an old landlubber like me knows better than to stand up in a boat, thought Lute Jonson, *especially this decrepit canoe*. But as exhilaration flooded his mind and drowned his good sense, he raised himself carefully in the bow, and stood with his legs spread as far as the canoe's ribs allowed.

"Oh, my God," he whispered.

His companion's voice cracked the stillness from the back of the small boat. "Is not Alaska in June more beautiful than anywhere else on earth?"

Lute stared north up a stretch of the quarter-mile-wide Yukon. He lifted his gaze slightly from the river's cold clear surface to a perfect Midnight Sun, just beginning to skim the flat and treeless horizon, ready to rise seamlessly into dawn within minutes. The blended blaze of orange-red sky raised gooseflesh all over his skin. His arms elevated until they were straight out, palms facing the sun in an unselfconscious embrace of the pristine landscape before him. He breathed in pure river air.

"Oh, my God," Lute prayed again, this time with a soft voice that broke the silence. "You have safely guided me into Your wilderness. You have let me taste this perfect peace, prepared me to reveal Your astounding news tomorrow, steeled me for the reactions of a billion Christians who'll be shocked by this final Dead Sea Scrolls secret."

Arms open wide, eyes fixed on the horizon's extraordinary solar event, lungs full of unspoiled oxygen, Lute was startled by his companion's words, especially the unmistakable anguish in their tone: "God forgive me for this." The click of a revolver cocking completed the meaning.

Lute's arms chilled instantly. *Oh Lord God, NO! This is Your answer?! This is how it ends?*

CHAPTER 1

TRUTH OR CONSEQUENCES

One week earlier: Friday, June 14, 1991
Offices of the International Dead Sea Scrolls Study Team
Rockefeller Museum, Jerusalem

The two co-directors of the International Study Team walked to the end of the hall and stopped at the door. Father Sean O'Derry, whose name was stenciled on it, unlocked the door and ushered his colleague in.

Dr. Luther Jonson—just "Lute" to all who knew him—preceded Sean through the empty secretary's office and on into the old priest's private study. Tall and slender, Lute's Nordic blue eyes were deep-set into a lean and smile-creased face. At age 68 he still had a full mane of white hair brushed back over his ears. He wore light gray slacks and a blue blazer, his daily uniform year in and year out.

He sat on the couch by the window and watched through the inner-office door as his short, balding colleague re-checked the lock on the outer-office door. Sean then followed Lute into the inner sanctum and closed that door. Lute caught himself grinding his teeth; he forced himself to stop and to relax his tense shoulders.

"Ye need to talk about this *kairos* thing again, Lute?" Sean's smile was tight and tired-looking. He pulled his drooping khaki work pants up from under his paunch and tried unsuccessfully to cinch his belt another notch. Despite the girth he had acquired over the last 69 years, the leather strap was long enough that the silver-tipped end hung down three limp inches in front.

Lute sat forward on the couch. "Yes. Look, you said last week you can't agree to this, but that's just not acceptable. We have to go public. I'm scared, Sean. You and I aren't getting any younger. What would happen if both of us keeled over with heart attacks? It's inconceivable that those seven fragments might be lost for another two thousand years. Lost or destroyed because of how we've hidden them."

Sean settled himself at his desk and ran his finger behind his loose Roman collar. He looked up. "It pains me to say it, my friend, but you've become obsessed with this *kairos* idea."

"But they *are* a *kairos*! In every scriptural story when God broke into our time from His, He had to tell the quivering little human beings, 'Fear not!' And He's breaking through again in the words on those ragged little parchment scraps. You know it, Sean. It's indisputable. Do you need an angel to walk through these locked doors and say the same thing to you?" Lute sighed deeply as he realized how these repeated arguments had entrenched their disagreement rather than bridging it.

Sean shook his head. "I still cannot agree. After more than forty years, you've all of a sudden got a bee in your bonnet about revealing them to the world. How many times do I have to say it? *People just aren't ready*. It's just too explosive. Why rush? Someday people may be much more progressive … that'll be the time for this news."

Lute shook his head and clenched his fists. "We never should have hidden them, Sean. Sorry I ever suggested it."

"If these parchments *are* a *kairos* event like you say, who says they should now be yanked into '*chronos*'?"

"*I* say so. But better yet, *we* should say so. Imagine: the two of us standing up together and announcing it to the world. Seven long-secret Dead Sea Scrolls fragments, containing some of the most astounding words ever written, are now going to be released for everyone to read."

Sean shook his head. "Nope. Sorry. We have a split decision, and that always means we stay with the status quo."

Lute stood up and approached Sean's desk. "What in hell are you afraid of? Don't you think they're authentic? Don't you think they're important? Don't you think God's people can handle the truth?"

One by one, Sean touched the four fingers on his left hand as he ticked off answers to Lute's questions. "'Everything.' 'Yes.' 'Yes.' 'I don't know.'"

Lute rolled his eyes. "You *do* think they're authentic. You *do* think they're important. You *don't know* if Christians can handle the truth in them. And you're afraid. Afraid of everything. So we risk letting them stay hidden for another two thousand years. Or forever, since they're under lock and key."

"Three locks, no keys," Sean corrected.

"What are you *most* afraid of?"

Sean took a long look out his office window before reciting the answer Lute had heard repeatedly in recent weeks. "Those words will destroy the faith of conservative Christians all over the globe. So what am I most afraid of? The future of Christianity."

"Well, no wonder you can't move forward," said Lute. "You're carrying the weight of the world on your shoulders."

He leaned toward his colleague. "Why don't we let God handle the consequences? These are His revelations, Sean! They're completely in character with Jesus' radicalism. How many times have we talked about His proclivity for pissing off religious authorities? If the news of these fragments riles some people up, who are *we* to say it isn't God's will? You and I have stood in His way by hiding this *kairos* for four decades. In courts in the States, a witness has to swear to tell the truth, the whole truth and nothing but the truth. We're not telling the whole truth. As researchers, how can we continue to cover up what we know? I'm sorry it has taken both of us since 1951 to come to this conviction, but I for one have to end it. Compelled as a Christian. By John 8:32, no less. And by the psalm about not hiding the truth."

"Psalm 40. Ah, you missed your calling, Lute. You should preach. You're eloquent and convincing. But there's an objection you have no answer for."

"What?"

"Who'll pay the consequences? This time, *we* may have to. 'Killing the messenger,' you know? I don't know if *your* life would be at risk, but the Vatican would remove all hope of eternal life for *me*. Maybe temporal life, too."

Lute's hopes for a mutual agreement sank; each successive attempt he'd made in recent weeks solidified Sean's resistance. *Still, there has to be something I can say that would change his mind.*

Sean spoke again. "And you think we've taken grief up 'til now from the academic community for our unwillingness to release the Scrolls? You'll get crushed in the stampede if the first fragments you release are these seven pieces."

"'*Que sera sera.*' 'Let go; let God.'" Lute looked expectantly at his co-director even as he regretted the inanity of his choice of words. He added what he hoped would be the *coup de grace.* "'Thy will be done.'" His colleague registered no reaction.

Sean looked at his folded hands on the desktop a moment, then stood up. "I'll think about it."

Lute sat back on the couch again. "I'll wait."

Sean walked to the door, opened it, then turned and held it open for Lute, who didn't move. "Really, I'll pray about it," Sean insisted.

"That's what we said for the first two years. Remember? From '48 to '50, we just kept delaying what we knew we had to do. Next time we talked about it seriously was that time in '62 or '63, when we were so caught up in Vatican II. Since then, all we've done is think about it."

The old priest shrugged. "What else can I say, Lute? I don't believe you're right, but I'm willing to pray and stay open to whatever God says."

"God has already spoken!" Lute caught himself, and lowered his voice to a more civil level again. "Others have a right to know what He said in these ancient fragments."

"These aren't God's words. You know that."

"I don't know that, and neither do you. Are the letters of St. Paul 'God's words' or just a Tarsus Jew's reflections on Jesus' life? Of course they're God's Word. For crying in a bucket! So what about this unknown scribe? Why aren't his eyewitness revelations about Jesus' life in Qumran also *God's words?*"

Lute locked eyes with his longtime friend. Finally Sean looked down at his watch and shuffled into the outer office. Over his shoulder he said, "Got a meeting. Lock up for me, would you?"

Lute watched Sean leave. His teeth began grinding again, and a mental list of sins he was about to commit formed in his mind: lying, forgery, burglary. *Ironically, all*

to complete one great act of truth-telling before I die. Damn it.
And damn this nagging question I can't seem to shake, Lord: Is
this Your will? Or am I trying to tell a story You purposely buried
two millennia ago?

John 8:32

Then you will know the truth, and the
truth will set you free.

Psalm 40:7-10

I proclaim righteousness in the great assembly; I do not seal my lips, as you know, O
LORD. I do not hide your righteousness in
my heart; I speak of your faithfulness and
salvation. I do not conceal your love and
your truth from the great assembly.

CHAPTER 2

A Purloin of Great Price

Sunday, June 16, 1991
11:40 p.m. Israel Summer Time
Lower level, Rockefeller Museum

Lute quietly entered his access code into the electronic lock and opened the cellar door. He stepped through, clicked on his flashlight, closed the door behind him, listened for the click that reassured him it was again secure from outside entry, then eased down the dozen steps. He crossed to the far end of the small rectangular room, set his briefcase down, and squatted at the edge of an old braid rug.

One last time, he thought. *I'll never return these scroll fragments to hiding again. Four decades is long enough.*

He aimed his flashlight beam against the white wall ahead of him, and the small area brightened. Once more he cocked his ear toward the stairwell for any sound of the security guard. Seconds of silence eased his concern, and he returned to the task.

Lute carefully lifted the first-century water jars off the rug one by one, moved them off to the side, and pushed the rug itself to the right. He brushed dust from the newly-revealed, small steel cover plate sunk into the concrete floor. Drilled finger holes in each end of it allowed him to remove it easily, and he set it aside. Yet again he cocked his ear toward the door at the top of the steps. *Footsteps!* His heart raced and his palms turned clammy while he watched the bottom of the door for changes of light or shadow. The sound of approaching footsteps in the terrazzo hallway above was slight but unmistakable. Then they stopped. Right outside the door.

Damn! Yosef is on tonight. He's down on this lower level. Why couldn't it have been Iggy, who probably sleeps through most of his shift? Lute's pulse raced. He ran the back of a hand across his forehead and silently wiped sweat on his pant leg. *What the hell am I doing here? Does he have access to this basement storage room?* He fought down a rising sense of guilt. *This isn't stealing. This is* not *stealing. The world owns these scroll fragments, not Sean O'Derry.*

It seemed an interminable time for the guard to have paused up there, and an unlikely place since there was no chair or bench nearby. *Lord, what can he see? Did I leave something outside the door?* His eyes darted to his briefcase on the floor, and then his hands patted pockets for keys and wallet. *The light! He sees the light under the door!* Lute looked at the flashlight and considered slowly covering its beam. *That would just confirm there's someone down here, if he does see it. And I don't think he can—the climate control system required high-grade weather strips around doors into all acquisitions and collections areas. But what else could it...*

His thought was interrupted as the doorknob rattled once and then the footsteps resumed, soon fading away down the hall.

Damn it, Lord! Is that supposed to be a sign? If you don't want me to go on with this, make it plain but don't scare the bejabbers out of me again. OK?

He dried his palms and forehead with a handkerchief as he listened to make sure he was alone again in the night. Finally he turned back to the cavity in the floor and the now visible safe that was sunk into it.

Lute re-aimed the flashlight to the dial on the top. He turned the wheel in its unlocking sequence: left to 18, right a full turn to 6, left to 15. A reassuring click confirmed that the foot-square vault was willing to give up its secrets. He used the single handle to lift the top completely off and to set it aside.

He reached into the reinforced steel hole and withdrew a black lacquered Chinese puzzle box. Fine craftsmanship had produced no apparent seams. Only a person who knew the exact placement of the box's moveable bands and the pre-scribed order for executing the moves could retrieve its contents. And no one who knew or suspected the fragility and priceless worth of those contents would even consider using anything else—from blunt force to bandsaw—to circumvent the secret process of this ancient Oriental technology.

His hand muscles tensed; it took two attempts for his thumb to locate and push the first strip of wood that allowed the next move. Lute proceeded quickly through the next steps. The fourteenth move freed the lid. With a practiced hand, he withdrew the contents and counted the plastic document sleeves: one, two, three, four, five, six, seven. All present. No surprise, of course, but given their value, he sighed in relief nonetheless. Only Sean and he had access to this subterranean storage room, and no one who visited would have reason to suspect it housed more than the Herodian pottery, coins, and oil lamps arrayed on the floor and shelves. As he squatted holding the price-less scroll remnants, Lute mentally rehearsed the goodbye speech he could never give to his friend and colleague of half a lifetime.

I'm sorry if you feel betrayed, Sean. All the decades you and I kept these secret, we were wrong. They don't belong to us. They belong to the world. I've thought it through for months. I tried to get you to cooperate even knowing it would probably come to this. I've got to get them out of Israel and hand them over for independent examination. These secrets can't die with us.

Lute whispered into the darkness. "Lord, stop me now if this is not Your will." With no thunderclap or divine basso profundo to restrain him, he quickly opened a false back in his briefcase, placed the ancient treasures inside, and closed it up. He replaced the Chinese puzzle box in the safe and returned all the camouflaging. He lumbered to his feet. Retracing his way to the top of the stairs, Lute placed his ear to the door, eased it open, and stepped through. It was only after it closed and locked behind him that he heard the returning footsteps.

CHAPTER 3

BLESSED ARE THE THIEVES

The security guard rounded the corner, and his surprise was evident both in his voice and in the instantaneous appearance of a Browning 9mm pistol from the holster at his belt. "Who's that?" he growled. "Dr. Jonson!" Lute stared wide-eyed into the threatening muzzle, and the guard's voice offered no hint of friendliness to accompany the recognition. "What are you doing here at midnight?"

Lute looked up to his face. "Hoping to steal something, Yosef."

The guard froze in his offensive stance for a long moment. Finally he lowered the handgun, and when Lute saw the hint of a smile on Yosef's pock-marked face, he breathed again.

Yosef grunted, "Thank God. I thought it was something serious," but then the smile disappeared as quickly as it had appeared. "Why *are* you here?"

Lute parried again. "I was hoping to find your dinner sack and lift some of those cookies Sara makes. The white chocolate ones with macadamia nuts. Now I've blown my cover."

"It don't take a genius to see you liked that one I gave you. She has to hide 'em from me at home, too, or they're gone in a day. Tasty little buggers."

Lute nodded. "Did she send more than one with you tonight? I would pay, you know."

The guard shook his head. "Nope." He turned serious again. "What's up? You put in long hours, but I don't think I've seen you here this late in the last few years."

Lute hoped the retired Israeli soldier's demeanor indicated concern, not suspicion. "Couldn't sleep, Yosef. Been worrying over a publication deadline I have coming up." He began walking down the hall in the direction the guard had come from. The middle-aged guard turned and fell in step.

"But you haven't been up in your office. What's down here in the tombs?"

Lute hoped the low-level security lights didn't reveal the flush he felt in his cheeks. And he quickly put a check on his rising sense that his employee's questioning was approaching an inappropriate level of insistence. If Lute displayed any defensiveness, he knew, his departure plan could be destroyed.

"Actually, it *is* hunger that brought me out so late. Not for food—an old widower can make a late-night sandwich if need be. It's another kind of hunger. But hard to describe." He hoped his unwelcome and now disarmed walking companion would let the subject drop at that.

But Yosef pursued. "A hunger for...?"

Lute stopped and drew in breath. "For understanding, I guess." Again he hoped that would satisfy the stocky guard, but a quick look at Yosef's raised eyebrows forced him on, further down the hall and deeper into his motivations. At least those that he could safely reveal. "You know we're under a lot of pressure from antiquities scholars around the world to release more of the scroll fragments. Pictures, translations, all that. You know?"

The guard nodded. "O'Derry told me that recently when he explained I need to go on high alert around here. Said there are people who would actually steal artifacts and fragments from the collection and never think twice about it. That's why I check everyone and everything."

Now Lute understood. "Good. That's very good. We definitely have to be on high alert. The consequences of any failure would be terrible. That's part of what's been making me restless at night the last couple of weeks. Trying to figure out how to safeguard what we've learned so far, and how to share it at the right time."

"So he said to check everyone and everything," Yosef repeated.

Lute looked over to Yosef's face as they walked. The security man's eyes snapped up from the glance he had stolen at Lute's briefcase. Uncertain, Lute looked ahead again and continued to walk as he spoke. "So it's a hunger to know what's right, and how to do it, that brought me back tonight. I've been walking the halls downstairs, looking at some of the oldest acquisitions in the collection, trying to figure it all out."

"Praying?"

"Yes," Lute answered with mental reservation. *Wait*, he thought, *it's not a lie. I did pray before stashing the parchments in my case.*

Yosef said, "I think it's good how we Jews can work alongside you Christians here. Respectful like. I figure you can worship God in your way, and I can worship Him ... in His way."

Lute knew their Jewish colleagues were fond of the joke, always with the identical pause in timing, so he laughed despite its hoary age.

They reached a niche in the hallway where one of the Qumran scriptorium tables had been placed. A museum glass cover made it safe to actually use the surface, and Lute laid his briefcase on it. "Yosef, take a look here." He unsnapped the hasps, opened the cover, and waved his hand over the half dozen file folders and loose documents in the case.

Yosef looked at Lute, hesitated, then approached the case and looked in. As light levels were low in the halls overnight, he trained his flashlight into the case, looked down the folder separations in the lid, and lifted a few piles to look underneath in the bottom.

Lute prayed silently that the false back would not pop open. *And yet, Lord, this is one more chance for You to stop me if I am about to violate Your will. Let those fragments spill out right now if You want me to miss that plane in Tel Aviv. I'm not asking for miracles for myself, only that You let me know whether these pangs I have are a hunger for the truth, or for my own glory.* Lute added a silent thanks that he had left in the car the few spare clothes he was taking on his rapidly approaching international flight.

Yosef closed the case and grunted a signal he was done.

"Thank you. I'm impressed with your dedication, Yosef. I think you, too, might have a hunger like mine tonight. A hunger for righteousness."

"Yeah. Right." The guard frown-smiled as if to say *Whatever*, then nodded goodnight and strode away.

Maybe it is righteousness I'm famished for, Lute thought. *Maybe Sean and I have been on a 40-year fast by hiding the truth. I wonder if the world will find this* kairos *to be a feast. Or a potion too bitter to swallow.*

He checked his watch: almost 12:20. The airport should only be forty minutes away in sparse overnight traffic, leaving him just an hour and fifteen minutes to park his car, check in, and get to the gate for the flight to New York's JFK International. *No room for error. Time to go. Just a little more* chronos *time before a major* kairos *breaks through.*

Proverbs 6:30

Men do not despise a thief if he steals to satisfy his hunger when he is starving.

CHAPTER 4

THE BEN GURION GATE

Monday, June 17, 1991
1:30 a.m.
Ben Gurion International Airport, southeast of Tel Aviv

Lute slumped in an El Al lounge seat, scanning a smudged copy of the Sunday Tel Aviv *Ha'aretz* and waiting for the security stations to open. As he read about the violent volcanic eruption of Mt. Pinatubo in the Philippines the day before—"after 500 years of dormancy"—he wondered if his own news about these Dead Sea Scroll fragments might have a similarly explosive effect on Christendom within the next few days.

He pressed his ankles against the briefcase on the floor. Reassured that his precious cargo was in this carry-on luggage, he mentally checked off the last minute items he had replaced the file folders with after leaving the Rockefeller Museum: a fresh shirt, two changes of underwear and socks, a small shaving kit. Airline giveaways would get him through the eleven-and-a-half-hour transatlantic flight. Even though he had decided to fly directly on from New York to America's West Coast to get his only sister's help in setting up a news conference, this light packing should see him through until there was time to find a clothing store.

He silently rehearsed his answers for the security agents, and looked again at the fake passport he had acquired two months before. Never in all his life had he even thought about taking such an illegal step, nor could he have guessed how to connect with anyone capable of providing it. Increasingly frustrated with Sean's inflexibility about releasing their secret scrolls, he had begun to realize he could not do so in country, and traveling on his own passport would have left an easily followed trail. How extraordinary that an innocent joke about fake passports, which manager Bruce Reed told him at his neighborhood Be'er Sheva Café, would end up in his acquiring documents like this one. With his own picture next to completely fabricated information on an American passport. Although it looked like his real passport, his pulse raced a little with the recurring fear they would detect a forgery, throw him in jail, and frustrate his commitment to truth-telling before mortality took away that option.

Finally, three agents approached the security stations and armed guards allowed passengers waiting in the great hall to queue up. With only his briefcase to carry, Lute was soon standing at one of the elevated platforms, looking up at the female agent through heavy plate glass.

"Name?" Her tone was clipped, and during the short exchange her eyes darted back and forth from picture to face to passport to a passenger manifest to another typed list.

"Karl Rose."

"Occupation?"

"University professor."

"This is your address?"

"Yes, ma'am. Minnesota. Going home."

"You arrived here three months ago. What have you been doing in Israel?"

"I teach Middle Eastern history and religious studies, so I spent my sabbatical at the Jerusalem Museum, and in Qumran, and primarily on an archaeological dig west of a kibbutz near Lake Gennesaret."

"Which one?"

"Nof Ginosor."

"Mmm. Luggage?"

"I shipped everything back yesterday except this overnight case. It'll get me through New York and on to Minneapolis."

She studied the information in front of her. He began to relax. *Thank you, Lord. You're making the path straight for me.*

"Minnesota?"

"Yes ma'am."

"Where do you teach?"

"St. Olaf College. In Northfield. It's about half an hour south of Minneapolis."

"Where are you going from New York?"

"On to San D..." Lute stopped and swallowed hard. "...to *Saint Olaf.*" He was sure he was turning crimson. One small detail accidentally thrown into his rehearsed answers was now grinding the wheels of his escape to a halt. He feared it had set his face to burning.

"Because your ticket is just to New York."

"Yes, well, ah... What happened was, when I reserved the ticket, I thought I would stay awhile in Manhattan. See some plays." *I'm talking too much.*

"But?"

"But, well, I thought I would...I mean I want to get home, so I'm going straight through."

"Your ticket to Minneapolis, please."

Lute set his briefcase between his feet, his mind racing and heart sinking. *How could I possibly have screwed this up?* His head down in shame, he finally spoke.

"After my travel agent closed today I realized the dilemma I have put myself in. El Al doesn't fly to Minneapolis, of course, so I realized all I can do is get to New York and stand in some line until I can get on a plane."

He lifted his eyes to hers in an unsuccessful attempt to gauge her B.S. detector.

"You know you'll pay a high price for the lesson you just learned?" she asked. "You know how expensive same-day tickets are?"

He hung his head and nodded.

She studied him a moment, then passed his ticket and passport through to him.

"Have a good flight, Dr. Rose. Good luck getting to Sandy Olaf."

He gathered the documents and walked through the little station. When he turned back to nod "thank you" to her, she was dialing a telephone and looking up toward the supervisor at the luggage x-ray machine where he was headed.

With nothing metallic inside, his case rang no alarms, but an agent took him and the case aside anyway. At the agent's direction, Lute unloaded the contents onto a table in a private cubicle. The uniformed man poked through the documents without real interest, and then looked closely at the bottom of the case. He used a small screwdriver to pry gently at the bottom, with no result. He pushed the top, and looked up unexpectedly at Lute's face. After the experience at the passport booth, Lute had re-summoned his self-control, and looked back at the agent with a calm that did not betray the inner fears. The agent pocketed his screwdriver and pushed the case back toward Lute.

"That's it," he said, and moved back toward the x-ray machine.

Having repacked his belongings, Lute began the long walk toward the assigned departure gate. It was over! Years of consciously controlling his nerves before speeches at conferences paid off. Lute wanted to stab his arms into the air in victory.

The plan worked! I'm through the gauntlet! Nothing will keep me from releasing these incredible scrolls now. San Diego, here I come!

II Kings 18:19-20

`This is what the great king ... says: On what are you basing this confidence of yours? You say you have strategy and ... strength— but you speak only empty words. On whom are you depending...?'

CHAPTER 5

MISSION SAN DIEGO

Over San Diego
Monday, June 17, 1991
10:20 a.m. Pacific Daylight Time

Lute checked his seatbelt as he heard the flight attendant's familiar refrain, "...and make sure your seatback and tray table are in their full upright and locked position." As the United Airlines jet approached Lindbergh Field just west of downtown San Diego, he was disappointed to discover that brown air had migrated south from Los Angeles since his smogless visit twenty years earlier. Still, the urban scene a thousand feet below eerily mirrored his own emotional landscape: orderly homes ostensibly serene with manicured green lawns and still blue pools, all bravely set against a wild, sandy terrain surrounding them.

"Sir?"

Lute's gaze snapped from his window view to the aisle as a husky voice broke into his thoughts. His pulse slowed again when he realized the steward had addressed not him, but the young man in the seat beside him.

Lute wondered if the tension of the past twenty-two hours—theft from the Museum, precarious moments at the airport, eleven hours of transatlantic flight, and a rushed transfer to this cross-country flight at the terminal in New York—would dissipate after he got some rest. He instinctively squeezed his feet together again to confirm that his briefcase was safe.

He looked back at the Gideon Bible he had found in the magazine rack, and read the verse his finger rested on. "Do not let your hearts be troubled," Jesus was saying to the disciples just before His arrest in the Garden of Gethsemane, "and do not be afraid." Lute nodded almost imperceptibly, and placed the book into the seat pocket.

Lute turned to the fellow beside him. "You know," he said with a grin, "you were supposed to have been better-looking. When I called for reservations they promised me a curvaceous blonde for a seatmate."

The young man looked with surprise at the elderly gentleman next to him, but quickly returned the smile and answered, "Yeah, me too. Maybe you'll get lucky in Tijuana."

As Lute walked up the jetway ahead of the fellow a few minutes later, he thought he could feel the handsome young man's gaze running up and down his back. *Jeez*, Lute admonished himself silently, *get a grip. This thing is getting to you.*

* * *

La Jolla, California
Two hours later

"Lute?" his sister cried out. "Lute! Oh, Lute!" She came through the open front door to enfold him in her arms, and they locked in embrace.

"Praise God!" she said, stepping back to look at him a moment. While she closed her eyes and folded her hands for a few seconds, he turned briefly to flash the OK sign to a taxi driver, who then backed out of the driveway. Lute turned back to wait through his sister's silent prayer, reflecting on the deep religious faith she held. As uncommon as it was in contemporary society in one so sophisticated and well educated, her fundamentalist faith had been a constant in life for six decades. She opened her steely blue eyes, smiled at her brother, and voiced a hearty "Amen!"

"Buffalo, Buffalo, rise and shine, you belly-hookers!" Lute chanted their childhood's nonsense mantra.

Christiana Hansgaard laughed. "You old rascal! Why didn't you tell me you were coming? I can't believe this! What are you doing here? Come in," she added, pulling him out of the damp warmth of the Pacific beach June morning and into her elegant home. A step behind, he looked her over approvingly. From her casually elegant hairdo to her trim California figure, his only sister was still the beautiful woman he remembered. Neither her 65 years nor the strain of her medical profession had aged her. And yet, as he looked closely at her eyes, he noticed as he had many times before how heavy they appeared. Even when she spoke of the joy her Savior brought—an oddly frequent subject for a well-to-do M.D. in hedonistic Southern California—the smile on her lips was usually too tight to reach all the way up to her eyes. Lute wished there was more playfulness in her joy, but he loved her without requiring changes.

"What's up?" she asked as she poured mugs of coffee. "How long are you in town?"

Lute grinned. "Well, I can't stay more than a couple of months." She smiled and quietly waited for her curiosity to be satisfied.

He stood at the expansive window wall and studied the rich person's Pacific Ocean view. He was pensive too long.

"Lute? Are you OK? You're not ill?" Christy leaned forward.

"No, I'm healthy," he said, mentally waiving his doctor's recent cardiac cautions. He ran a hand through his hair. "You'll have to wait a long time for your big brother's inheritance."

"You're in the United States for a conference?" Then, animatedly, she added, *"You're ready to publish the Scrolls?"*

"We're *almost* ready," he teased, and both of them laughed. While he was somewhat sensitive that translations of the Dead Sea Scrolls still hadn't been fully published by their International Study Team even after forty years' study, Lute had learned to tolerate the drumbeat of jealous criticism from those who railed against 'the intransigence of the privileged Jerusalem scholars.'

He turned toward Christiana and plunged in. "Do you know the word *kairos*?"

She shook her head, watching him intently.

"It's Greek for 'God's time' or 'a breakthrough of the divine into the human.' Here, let me show you." He pulled the airline ticket jacket from his inside breast pocket, removed all the contents and placed those on the glass-topped coffee table. He held the folder on the palm of his upturned left hand. "Imagine we all lived in a two-dimensional world like this," he explained, "and all we knew was life on this flat plane. We would simply be drawings, right? And all we could possibly know would be what we experienced on this surface. Everything would be limited to length and width."

She nodded, her eyes moving from him to the paper folder and back.

"Then if God, from a *third* dimension, stuck His finger through our world like this"—he jabbed his right index finger through a slit in the paper—"we would be amazed, right?" He slowly pulled his finger almost out of the hole, then lowered it in again.

"One would just know it as a cross-section," Christy volunteered. "It would seem to grow larger and smaller in diameter, magically."

"Very good, doctor! My sister, the brilliant M.D. You might someday convince some of us men that women are almost equal."

She rolled her eyes and pushed on. "So how is that related to...what did you call it?...*kairos*?"

"Yes, *kairos*. To the two-dimensional figures in the world of this plane, the mysterious appearance of my *three*-dimensional finger would be a *kairos*, a breakthrough, literally a breaking-into-their-world by a higher power. It would be perceivable, but not understandable. At least not in any depth."

"So to speak," Christy said.

Lute grinned and looked down at his teaching tools. In one brief moment that surprised both of them—completely out of character when he was with anyone except his poker buddies—he raised an eyebrow wickedly and humped his finger in and out of the hole in the folder.

"Lute Jonson!" she scolded softly. Her face tightened.

"I know, I know," Lute apologized, averting his eyes and pursing his lips. "That's for marriage only, right?"

She crossed her legs and folded her arms. "Yes. Some of us still hold to the Biblical values proven throughout the ages. You and I had a good upbringing, brother Lute, and our duty is to pass the truth on to succeeding generations." She added an echo of his own question: "'Right?'"

Lute nodded briefly, then gathered the contents of the folder and returned it to his pocket.

"Anyway, is that why you came to San Diego?" she asked. "To teach me an interesting Greek word?"

He turned his gaze back through the plate glass window to the restless ocean, and fell silent.

She watched him a long moment, her brows knitting tighter, then rose and joined him at the window. Her hand kneaded his tight neck. "Lute?"

"You're still Christian?" he asked, one of those time-filler, assurance-seeking questions that don't truly need to be verbalized between people who know each other well, but which serve to delay or soften a difficult conversation.

"Until He takes me home," she said.

"Then we both believe that Jesus' coming to earth was a *kairos* event."

"Yes." She added, "Aha! So was the Burning Bush, then, God's appearance to Moses. And the Tongues of Fire, the first appearance of the Holy Spirit at Pentecost." She appeared to mentally catalogue other instances when Judeo-Christian scriptures said that God had intervened in human history. She smiled and pronounced her new term aloud. "*Kairos*. Rhymes with 'high dose.' Thank you! I like it."

"It's been quite a while since a new one has been found in ancient scriptures," Lute said. The room was still as both looked out over the crashing Pacific waves.

Christy's hand tensed on his neck. "Lute?"

He turned to face her, and nodded gently. "I believe God is poised for *kairos* again. Here in America. This week."

Lute watched the eyes of his normally imperturbable sister widen in amazement. But a gnaw of fear and a history of sibling honesty compelled him to chill her with a post-script.

"If I live to tell the story."

CHAPTER 6

QUMRAN RUINS, ISRAEL

Fourteen miles southeast of Jerusalem
Monday, June 17, 1991
4:30 p.m.

Father O'Derry excused himself through the group of tourists that was assembling near the west end of the Qumran ruins. He flashed his hearty Irish smile to the security guard at the entry point.

"Top o' the day, me brother," Sean said with a brogue thick and sweet enough to cover a stack of pancakes.

"And t' ye, father," replied the uniformed Israeli guard in a respectable Irish accent, completing the light-hearted antiphon the two had begun years before. Today he added, "How's me favorite Dead Sea Scrolls Study Team Director?"

"Right as rain, lad," grinned the old priest. He winked. "But I'll bet ye say the exact same words to me pal Lute whenever *he* visits."

The smiling guard stepped aside and Sean, along with his assistant Richard McGuire, walked through and then up the small rise into the familiar ruins. They strolled by the raised rubble of the defense tower, and through the maze of excavated half-walls that had enclosed various chambers some two thousand years ago. The cleric's left leg faltered occasionally during the walk, attesting to the onset of arthritis. Once past the guard, his smile disappeared and a frown creased his face. He stopped in the heart of Khirbet Qumran, at the scriptorium.

"Richard?"

Sean's 24-year-old assistant scurried to catch up. Looking as if his graduate assistant's stipend afforded only one meal a day, McGuire's lank six-foot frame contrasted with his mentor's corpulence.

"Is that radio thing turned on?"

"Yes, Father." McGuire pulled a cellular phone out of its black pouch at his waist and showed it to the priest. "Do you want me to call the office?"

"No, no. It will ring if they call us?"

McGuire nodded. "It sort of buzzes."

"I need to know, the minute they locate Lute. It's not like him to be gone without telling anyone." Sean looked closely at his clean-cut assistant. "You're sure he didn't talk to you?"

"No, sir. Dr. Jonson said nothing to me about leaving."

"Even if he swore you to secrecy, you know, you must tell me. He has a ... well, a condition that we haven't discussed with anyone, and he may need treatment." The priest searched the younger man's eyes, wondering if he were lying. Or worse, if McGuire could tell that Sean himself was. "If anyone on the staff knows where he's gone, or why...?" Still no sign of comprehension showed on the thin face, so the priest's shoulders sagged.

"Are we looking for anything specific today?" asked the jeans-clad assistant, his gaze sweeping the rocky landscape, and then across the kilometer or so to the northwestern shore of the salt-saturated Dead Sea.

"A little peace. Just a little peace for me weariness."

McGuire rested his hand on his mentor's shoulder. "I'm sure he's OK, Father. Don't worry. There's gotta be a logical explanation."

Sean wiped his forehead with his sleeve. "It's so hot. Could you sneak us a couple of Cokes out of the gift shop? As long as *they* don't see us," he waved toward the tour group just beginning its carefully restricted walk, "it's OK."

McGuire nodded and left.

The priest prayed silently. *Holy Mother of God, please intercede and send Lute back. Let him see his error; curb his loosened tongue. Chasten him, Blessed Virgin, and bring him back to me, to his friend and colleague of these forty-plus years.* Sean's open eyes glistened. *Or, if it is the will of the Heavenly Father, give me strength to do whatever His Kingdom requires.*

A small gecko darted out of a crevice near his boots. Momentarily startled, the priest stood and watched as the lizard initially ran from him, then stopped in its tracks. Sean moved closer. His eyes focused into a faraway place; his jaw muscles clenched. The creature's attempt to get away brought his attention back. Awkwardly, he stretched to step on the creature, but then checked his stride and let the little reptile scamper away.

CHAPTER 7

MANUSCRIPT 1Q-CETHER-1:
BOY YESHUA

"Our notes on this fragment: From Cave 1 at Qumran. This was the first scroll fragment of the seven found by Abouid Mhoamm, goat-herder, and sold to O'Derry on December 22, 1948. Translated by Jonson. Fortunately we didn't share them with anyone until we realized they were distinctly unlike most of the other discoveries. The vast majority of what we're now calling the Dead Sea Scrolls were copies of scriptures, scripture commentaries, community rules, or testaments against the Sons of Darkness. But so far, these seven are the only journal-like writings found. Because they mention Yeshua—Jesus—we are keeping them in hidden files. None are included on our inventories, nor have we even mentioned them to our colleagues. For now we're listing them 'secret' (hence the Hebrew 'Cether'). L.E.J. 4-10-55"

THE KNOWLEDGE OF THE [YOUTH] YESHUA FROM [ARRIVAL] TO INITIATION.

EILLO, ONE OF THE SONS OF LIGHT, RECEIVED WORD HIS BROTHER JOSEPH FELL ASLEEP IN NAZARETH, LEAVING A SON OF 14 YEARS. EILLO RECEIVED PERMISSION TO ATTEND JOSEPH'S AFFAIRS, AND BROUGHT YESHUA WITH HIM ON [HIS] RETURN. STILL AFTER [MANY DAYS] EILLO WEPT. YESHUA DANCED.

THE YOUTH JOINED RITUAL CLEANSING CEREMONIES, STEPPING DOWN INTO FIRST BATH BE[FORE THE] SECOND AS INSTRUCTED. THE SOIL OF PRECEDING [MEN] IN THE FIRST BATH DREW BACK FROM WHERE YESHUA ENTERED, AS TOUCH OF LYE CLEARS WATER SURFACE. ALWAYS THE UNCLOUDED WATERS FOLLOW.

ELDERS INSTRUCT YOUTH IN TORAH WITH . . . . CLEARLY . . . . . WITH QUESTIONS . . . . JERUSALEM . . . . . WRITING IN DIRT AT [HIS] FEET

   . . . SONS OF
   . . . EVIL SP[IRIT]

CHAPTER 8

A KAIROS DECLINED

La Jolla, California
Monday
12:35 p.m.

Lute breathed deeply, looked squarely at his sister, and began. "Christy, it's not scholarly stubbornness that has kept us from releasing all the Scrolls. Even academics on government grants don't take forty years to piece together and translate ancient Hebrew parchment scraps. There's a more difficult reason for our delay."

A dry cough choked off his speaking. He shook his head, cleared his throat, and drank from his coffee mug. There was silence in the room for long moments beyond his throat's recovery. Finally he began again.

"The real reason for our delay is because of seven scroll fragments which we have never before acknowledged, Christy. Once we found these seven, we delayed releasing *any* translations, for fear something in one of the many others would somehow point back to the existence of these seven."

"Oh, Lute. What...? Can you tell me what they...? Are they secret...?"

"Yes, they're secret. They're so secret you're only the third person to know they exist. At least, I *believe* you're only the third person. Sean and I bought them with the first fragments in 1948. Late in the year. They were some of the most perfectly preserved and longer pieces, so the two of us translated them right off. As soon as I read them, I knew my life was changed forever." Lute reached down for his briefcase beside the sofa, but stopped. He looked at his sister a moment, then folded his hands in his lap and continued.

"We were so exhilarated we could talk of nothing else, but also so scared and astounded we felt we had to hide them and not discuss them with anyone. At least until we could decide what to do with them. We delayed a week at first, then a second, then we set ourselves a deadline of making a decision by New Year's Day, 1950. But Sean had to return to Belfast to conduct his sister's wedding about then, and we just kept on delaying. It's like a terrible chore you keep putting off until finally you realize you can live with the problem more easily than with any solution you can imagine."

Christy nodded understanding but pressed him to get past the introduction. "What in the world do they contain? I've never known you, brother—champion of academic freedom and robust scholarly inquiry—to be so...well, so secretive. What are you afraid of?"

Lute's throat constricted as he coughed once more. He sipped his cooled coffee. Concerned, Christy stood to help her brother but he waved her away and said, "It's just nerves."

"Can you tell me what the Scrolls say, or would that be breaking a confidence?"

"*Yes!*" he snapped. "Yes, I'll tell you what they say, and yes, it will break four decades' code of silence!" As if he'd been listening to himself, he cocked his head to one side a moment and then looked back at his sister. "Christy, I'm sorry. Please understand, I'm not upset at you. It's just ... this may be extremely difficult."

She nodded, her eyes full of patience and concern for her one remaining blood relative. Lute breathed slowly and focused his eyes on the middle distance, gathering strength to complete the unveiling he had begun. Christy rose from the elegant white sofa and took their coffee mugs to the kitchen. She returned with steam rising from the refills and set them on cork coasters on the glass coffee table between them.

"Why will it be difficult for you?" she prompted.

Lute said, "Not difficult for *me*. It's for you, for the rest of the world. I don't know if you're ready for this, my dear. There are so many who may find offense in this." He studied her face; she met his gaze, absently rubbing her index finger on the knee of her teal-and-gray slacks. He continued. "It has to do with our faith. *I've* come to see my news as a great revelation, but others might not see it as positively. Not at first, anyway."

Her eyes hardened. Once again she stood up. She walked to the breakfast bar separating the living room and kitchen. A tall rattan stool was pushed back from the bar where a luncheon plate sat on the surface next to an open Bible. She brought the black leather-cover book back to the sofa with her, clutching it tightly to her breast. A firm Nordic stoicism enveloped her body like a Northern Elk parka.

"The Scrolls tell of a young man who lived in the Qumran community of first-century Judea. His father was a carpenter from Nazareth. The residents there came to believe he was divine. His name was Yeshua—Jesus."

The two locked eyes in silence before she reacted.

"Lord now lettest Thou Thy servant depart in peace, according to Thy word," Christiana chanted from the Gospel of Luke and her beloved Lutheran liturgy, nearly levitating off the sofa again. "For mine eyes have seen Thy salvation, which Thou hast prepared before the face of all people, a light to lighten the Gentiles and the glory of Thy people Israel."

The Scandinavian reserve was thrown off, and the 65-year-old physician nearly danced across the plush pile carpet. "Praise God. Oh, praise God!" she murmured in barely-controlled euphoria, raising her Bible slightly toward the heavens and returning it to her bosom.

Finally stopping beside the breakfast bar, Christy had to confirm what she had heard. "He lived as a man there, where they wrote the Scrolls?"

"Yes."

"They've been carbon-dated as two thousand years old?"

"Every fragment we *have* tested was. We only tested one small blank section from these seven, but it was lab-proven as somewhere between nineteen hundred and twenty-three hundred years old, same as all the other fragments we tested that we didn't consider this sensitive."

"He was considered by the members of that community to be divine?"

"One of the seven scrolls calls Him 'God's own Child,' and 'The Anointed'—the same word we use for Messiah."

"And he was called Jesus?"

"In the Aramaic language of His day, 'Yeshua.' In English, Jesus."

The elegant woman returned to her dance-walk across the room. She appeared to have entered a trancelike state, hugging her well-worn Bible, moving with more peace and gentle grace than Lute could ever recall. He wondered if she might be raptured directly to heaven before his eyes.

Suddenly she stopped in front of him, and the sound of judgment he had heard before returned to her voice.

"How could you possibly have kept this from me? From the entire world? I am a scientist! I wanted proof in my religious life as much as I expect it in my profession, but in its absence I have lived in faith anyway. You've had evidence that *proves* what millions of us have *believed?* For over forty years, you have *known* and haven't *shared?*" She shook her head in judgment, but softened immediately. "It doesn't matter now. I forgive you, Lute; I cannot feel anything but ecstasy. My faith is complete!"

"Christiana, the Scrolls say something else."

The tone of his voice curbed her elation. She stared at him and rubbed her exposed arms as if they had suddenly turned cold. He reached a second time for his briefcase and pulled it to his knees. Dropping a file folder flap from the top cover, he used his fingernail to pry open the simple false back. From that compartment he carefully withdrew the clear plastic document sleeves. A yellowed scrap of parchment was visible inside the one on top. His eyes caressed the ancient manuscript as he spoke again.

"They reveal a secret about the Savior that may surprise you at first. Somehow this part of His life almost got lost, and Christians have misunderstood it through the ages. This new *kairos* brings us more light."

Silence reigned. Christiana made no move to see his treasures. Finally Lute finished.

"They say Yeshua ... that He was not a virgin."

Neither of them breathed for a long moment. When Lute looked up at his sister, all gentleness—let alone rapture—had drained from her face. He couldn't remember ever having seen such emptiness in her eyes. She moved listlessly around the corner into the kitchen. Through the open space between the breakfast bar and the cupboards above, he saw her standing in slumped silence and then reaching a dispirited hand out for the Waterford glass beside her lunch plate, tiny slivers of ice in it now almost completely melted. His gaze dropped sadly for a moment, but snapped back to her at the sound of crystal shattering on the ceramic tile under her feet.

CHAPTER 9

THE WARRANT

Rockefeller Museum, Jerusalem
Monday, June 17
10:00 p.m.

"Father O'Derry?" The whiny voice always irritated Sean, and even more so when it was spiked with static over the intercom. Tonight, however, his heart leapt to hear it, hoping there was word.

"Yes, Izbaca?"

"Father, Mr. Staumper is here. He says he needs to see you immediately. Also, I finished typing this new draft of your speech, and I'm nearly falling asleep. I'm leaving now, OK?"

The priest was up and over to the door before his secretary finished her message. He yanked it open to find the museum's security chief sitting in the outer office. "Come in, Morrie. Come in." He turned to address the haggard woman at the desk nearby. "Yes, goodnight, Izbaca. Thank you for staying so late."

Morris Staumper looked up at his supervisor from the wheelchair he occupied. His face betrayed no emotion, but his fingers moved imperceptibly to start the battery-powered chair moving toward the office door.

Staumper's 61-year-old body slumped in the chair, but he gave the impression he could have jerked upright and flattened anyone who might have offered him help, solicitously or not. His eyes moved quickly to take in every detail around him; his chin jutted with the power of an unshakable inner self-confidence; his starched khakis and white tab-collared shirt bespoke precision and conscious attention to appearance.

The two entered Sean's private office, and the priest closed the door before sitting down on the couch to the left of his desk.

"We have located him." The Israeli's words were as welcome to the cleric as a cold beer after an August jeep drive in the Negev desert. "He is in the United States. San Diego, California."

"Morrie!" Sean shook his head with gratitude and relief such as he had not known in many years. "You'll never know, my loyal friend, how much I appreciate your brilliant work for us here. Regardless of what I ask, you always accomplish it without hesitation, without failure."

Staumper continued his thought. "It appears he is at the home of his sister, a physician, in a suburb of San Diego. He had departed Ben Gurion International for New York, as I told you shortly after you inquired about his whereabouts. Had we talked earlier, we could probably have had his El Al flight met at JFK in New York."

Sean did not answer the implied criticism, though he mentally chastised himself once more for having waited so long to report Lute's absence. It should have been clear, after all, that Lute was not going to agree to wait. Sean knew he should not have ignored Lute's recent obsession with the old Greek concept of "God's time."

"And he flew on to San Diego?" prompted Sean.

"That's what took so long. He didn't use his own name to get to New York or to San Diego. We checked the manifests for outbound flights from Ben Gurion, then El Al sources for passengers matching his description. Because of several factors—the timing of the ticket purchase, among others—we're virtually certain that a 'Dr. Rose', Dr. K. Rose, was actually Dr. Jonson. And if that's him, he flew to San Diego on United Airlines less than two hours after his arrival in New York."

A surprised "Ah!" escaped from Sean's throat. "K. Rose. '*Kairos*.' He's spoken of that so often these past two months. Perhaps he really wants me to find him. I think he does, Morrie; I think he wants me to bring him back before he does so much harm."

"Sir?"

"Never mind. So he didn't have to use his passport in the U.S.? He just paid cash and walked onto the plane?"

"Once he was in the country, he only needed a driver's license. So either he has a contact there who helped him, or he acquired identification here before he left."

Sean shook his head in disbelief. "Does this sound like our friend? He wouldn't even *know* anyone in Israel he could get phony ID from, let alone actually do it."

"He spoke at four international conferences in the past year," offered the security chief. "One meets all kinds of people."

Sean nodded agreement but his eyes continued to show confusion as Staumper continued.

"Father, have you told me everything you know that will help us trace him? Have there been recent changes in Dr. Jonson's behavior?" The paraplegic's tone was clinical; it lacked even a hint of personal interest. The priest paused only a moment before shaking his head, hoping—as he had earlier with his graduate assistant—that his lie was convincing.

"Where do y'think he's gone to in San Diego?" The brogue slipped back into Sean's voice, as a pacifier brought out for an infant's quieting.

"He has a sister there, sir."

"Ah yes, so you said. And have you ... gone to him?"

The security chief's eyes narrowed and his crippled body stiffened. "I have people en route. We'll have him shortly."

Sean pushed himself up from the Naugahyde couch in his office. He turned around toward the window overlooking the patchy garden in the hub of the museum. The security officer's respectful silence filled the office a long moment before Sean spoke again. "Morrie, he *has* to come home."

"Sir?" Sean realized that Staumper seemed to find that a convenient question, far more eloquent in its brevity than many more long-winded options. He used it often.

Sean cleared his throat and clenched his fists a couple of times. "You simply have to bring him back, Morrie. He has a condition. We haven't discussed it with anyone, but it's serious and he needs to be treated here. You must also send word that he's prone to spells. Without his medication, he occasionally talks nonsense, but without appearing the least bit incoherent. He sounds totally sane, but he tells wild tales, which is the great problem. So your people simply have to find a way to bring him back. Quietly. Without fuss."

The former Mossad agent's eyes narrowed. He pushed a knob and his chair whirred toward the door. With his hand on the doorknob, and without turning back toward his employer, Staumper asked in a low, steady tone, "And what if he begins to tell what he knows? Do you want to see your friend again? Or is it more important that his voice be stilled?"

He waited for an answer. The two men faced opposite directions in the musty room: one looking out a window toward an untended flower patch of the central courtyard; the other poised in his wheelchair to open a door and escape the dark paneled office. Still, no answer.

"Father, do you wish me to 'rush medicine' to him?"

Sean could hear the disbelief in Morrie's question. "He *has* to come home."

"And if he will not come willingly?"

"He will come. My friend of forty years will come home."

"Sir?"

Sean sank to his knees, held his head in his hands, and his shoulders sagged.

"I'm sorry, sir. Your instructions?" said the Israeli with no emotion but insistence. Finally Sean spoke.

"Oh, Blessed Virgin, gird up my soul. Almighty God, Thy will be done." The scholar-priest's throat constricted and the pitch of his voice rose a bit as he answered, "Ecclesiastes, Morrie. Ecclesiastes three and three."

The old priest shook his head wearily again, and his subordinate powered his wheelchair out of the room.

Ecclesiastes 3:1-3

To everything there is a season, and a time to every purpose under heaven; A time to be born and a time to die; A time to plant and a time to pluck up that which is planted; A time to kill and a time to heal....

CHAPTER 10

DAYMARES

La Jolla

The crystal shards on the kitchen floor cracked and snapped as Lute walked Christiana back around the breakfast bar and into the living room.

"Oh, Christy," he consoled. "Please don't cry. What I'm telling you is *good* news, not bad. It's *kairos*. You're coming face-to-face with God; don't be afraid."

Lute steered her toward the sofa, but she wouldn't sit. She gently pushed away from him and walked toward the window wall. She opened the sliding glass door beside the picture window, and he followed her out onto the sunny deck.

"I can't believe this, Lute."

"Can't believe what?"

"How could you say Jesus was not a virgin? Are you saying he was married?" The flesh of her face turned into white marble.

Lute shook his head slowly from side to side.

"Then you're saying he was a *fornicator*. You're saying the Son of God was *immoral*. There's a good old-fashioned word for what you've said, you know. It's 'blasphemy.' It may not be chic in today's society, but I've believed you've held onto the faith of our fathers, Lute. As I have. Committing blasphemy like that should strike fear in you."

Lute turned to the redwood railing and peered out over the white-tipped waves of the Pacific. He felt overpowered by doubt. *This is it,* he thought. *This is exactly what will happen when some of these people hear. Anger. Fear. Denial. I don't know if I can go through with this. I've had forty-three years to think about it and it's still amazing. How can I expect people to hear the big secret and then calmly go on with their lives?*

He turned back to her. "What can I say to help, Christy?"

She attempted a smile, but Lute was struck by how his well-educated, affluent, professional, late-middle-aged sister suddenly looked almost childish in her nervous plea. "Say it's a bad joke and you're sorry," she said.

"'It's a bad joke and you're sorry'." He knew the moment the words were out that his attempt at humor would fail miserably.

Her face hardened again.

He tried another tack. "Remember what the annunciation angel told Mary? And what the angels heralded to the shepherds at Jesus' birth? And what the angel at the tomb said to Mary Magdalene? It was always the same message: 'Fear not.' Christiana, in almost every story when Scriptures tell of times when God approached human beings, His message *began* with the same words."

Her set jaw and lowered eyes were unmoved.

"Do you remember the first words out of Moses' mouth in Exodus, when he came down from Mt. Sinai carrying the Commandments God had given him? 'Do not be afraid.' Or what the angel said to Hagar, Abraham's slave sent into the wilderness? The same words. And when the disciples were terrified by the sight of the Lord walking on the water?

He said, 'It is I; be not afraid.' I feel like I'm beating the evidence to death, but what were His most tender words the night of the Last Supper? 'Do not let your hearts be troubled.' He said it *twice*. Or how about the incredible moment when He first appeared to the disciples after His resurrection! He said nothing else before the words, 'Greetings. Do not be afraid.' Sis, whenever God broke into human time from His, the immediate *kairos* greeting was the same!"

Motionless beside him at the railing, Christiana's arms were wrapped tightly around herself.

He ached because of her anguish, because of the threat his news posed to the literalism of her fundamentalist faith. He shook his head slowly as he realized how one sentence—"Jesus was not a virgin"—could disturb her profoundly-held belief in the purity of the Son of God. Lute realized his revelation left her with two terrible choices: either to accept that a basic tenet of her faith was flawed, or that her own brother was spreading an unspeakable heresy. Seeing evidence of the momentous churning he was causing her, Lute's resolve began to falter.

As he repeated the words "Do not be afraid," the phone rang indoors.

She returned to the living room and picked up a cordless phone from the coffee table. Regaining her composure, she let it ring twice more before pressing a button and saying, "Hello?"

"Oh, hi, hon." Lute watched as she turned to him and mouthed the words, "My husband." Lute turned again to study the pacific scene spread out to the horizon.

"Yes, he's here. How did you know?"

Moments later Christiana rejoined her brother on the deck. "That was Hjalmar. Would you excuse me a moment so I can clean up the mess I made in the kitchen? You're going to have a visitor in a few minutes."

He whipped around, and his eyes bore into her. "Who?"

"Someone called his office for our address, and since Hjalmar was standing by the receptionist, he took the call. Our home phone is unlisted, and most of us La Jollans don't give out addresses unless it's something like this."

Lute nodded quickly. "Who's coming?"

"Someone from the airlines. They called and said you left a bag there; they're bringing it out."

His heart racing, Lute grabbed his sister by the hand and pulled her through the house toward the front door.

"We have to go, Christy. Quick. Where are your car keys?" She pointed to a set on the hall table. He grabbed them and opened the door, but stopped abruptly.

"Wait. How much cash do you have?" Her answer was too slow in coming. "Please get it—all of it in the house. This is an emergency. I'll pay you back."

Her eyes wide in astonishment, Christiana began to walk down a side hall.

"Please *hurry*, Christy. We need to get out of here immediately! The garage is open; I'm getting your car out."

Less than a minute later Lute was at the wheel and careening up Torrey Pines Road and across Ardath Road toward Interstate 5. Intent on speeding back toward downtown San Diego, Lute was oblivious to his sister's confusion.

"Lute?" she began. "What's going on?"

He glanced at her. "Sorry. Look, for one thing, that couldn't have been the airline that called Hjalmar, because I didn't *have* another bag, only this one." He nodded toward the oversize briefcase on the seat between them. "And for another, they didn't even know *my* name, let alone yours or Hjalmar's. I used a false name so nobody *could* contact me out here. What a fool I am; I should've guessed they'd start the search with you, my only living relative. Damn it. I thought I'd have a little more time."

With jaw clenched, Lute cut in front of a Mazda on Interstate 5 and then searched his rear-view mirrors for signs of cars following them. The college-age Mazda driver leaned on his horn in irritation, but Lute was preoccupied as he pulled off onto the Laurel Street/El Prado exit downtown. Following prominent street signs toward Balboa Park, he had them in the San Diego Zoo parking lot within minutes. He found an empty spot under a light stanchion bearing a sign with a giraffe's silhouette.

Christiana broke the tense silence. "Shall we have lunch and wait until they're gone?"

He shook his head. "I don't think you understand how serious this is. I have to get lost for a while. Do you have the money?" She pulled a fat bank envelope from her purse and handed it to him. "Here's five thousand dollars. It's my mad money."

"I don't think I've ever been five thousand mad. Have you?"

"I'm a southern California doctor nearing retirement, Lute. Did you think I'd keep a fifty dollar bill hidden in my dresser?"

"*I'm* a poor old researcher, Christiana. Did you think I'd keep more?" Then he remembered his manners. "Thanks, sis. You'll get it back soon."

He got out of the car and gestured for her to come around to the driver's seat. "Go shopping or something. Use your credit card. Go home in a few hours. If anybody asks, just forget that you saw me. If you can't lie about it, tell the truth: tell 'em we visited a little while and I left without telling you where I was staying in town or when I would be back. Or *if* I'd be back. They'll leave you alone once they know I'm gone. And if they frighten you, call the police."

She looked very confused, and didn't move from the passenger side.

"Damn it, Christiana, get over here and drive this thing outta here. You have to leave. Fast. They can't find me in a city this size. Not until I've done what I have to do."

He started jogging in the direction opposite the zoo entrance, into acres of cars left by thousands of mid-summer visitors.

He stopped two rows away and turned to see his dazed sister walking around to the driver's side of her car. He called out, "Fear not! There are tidings of great joy." Before she pulled the car door shut, he added, "And I love you, Christiana."

Exodus 20:20
And Moses said unto the people, Fear not: for God is come to prove you...

Judges 6:22-23
When Gideon realized it was the angel of the Lord he exclaimed, "Ah, Sovereign Lord! I have seen the angel of the Lord face to face." But the Lord said to him, "Peace! Do not be afraid. You are not going to die."

CHAPTER 11

MANUSCRIPT 1Q-CETHER-2: YESHUA

"Re the fragment in this binder: Second of the seven manuscripts from Abouid Mhoamm the goatherder. O'Derry argued from early 1950 that we should release this one and 1Q-Cether-1; Jonson strongly disagreed, on the 'where-there's-smoke-there's-fire' theory: if these scrolls were known to the Church, we would be forced to open up all scrolls immediately. Probing ... references we haven't found yet ... something might endanger the confidentiality of the more sensitive ones (all our *Cether* list), but also threaten the integrity of the entire international team's study process. Sean has so far agreed. L.E.J. 4-10-55"

In another pen and a more casual handwriting: "*Reluctantly* agreed. One factor being the dramatic difference between these seven scroll pieces and all others we have translated so far. The personal reflections of scribe(s) vs. copied scriptures, community rules, war documents, etc. The emphasis on one named individual is a striking departure from emerging norms. (But then, so was the person of Yeshua.) S.O'D"

YESHUA'S APPETITE [HAS IM]PROVED GREATLY SINCE HIS ACCIDENT.

THE SONS OF LIGHT MOANED AFTER HE DISAPPEARED FOR [ONE] DAY AND REJOICED WHEN THEY FOUND [HIM] IN THE CAVE. NURSED HIS LEG BACK TO STRENGTH.

YESHUA [HAS] ALWAYS BEEN LAMB-LIKE. [HE] HOLDS LIGHTNESS OF SPIRIT. WHEN OTHERS TIRE AT DARKNESS, [HE IS] STILL PLAYFUL, EVEN AS HE NEARS 15TH YEAR. IN GAME OF [HIDE AND] SEEK, YESHUA REMAINED HIDDEN MANY MINUTES BY FOLLOWING RAMAH'S BACK. IN WRESTLING HE PLAYS WITHOUT ROUGHNESS AND DOES NOT [PIN] OPPONENTS. THE TEACHER SAYS WRESTLING NO LONGER RAISES THE FIRE INSIDE, SINCE YESHUA'S [WAY] FLOWS WITH PEACE.

EVEN IN BREAKING COMMUNITY RULE OF SILENCE DURING MID-DAY MEAL, YESHUA CHARMS. ACCEPTING PUNISHMENT HE FLOATS ABOVE [IT]. YESHUA'S APPETITE VERY STRONG [AND] HE LOVES EVEN THAT [COOKING] OF BEN-ZARTHAN. YET HIS SUPPLENESS REMAINS. THE SMELL OF NEW WINE WAS ON HIM AFTER TREK INTO WILDERNESS BUT [WITH]OUT AGGRAVATION OR DRUNKENNESS.

YESHUA SMILES. HE LAUGHS.

THE PEOPLE CLUSTER WITH HIM DURING STUDY PERIODS, AS [HIS] IDEAS CRACK SHELLS

OF OLD TRADITIONS TO REVEAL SEEDS OF NEW [LIFE]. MANY OF THE NEW MEN IMITATE YESHUA HABIT OF DIRT-WRITING. EVEN THE ELDERS WONDER AT [HIS] UNDERSTANDING.

WHISPERS TELL OF HIS NIGHTGLOW IN SLEEP, OF BRAMBLE SCRATCHES DISAPPEARING IMMEDIATELY, OF CISTERN IN DANGER[OUSLY LOW SUPPLY] REFILLING, OF SMALL DEVILS BLOWN OUT NOSES OF HIS COMPANIONS, OF A STONE-CRUSHED SNAKE INFLATED BY YESHUA'S BREATH AND SET LOOSE BUT WHICH WOULD NOT LEAVE HIM THE DAY.

HIS [DUNG DO]ES NOT SMELL BEFORE IT IS COVERED.

CHAPTER 12

A FATHER'S FURY

Jerusalem
Tuesday, June 18
6:30 a.m.

Sean awoke at his usual hour despite having lain awake most of the night. He stared at the plastic glow-in-the-dark stars hanging above his bed, but without the gentle pleasure they usually brought. His eleven-year-old grand-niece had carefully installed them two years before on a visit, and Sean awoke most mornings to the memory of that pleasant week with his sister and brother -in-law, their daughter Janet, and her daughter Sue, the star-hanger.

Suddenly Sean threw the covers off and rolled out of bed. The cold morning floor jolted his feet as the recollection of the previous day's difficult situation awakened his mind.

He opened his bedroom door and called down over the railing to the housekeeper. "Mrs. Naza?"

"Good morning, Father," the woman called up to him, and emerged through the kitchen door in an apron imprinted with the words "Have you hugged a Presbyterian today?" It amused the cleric that a tiny Israeli woman working for a Catholic priest in the heart of Jerusalem would sport such attire.

"Can you smell them? There are fresh cinnamon rolls in the oven," she said cheerily.

"Mrs. Naza, please call Morrie Staumper and tell him to meet me at the office as soon as he can. Will y'do that?"

"He's waiting for you there, Father."

"He already called?"

"Almost an hour ago. He told me to wake you up and I told him no, you needed your beauty sleep. Desperately."

Sean ignored the woman's good-natured mothering and whispered "Damn it" through his clenched teeth. Aloud he added, "Did he say he had news?"

"Did your crippled clam open up and tell me something? Did he even so much as say 'Good morning' when he called before God's Breakfast?"

"No, eh?" Sean finally grinned a tight little smile as he headed toward the bathroom.

"Thanks," he called over his shoulder. And then, sheepishly, "And good mornin'."

Within minutes, having braved Mrs. Naza's exasperation that he wouldn't wait to sample the first batch of homemade sweet rolls, Sean sped up HaNevi'im Street in his Fiat, heading toward the Rockefeller Museum and his office. He was waved through security as usual and parked in his reserved space next to the employee entrance in back. He hurried inside.

"Morrie?" The priest called into the stillness for the security chief. "Morrie, are you here?" The stone hallway's chill gave him the shivers and he rubbed his arms as he walked past the Qumran scriptorium tables exhibit.

Sean's stomach muscles tightened. It was unlike the ubiquitous Staumper to play hard-to-find. Crazy thoughts crossed the priest's mind, cloak-and-dagger thoughts of violence and untimely ends. He couldn't untangle whether his premonition of blood and mayhem concerned his crippled security chief—waylaid somehow, somewhere, for some unexplainable reason—or whether it was a foreboding of imminent danger to himself.

Foolishness, he thought. *Damned foolishness. I am the hunter—as strange as that role is to me—not the hunted. And yet there is Matthew 26 and 52. Oh, sainted Mother of God, be with us all.* He shook his head in confused wonder at how life had changed so dramatically in just one day, and an involuntary shudder ran through his extremities.

"Father?" The voice came from behind him, and Sean started. He turned and saw Staumper approaching.

"Morrie, are you all right?"

The man in the wheelchair looked up quizzically. "Sir?"

Sean realized that his fantasies and fears had soared over the head of real life, and he made "never mind" motions with his head and hands. He led Staumper toward his office where they began their conversation again behind a closed door.

"What's happened?" demanded the priest. "Have you ... have we ... well, has Lute been picked up in San Diego?"

"No, sir."

Sean waited for an expansion of the answer, but Staumper seldom offered more answer than the question asked. "Damn it, Morrie, tell me what you know."

"We have had a temporary setback, Father. Dr. Jonson was not at his sister's home when our associates arrived. I suspect one of them was less than adept in his investigation and may have inadvertently alerted the household somehow. I'm looking into the cause and it won't be repeated. The bottom line is that we know he is in the San Diego area and we're closing in on him. These are considerable accomplishments in the twenty-four hours he has been gone."

"You had him and you lost him?!" the priest cried out angrily. He lowered his voice but it was still powered with fury as he continued, "You found him with pinpoint accuracy halfway around the world and did not hold onto him?"

There was silence between them. Staumper met the priest's fiery stare with his own cool gaze.

"Did I understand you correctly, Morrie?"

"We were virtually certain we knew where he was about ten o'clock last night—noon in San Diego—but he was not there when the agents arrived shortly afterward. If that is your understanding, you are correct."

"Damnation." The expletive was mouthed but not voiced. Sean was regaining self-control. "Where is he now?"

With a condescending patience, Staumper answered, "Somewhere in San Diego."

"I know that, goddammit, *where* in San Diego?"

Staumper fixed his eyes on the priest and briefly shook his head to indicate he had no answer.

Sean felt a fury erupt in his gut. He looked at the closest wheel of his employee's wheelchair and wondered what it would take to break it. The spokes seemed sturdier than on other wheelchairs. He looked back at the stocky occupant of the device, at the well-developed biceps filling the sleeves of his shirt, and only then down to the obviously withered lower limbs. He turned away and stomped toward his desk. He sat and calmed himself by staring into empty space. Finally he leaned his elbows on the polished cherry-wood surface and lowered his head into his palms.

"What will your people do now? How do you pick up a trail again?"

"We think like he is thinking, then go where he thinks he'll be safe. We talk to friends we already have there. We rent new ones. We keep close watch on transportation: airlines, buses, rental cars. Computers are the worst enemy of those who are running away. Speaking of buying, I do not need to know where the cash you gave me yesterday came from, but I may need to know shortly if there will be more available. I have not questioned your expanding my department's responsibilities to include these operations, but there will be costs."

"If there has to be more, it will be available." Sean wondered if Lute realized their $475,000 acquisition fund, cash accumulated over many years from four privacy-obsessed benefactors, was now being employed against him.

"What do you think he's trying to do, Morrie?"

"Sir?"

"What makes you think he's running?"

As soon as he spoke those words, Sean regretted them. They had provided the security chief a flashlight view into the dark recess of Sean's own mind. He had meant, "What do you think Lute's trying to do?" in the sense of 'Where's he trying to *go?*', but his actual language reflected his deeper fear: that Morrie knew the secret. Staumper had apparently recognized the ambiguity, asked for clarification—which Sean offered from his subconscious—and the security chief thereby avoided answering the wrong question. *He knows his business,* thought Sean. *Now he has another piece of the puzzle. He takes it all in: he listens and observes and questions, and only loosens the grip on his own information when he has to. He'll find Lute.*

"Why do you think he left?" Sean asked again, now that the subject was on the table.

"Do you want me to look into that, Father?" asked the security chief, coldly matter-of-fact.

This time, Sean would not be drawn in. "Have you no idea?" he asked.

"You said it was because of a condition he has. Is there more?"

Sean studied his colleague's face. *He is masterful. Even if he doesn't already know—and I'm sure he couldn't—then he suspects something close to the truth. I can't lose him. I've got to keep him with me on this.* Finally he answered. "There *is* more, Morrie, and we'll discuss it soon. But while the trail is hot...?"

Staumper's slight nod acknowledged that he had important tasks to be attending. He turned his motorized chair and approached the door toward the outer office. Before opening it and leaving the priest, however, he spoke again. "If it's something that would drive Dr. Jonson away from his home here, it's probably something I need to know in order to locate him. Unless I know his motivation, I can scarcely guess his next steps."

He waited. Sean struggled to decide whether to reveal the secret he considered to be in the life-and-death plane. Thirty seconds stretched to a minute; one stretched to two. There was a rustle from the priest's direction and Staumper turned his chair around. Sean was on his knees at the simple wooden prie-dieu in the corner, his hands folded, his head drooped in defeat.

When the priest's second sigh in as many minutes suggested the prayer would not be brief, the security chief turned his wheelchair once again and departed, closing the door softly behind him.

Matthew 26:52

Then said Jesus unto him, "Put up again thy sword into his place: for all they that take the sword shall perish with the sword."

CHAPTER 13

PACIFIC OUTPOST

Seattle, Washington
Tuesday, June 18
1:00 a.m. Pacific Daylight Time

Lute waited for all the other passengers to get off United's Flight 111 before he got out of his seat and rummaged through the overhead bins, feigning a lost bag other than the briefcase he had kept at his seat. A tired-looking steward and stewardess came to help him search, both eyeing the empty cabin and the exit twice until at last he shrugged his shoulders and lifted his hands in a gesture of surrender.

"Where do I report it missing?" he asked with a look so worried he thought he deserved an Academy Award.

He listened to their directions and finally eased his world-weary body up the jetway and into the north satellite of Seattle-Tacoma International Airport—"Sea-Tac" to travelers around the world. His ruse had worked. There wasn't a single human being in sight except one blue-uniformed cleaning man emptying trash containers.

The flight attendants and pilots who followed him through the jetway soon passed him on their way to the escalator.

"Good night, Mr. Porter," said one as they pulled even with him. "Good luck finding that bag."

By the time he reached the underground tram, he was certain no one had been waiting for a tall, white-haired scholar, regardless of nom-de-plane. His now rumpled gray slacks, wilted blue blazer and *probably smelly dress shirt,* he thought, belied almost non-stop travel for the past 28 hours. He was exhausted.

I'm panicking, he decided. *I could have just gone to the major newspaper in San Diego with this news. I should have. Coulda, shoulda, woulda. Damn the adrenaline. And now I'm delusional, flying all the way up the West Coast using the second false ID I got in Jerusalem. If Sean sent someone to San Diego for me, they didn't trace me by airlines. They probably still haven't figured out 'K. Rose.' Could they? No, they just got lucky and called my only sister. Now all my safeties are spent: no more fake ID's. Gotta find a connection in Seattle. I need sleep.*

Lute used a direct-connect phone at the hotel/motel kiosk and located an available room at the Sea-Tac Inn. The clerk on the phone told him it was the closest motel that still had a late shuttle running.

Thank God for Christiana's cash, he mused on the drive down Pacific Highway. *These same-day flights are expensive. I've got to go ahead with this thing, or else quit and go back to Israel with my tail between my legs. One or the other, and soon.*

His head drooped; he snapped awake as the shuttle braked quickly to avoid a swerving driver. *I'm so tired.*

Once more he lost control of his eyelids. The driver had to wake him when they arrived at the motel.

Barely maneuvering himself out of the bus, Lute shuffled to the desk, signed a registration card, paid cash, took his key, and somehow made it to his room. He fell into a chair to remove the shoes from his aching feet, and was asleep before he could move to the bed.

* * *

South of Seattle
Tuesday, June 18
1:55 p.m.

Consciousness returned slowly after he had slept twelve hours. Finally awake enough to remember where he was, Lute crawled from the floor—where he had slumped sometime during his long sleep—to the bedside. He pulled himself up to look at a clock on the table.

Almost two o'clock, Lute mused. *Must be afternoon here. Midnight in Jerusalem. The start of Ari ben Kader's shift for nearly twenty-five years; month in, month out, the most reliable security guard we ever had. I wonder what they've told him—told the whole staff—about my abrupt departure. Or if they've even mentioned it. Almost midnight there. A new day is about to begin in the Holy Land.*

The irony of the *kairos* thought caught Lute by surprise, and he chuckled aloud.

Finally on his feet, he looked around the nondescript room for his briefcase. He could feel his pulse quicken as the case was nowhere to be seen. Nearing a state of panic, he flipped on the bathroom light and looked there, to no avail. Returning to the main room, he picked up the telephone and pressed zero for the operator. In the few seconds it took before he was connected, Lute realized he had a small problem.

"Sea-Tac Inn."

"Operator, this is, ah, John Porter in room ... well, I'm not exactly sure what room I'm in. I came in so late last night."

"You're in room 160, Mr. Porter. I can tell on my readout here."

Lute chuckled. "Thank you. Listen, I was exhausted last night and may have left my briefcase at the desk when I checked in. Is it there, by chance?"

"There was a briefcase left in the office last night and it is locked safely away. But I believe it belongs to someone else, Mr. Porter."

Lute hoped there was no trace of anxiety in his voice as he answered. "The one I left is the thick, over-nighter style, it's black and has a luggage tag with a business card for 'Lute Jonson' at the Rockefeller Museum in Jerusalem."

"Just a moment, please," said the clerk, and switched the line to music-on-hold.

Lute waited, eyes wide, breathing shallowly, insisting to himself obdurately that such clear identification should avoid any problem in recovering the priceless package.

"Mr. Jonson?"

"Yes," Lute said quickly, then recovered. "I mean, yes, that's the name on the briefcase. I'm John Porter."

"Well, it's a little unusual, of course. Do you know the combination to the lock on it?"

Lute confirmed that he did.

"I suspect if you'll open it down here at the office that should suffice as proof that we can release it to you," the clerk said. "I hope you understand we need to be careful of releasing property, especially without identification matching the tags."

Lute said he certainly approved and was soon introducing himself in the office. The clerk placed the black briefcase on the counter with the handle facing his guest. Lute quickly rotated the lock-dial numbers on each of the two hasps, and released them. Nothing happened. He stared at the balky hasps which had not popped open, and felt his cheeks redden. The clerk's hand reached over to touch the rear of the case.

"Well…" Lute stammered. He rolled the lock numbers again, slowly and more carefully. With a lump in his throat he pressed the two releases again.

The clerk nodded and smiled as both hasps snapped open. "If you'll sign this property receipt form, it's all yours, Mr. Porter. Sorry to inconvenience you."

Back in his room, Lute immediately opened the briefcase and found the package hidden just where he had replaced it at Christiana's home. It clearly had not been tampered with. The precious scroll fragments were safe. He breathed a sigh of relief that the previous night's exhaustion had not cost him an incalculable loss, but he excoriated himself for such carelessness.

Lute spent the next forty-five minutes showering, shaving and attempting to make himself presentable. His one clean shirt from the briefcase was wrinkled, but hanging it and his slacks next to the steamy shower brought them back to life. He returned to the office to pay for another night, then followed the clerk's directions to a Denny's restaurant two blocks away to satisfy the stomach devils which had been growling.

By three-thirty, Lute was back in his motel room. Following the simple plan he'd decided on during lunch, he looked up a number in the Seattle phone book and dialed. His heart sank as the phone rang six times, seven, eight. He realized he had all his eggs in one basket in Seattle, and an omelet pan seemed to be descending toward that cluster. Nine rings, ten. With shoulders sagging, he placed the phone back in its cradle, but a split second before the disconnect, Lute thought he heard something. He quickly redialed.

"Hello?"

Thank God! Lute exulted silently.

"Hello, Harald Ericksen?"

"Speaking."

Lord, it's in your hands, now. If You don't make this work, I don't know what to do.

"Harald, how good to hear your voice. This is Lute Jonson, a voice out of your past. Do you remember me from St. Olaf?"

"Hello, Lute. Of course I remember. Perhaps you've forgotten that I attended a session you conducted at the American Archaeological Association conference in New York in ... when? 1972 or '73?"

Yes!

"Yes, I do remember, Harald. I do indeed." Lute drew a deep breath, suddenly unsure of how to proceed, and more than a little worried he might screw up this opportunity to do what he must.

"Where are you, Lute?"

"Well, I'm in Seattle, matter of fact, on a kind of no-forewarning trip. I'm here today and possibly tomorrow, and wondered what your schedule was like. I've followed some of your papers in the journals, of course, and have often thought about touching base again."

Harald did not jump in immediately with an offer of hospitality, but Lute remembered him to be quite reserved. Harald had been a straight-A student during their St. Olaf College days, studying when Lute was courting, and working for their mentor in archaeology when Lute was swimming to build back the strength that rheumatic fever had robbed him of in childhood.

"I'm honored," Harald replied. "It's not many old classmates who get to rub elbows with the world's premiere Dead Sea Scrolls scholar, let alone an old archaeology classmate."

"Let's both go easy on the word 'old,' eh?" laughed Lute.

"As luck would have it, my schedule is open today. My senior seminar meets Mondays and Fridays this summer, and I'm just puttering in my backyard this afternoon. I almost didn't make it in to answer the phone because of that. You called twice just now, did you?"

"Yes, that was me. Harald, are you sure you can spare a little time? It would mean a great deal to me. I mean, I need some help here in Seattle and you're the perfect person. But if it's any trouble...?"

Lute held his breath and once again chastised himself. *Damn it! He already said yes, so why press the issue? Why am I so fawningly concerned about imposing on people? And besides, if I'm going to conserve my remaining cash, I've got to ask him for transportation and food. Damn! I had the answer I wanted and now I may have screwed it up.*

"Don't be silly. May I pick you up somewhere? I won the department's split-club raffle this week and got a certificate: dinner for two at Ivar's on the waterfront. Interested?"

"If it's not too much trouble. I'm at the Sea-Tac Inn, near the airport at 192nd and Pacific Highway. And listen, I know it sounds odd, but I would appreciate your not mentioning my being in town to anyone. I'm on a kind of speculative mission."

"All right. Sounds mysterious. Shall I see you about six?"

"That would be wonderful. I'm in room 160. *Munga tusen takk.*"

Harald deflected Lute's Norwegian phrase for "many thousand thanks." "Your gratitude belongs to my departmental colleagues, not me. Besides, I'll have to translate the *'tusen'* for them. I usually just say *'takk'* or, in my more effusive moments, *'munga takk'*."

Lute chuckled, and they signed off. Like a child relieved of a great fear, the 68-year-old international scholar fell to his knees by the motel bed.

Thank you, Heavenly Father. Forgive me for ignoring the exhortation You repeated so often. From the first book of the Bible to the last. In Jesus' name, Amen.

Genesis 15:1

After these things the word of the Lord came unto Abram in a vision, saying, *Fear not*, Abram: I am thy shield, and thy exceeding great reward.

Revelation 1:17

When I saw him, I fell at his feet as though dead. Then he placed his right hand on me and said: "*Do not be afraid*. I am the First and the Last. I am the Living One...."

CHAPTER 14

COMMUNION BEGINS

The Seattle Waterfront
Tuesday evening

Ivar's Acres of Clams on Alaskan Way gave no hint of being the local landmark restaurant that it was. The blue and white exterior and awnings barely distinguished it, and even the three-foot-tall letters of the "IVAR'S" sign were not all that much more notable than others on the waterfront. Nonetheless, a line extended out the front door and more than thirty feet down the sidewalk. Although it still refused to take reservations after all these years, Ivar's had no difficulty attracting customers. Its fresh clams and other Pacific Northwest seafoods were legendary. The unpretentious ambiance and reasonable prices – and the culinary mystique of Ivar's Famous Clam Chowder – kept the locals and visitors coming.

"You don't mind waiting?" asked Harald as they drove past in search of parking.

"Not at all," Lute answered. "Do they have some quiet booths? We might profit from a little privacy for part of our discussion."

Harald offered assurances and they were soon standing like two well-dressed string bean professors at the end of the line of casually-clad and generally more portly tourists. Dr. Ericksen looked much like Dr. Jonson: at six-foot-three, Harald was two inches taller, but both were slender, blue-eyed, dapper, with normally serious demeanors occasionally broken by smiles. Or even by laughter, in Lute's case. Harald's light brown hair was crewcut to a length of about half-an-inch. He wore dark brown pleated slacks and a rich herringbone jacket. His tieless white button-down shirt was open at the collar.

The two old college friends continued the reminiscing they had begun on the drive in from the airport motel.

"How about Ole Christoferson?" offered Lute. "Do you remember him?"

"Clearly," nodded Harald. "Intro to Religion, Old Testament 201. I think we had him for other classes. Powerful teacher, one of St. Olaf's finest."

"And a great sense of humor. I still remember his first words in Religion 101. He said, 'I will not grade you on your piety, but on your knowledge. *God* will grade you on your piety.'" Lute grinned broadly and Harald smiled.

"What I remember," said Harald, "was him talking about the importance of *place* throughout human history. I'll never forget. He said the word *adam* meant *mud creature*, or *man* in ancient Hebrew, and *adama* meant *ground* or *earth*. To a young college student who couldn't wait to get away from his parents' farm, the close connection between the soil and humankind didn't ring true; matter of fact, it struck me as so odd I've remembered it all this time. To a retirement-age bachelor professor who took great satisfaction in getting my hands dirty in my garden this afternoon, it is profoundly meaningful. Whoever said education is wasted on the young was right."

Though he nodded with Harald, Lute was not quite ready for the conversation to turn serious. "And Thunk-Poof

Christians? Do you remember that?" Lute asked. Harald shook his head quizzically.

"Ole said, 'Some of you may have come from Thunk-Poof Christian homes, but we shall change that.' He could see we were all afraid to ask what that was, so he explained. 'Those are so-called Christian men and women who pull their unused Bibles down from the bookshelf once a year, first slapping the cover to raise the dust, and then blowing it away: thunk! poof!'"

Lute made himself laugh with his mimed recollection, and a young couple standing in front of them turned with grins to see who the comedian was.

"Lars Longaard. Remember him?" offered Harald.

"Of course: chapel organist. What hymns were his favorites?" Lute challenged his old classmate's memory.

"You'll have to make these trivia questions much harder," said Harald. "Who could forget Dr. Longaard playing 'A Mighty Fortress,' and 'For All The Saints, Who From Their Labors Rest'? Oh, and 'Once To Every Man And Nation, Comes The Moment To Decide'?" Harald began to lightly drum fingers on his crossed arms to the old standard melodies playing in his mind. Lute's eyes narrowed briefly when the latter title struck him as timely to his mission.

"Speaking of hymns," said Lute, "my pastor in Jerusalem announced several weeks ago that he had picked a non-traditional one for a baptism that morning. And yet the title seemed quite fitting: 'Oh For A Faith That Will Not Shrink.'"

Once again, Lute grinned broadly and Harald smiled. *He hasn't changed much,* Lute thought. *He was always more reserved than the rest. I'm not sure this is going to work.*

They were seated after a surprisingly short wait. They ordered a bottle of Washington State sauvignon blanc and their dinners; Harald asked for pan-fried Quilcene oysters, and after kiddingly asking the waiter if they had the much-maligned Norwegian delicacy *lutefisk*, Lute decided on the Captain's Plate sampler. Afterward, Lute knew he had to ease into the subject. He looked through their own dining room into a noisier and more open one, grateful that Harald had asked for a booth for conversation. Though the restaurant was quite full, they were secluded in a high, scalloped-back booth on the wall opposite large windows which overlooked the crusty, weathered Pier 54 sticking out into Elliott Bay. Most diners in both rooms had fixed their attention on the approaching Washington State Marine Highway ferryboat.

"What's happening, Lute? I must confess I am flattered that you would call and ask to see me. You've been such a luminary in world archaeology for all these years."

Lute cleared his throat but then paused as their server approached with wine, completed the rituals of approval, and poured both glasses. The young man nested the bottle in a wine bucket and left.

Lute peered into his wine glass. *Lord, don't desert me. Give me the right words. If You want me to do what I believe You do, don't let me fuck it up now.*

He almost laughed aloud at the earthiness with which he addressed his Maker, but choked that laugh down with the realization that his liberal language—let alone the incredible secret he was finally prepared to release—would not seem funny at all to most Christians. *You are closer than any friend to me, Lord. But forgive me—correct me—if my familiarity offends You. I'm just following your disdain for Picky Little Rules.*

Harald broke the silence. "You've turned quiet. I sensed from your telephone call that you're working on something very special. I assume it's related to the Scrolls...?"

Lute looked up and began. "Yes. Yes, it surely is. Do you mind if I ask a couple of questions before I tell you about that? It's quite strange, I know, for me to call you out of the blue and want to talk about these things. But if you still have that intellectual curiosity I admired in you at St. Olaf, we'll get to the rest. You willing?"

"I suppose so. Assuming they're not *too* personal."

Lute searched his old classmate's eyes for a sign of humor, but Harald looked quite serious. "They might *be* kind of personal, my friend."

Harald's eyes dropped to his own wine glass, and he began to worry its base in a gentle circle on the heavy white tablecloth. "In that case," he said looking up, "I'll assume this conversation is quite confidential." He added quickly, "I don't know why, Lute, but I always trusted you. Even though you were popular and gregarious, and I was neither, I trusted you. You seemed less shallow than others with those social qualities."

"Strange, isn't it?" Lute shook his head slowly. "Strange how we can be yanked back in time to another life we've led with other people—and can return to the same relationships with them."

"I don't think it's a matter of *can*," Harald said. "We *must*. We're forced to it, regardless of preference. I went back to Minnesota six years ago and saw some of our classmates at the fortieth reunion. It was like we never left Northfield. I *wanted* to be different with them now—I am at least *somewhat* more confident and social than I was in those days. But there was some kind of magnetic force holding me in the role I occupied in their company between 1941 and '45. I went back to being 'Harald the Outsider.' And since all of us guys at St. Olaf in those war years were rejects of a kind—physically ineligible for the military—I felt like I was outside the outsiders."

Lute nodded agreement, and then steered the subject back. "Thanks for what you said about trust. I'm about to need it. I hope you can answer these questions for me. Comfortably."

Harald lifted his glass in a mock toast and held it long enough to communicate "let the games begin."

"How's your faith?" Lute asked.

"Strong."

Once it was evident Harald was not going on, Lute laughed and explained, "No, no, this is not 'Free Association.' You get to answer with more than one word!"

"I have a strong Christian faith," Harald began. "I was a member at University Lutheran until six or seven years ago when it became clear to me that they had become much more, well, *humanist*, than I think a church should be."

"Really?"

"Yes. It seems to me that the Lutherans and the Presbyterians and the Episcopalians—maybe some others, I'm not sure—are veering away from the true Christian faith. I'm not comfortable with that. I still believe the gospels quite literally, for instance, and ... and this is so amazing to me: I'm beginning to feel like a minority."

"You don't think most Americans are Christian?"

Harald shook his head. "I mean I don't think most *Christians* are Christian anymore. The other, about most Americans, is true, too. It seems church attendance is far lower than it ever has been. But even church people seem to be softening on all the basic principles of our faith."

"So you have quit the church?"

"I quit the *Lutheran* Church. I visited many of the churches around the University District, and am now a member of a conservative independent congregation near my home."

Harald saw the waiter approaching with their dinner plates, and quickly added, "Forgive me, Lute. You hit my 'hot button,' as they say on the campus. I'm sure this is not what you wanted to discuss."

"Please don't apologize. It's exactly what I need to hear."

After the dinners were properly placed and the waiter dismissed with thanks, Harald folded his hands and bowed his head. Lute interrupted. "I haven't done that for a long time, out in public, I mean. Would you say your grace aloud for us?"

"I still say the old Norse prayer my father prayed on the farm in North Dakota." He bowed his head again and spoke reverently. Lute found himself remembering the traditional words' English translation.

"I Jesu navn går vi til bord."

In Jesus' name we go to the table.

"Å spise, drikke, på dit ord."

To eat, to drink, according to Thy Word.

"Dig, Gud, til aere, og oss til gavn."

To honor Thee, O God, and to benefit ourselves.

"Så får vi mat i Jesu navn."

So we get our food in Jesus' name.

"Amen," said Lute. "How good it is to hear those blessed old words."

The two turned to their meals and ate silently for a little. Shortly, Lute resumed his questioning.

"Family? You mentioned bachelor, so no wife or children?"

"Never found a woman good enough to overlook my bad habits," the old professor recited smoothly. "My only family were my parents, and they both passed in 1963. Father died of a heart attack a month before his 65th birthday, in March, and Mother's health deteriorated immediately. Classic case of a broken heart. She died the day after Christmas."

Lute nodded understandingly. The two lapsed into a comfortable silence for several minutes, eating and watching the marine and avian activity on Puget Sound. Then Lute began again. "Any hobbies?"

"Well, my gardening. And I work out at a health club now. I gave up smoking ten years ago, and have tried to live more healthily since. I have friends at the club, and at church, and at a Macintosh Users club I attend occasionally. But my real interest is the digs at Forks, out on the Olympic Peninsula."

"Aboriginal settlements?" asked Lute, his professional curiosity stimulated.

"Yes. Fascinating. We've carbon-dated what appear to be campfire remains back to 3500 BCE. Bones, charcoal, flint at the same levels." Harald looked at his scholastic colleague and found the glint of true interest in the traveler's eyes.

"Do you still get gooseflesh sometimes?" Harald asked.

Lute nodded enthusiastically. "Yes, of course. I think if I ever find myself too sophisticated to be astounded that I am holding—whatever the object, you know?—that was last held by human hands *thousands* of years ago, well, I'll retire. It's not something you think about all the time...."

Harald nodded agreement.

"...but when you *do*, if your skin doesn't pop, you're just not human."

Despite sensing a collegial safety growing between them, Lute began to fret. They had nearly finished eating, and he had barely begun to get at what he really needed from Harald. He realized that newly seated diners were now too close for comfort, and he didn't want to broach the *kairos* within earshot of strangers.

Lute suggested they continue the discussion back at his motel room, but Harald was reluctant. After the check was presented and Harald had given the waiter his certificate along with cash for the bar tab, Lute tantalized his old classmate.

"I have news about the Scrolls, Harald. Important news. I need your advice and help. And there is an urgency that I can't fully explain here."

"Then let's continue this at my home, shall we?"

Thank you, Lord.

"How long will you be in town, Lute?"

"Only a couple of days."

"Maybe you should save on your motel bill. I have a student apartment above my home which is vacant this summer. Would you care to use it? We could go back for your luggage first."

Lute decided not to explain that the only baggage he had been able to take on his rather hasty departure from Jerusalem was the briefcase he had between his ankles at the moment. He counter-offered: "Can we talk about that possibility when we get out of here? I'm stuffed. I would love to walk a few minutes before we head out. Possible?"

"Not possible. Necessary."

Again he corrects and improves my choice of words, thought Lute. *A true academic. When I show him the Scrolls, I wonder if he'll grade them.*

The two walked outside into an azure Seattle evening. As they passed the entrance, Lute noted the punning sign Ivar's was famous for: "Keep Clam."

Keep Clam. Fear Not. You keep sending the message, Lord. When will we hear?

CHAPTER 15

KAIROS INTERRUPTUS

Seattle
Tuesday evening

Lute Jonson looked over Harald's professional bookcase as one looks through photo albums at a family reunion. Many of the titles were familiar to the Dead Sea Scrolls scholar, even though they were concentrated on the archaeology of the Americas. It was the comfortable and learned study of an American professor in semi-retirement, kept at home now rather than on campus.

Harald returned from the kitchen proffering one wine glass for Lute and holding another. The two men raised them in silent toast and sipped.

"What's this wine?" asked Lute.

"It's a Château Ste. Anne Cabernet Sauvignon. Their vineyards are on the Columbia River in the southeast corner of the state. Someday they'll probably find this wine's so good because of nuclear radiation out of Hanford, the federal site down there."

Lute grinned. *The old boy does have a sense of humor! He'll need it before this night is out.*

Harald moved toward two overstuffed armchairs and motioned an invitation to his old classmate to sit on the right, facing the bookcase and desk. Lute looked into his colleague's eyes.

"Just a couple more questions, Harald. And then, an interesting story." *After that, I'll ask your forgiveness for the understatement of the millennium.*

"I guess the most important question I have for you is: how well-connected are you among Seattle media people? Do you know publishers, editors, news directors, reporters? In radio, TV, print?"

Harald squinted. "I knew the *Times'* religion editor, Andy Boren, fairly well." Lute brightened until Harald finished his thought, "But he died about a year ago. Don't know the new one. She's Jewish, I think. I don't think the *Post Intelligencer* has a reporter on the beat. And I've never met any of the beautiful people they call TV Journalists."

"Oh, my. You have no contacts at all, now? Nobody in the Seattle area who...?" Lute's voice trailed off in disappointment.

"I have met the general manager of the local NPR station a couple of times at Lutheran functions."

"NPR?"

"Sorry, National Public Radio—it's public broadcasting, non-commercial radio; it does excellent news broadcasts early mornings and late afternoons, and plays jazz the rest of the time." Lute brightened again. "Actually," Harald continued, "it's not the local station, which is connected to the University of Washington, but the Tacoma station. It has a strong signal here and seems to be very active in news. I often hear their local reports on the national programs."

Lute sat forward in his chair. "They do feeds for the national network?"

"Fairly frequently. I believe they are one of the network's prime affiliates on the West Coast."

Lute pressed. "And you know the general manager?"

"I have met her a couple of times. The station is located on the campus at Pacific Lutheran University down in Tacoma. Beautiful place. She had me speak about aboriginal sacred grounds at a forum there. About two years ago."

"She's still there? You could call and get through to her?"

Harald nodded. "Lute, please tell me what's happening. Curiosity is consuming me."

The out-of-towner again looked into Harald's eyes. *Lord, here it is. It's time. If it's not Your will for these Scrolls to be released, strike me dumb. Let us be interrupted; give me a stroke if You must.*

Lute realized his childlike imploring was irrational, but he knew his faith was, too. Or, more accurately, not "against reason," but "above reason." Supra-rational.

"I'm almost there, Harald." Lute waited briefly for God's sign. The quiet soon brought the sound of a hallway grandfather clock to the foreground of their attention. Its reassuring tick, tick, tick was punctuated shortly by Westminster chimes signaling the half-hour. Lute looked at his watch, now adjusted to West Coast time, and noted it was 8:30.

"Is it bad news, Lute?"

"Actually, I have come to realize it's incredibly *good* news, even though many people will have great difficulty with it."

The classroom professor exercised skills honed over many years of drawing out reticent students. "Can you start by telling me why you left Jerusalem? Did you have a disagreement with your colleagues?"

"No, no. I mean, Sean—that's my co-director on the international study team—Sean doesn't want me to talk about these things to anyone, so it's a disagreement from that standpoint. But we haven't had a blow-up or anything." Lute stood and walked to Harald's world globe. He turned it casually, stopping at the Middle East. "No, it's just that I've had an increasingly strong feeling over the past couple of years that this secret will die with me. And it can't. It shouldn't."

"Are you ill?"

Lute shook his head and his eyes met Harald's, registering appreciation for the concern expressed. "No, but a bus might hit me. A terrorist's bomb could make mincemeat out of my flesh. And this secret has been locked away, literally, for *forty-three* years. I think it *is* a growing sense of my own mortality that has brought this on. My Naomi died four years ago, you know, and ever since I've had periods of intense preoccupation about my own … well, death."

Lute's eyes focused absently as he remembered his wife. "She died unexpectedly when I was in London. We had agreed I wouldn't call during the three days of the conference I was attending, and they reached me with a message at Heathrow just before I boarded the plane to return to her. A meter reader had found her. It was a heart attack; she was sitting in a lawn chair in our secluded little back yard."

Lute's eyes welled up, and the painful recollections caused long pauses between the phrases he offered his old friend.

"She had lain there two or three days ... a chilly January 16th, but still ... the flies and insects ... they suggested I not see her." Lute turned away for a few moments and then back when he had composed himself. "Sorry. It hits you at the oddest times, you know."

Harald added, "And especially when you're tired?"

Lute nodded.

"I think you should take me up on my offer to stay here, Lute. The apartment upstairs is fully furnished, the linens are clean. I'm sure you're exhausted from travel—Jerusalem is what, twelve time zones away?"

Lute shook his head. "Just ten."

"How would a good night's sleep sound? A big breakfast, and maybe a drive to the Olympic Peninsula—God's crowning glory—while we talk about your news tomorrow. I could even run back to your motel for your luggage while you turn in, if you like."

Smiling again, Lute tried to match Harald's sensitivity. "But it's not fair to delay this longer. You already said your curiosity is high."

"So it is. But I get the feeling this is not a five minute explanation. True?" Lute nodded and Harald continued. "Then let's talk leisurely on a drive tomorrow. I'm happy to wait, if your schedule allows for that."

Relieved, Lute agreed, briefly explaining that no trip to the motel was necessary. Picking up the case from beside his armchair, Lute followed his host to the upstairs apartment, took note of where the towels and extra blankets were, and agreed he'd come downstairs whenever he awoke in the morning. Harald departed after wishing his guest a restful night, and Lute realized how fatigued he still was despite his long sleep earlier. He brushed his teeth and prepared to retire. Finally, approaching the queen-sized bed with its tan, corduroy-covered comforter, Lute sank to his knees, folded his hands and closed his eyes.

Oh, God, I'm tired. I know You'll love me even if I ramble. I love You, Lord. I worship You. You know my heart, and I beg you not to allow me to do anything contrary to Your will. Purge all delusions and false teachings from me. If, indeed, it is You—not me—who wills this kairos *for Your world, then give me courage for the task, and relief from the agony of these doubts. I fear people's reactions to Your* kairos *and how they'll treat me, your messenger.*

Yes, just as You say. You repeatedly say "Fear Not," so I'll try. Good night, Lord.

Lute Jonson pulled himself into bed and lay in perfect repose. He reached down to touch himself. *Thanks for every good and perfect gift. Including this one.* He smiled. Too tired to finish, the world's foremost Dead Sea Scrolls scholar turned onto his stomach and fell asleep thinking of the only woman he had ever loved.

CHAPTER 16

NAOMI

Jerusalem
1952

As Naomi Rosheva silently read the page Lute Jonson had just given her, his thoughts raced through the events of the prior evening's intense discussion. How he had "called the question" to her, blurting out that he could no longer continue their breezy dating conversations—staying at the shallow end of the emotional pool—since his heart was suddenly finding depths he had never known before. How she had then confessed she had been feeling the same, but had continued being light and playful, for fear that turning serious would have driven him away. How she had said *she* had fallen in love, but worried *he* might merely have fallen 'in like.' What a night! They had hugged and cried and prayed. He could not remember the walk home from her apartment after that chaste event, except for a sense that he had literally floated above the sidewalk.

Lute studied her now across the small restaurant table where they sat. *She's beautiful*, he thought, *and an answer to my prayers*. Twenty-three years old, stunning brown eyes, blonde hair in an understated but stylish bouffant, the kindest face that he had ever known—eyes and mouth, mostly, but also the little button nose that made every other woman's look large. He loved the way she struggled to "stay cool" when she laughed, hunching her shoulders up and covering her mouth with her hands, but never able to keep from exploding with laughter. He loved her spirit: enthusiastic about any activity she engaged in, genuinely interested in whatever person the world put in front of her, neither cowering before rich people he had introduced her to nor condescending to street vendors they had passed on their walks.

Her voice interrupted his silent adoration; she read aloud the poem he had written in the wee hours of the previous night.

"Today I stood and paced, and sat and thought,

And finally prayed alone:

I asked to know which way to go? Whether to call, whether no?

At last the Hamlet-mantle fell; I made a desperate call.

At last you came and talked with me. And that has changed it all.

Tonight *we* sat and talked, and stood and kissed,

And finally prayed together.

The *you* and *me*, the *he* and *she*,

Now useless words. Thank God it's *we*."

Naomi looked up from the poem on the sheet in front of her, into the eyes of young Dr. Luther Jonson. "It *is*, now, isn't it? It's *we*."

"Turn it over," he said.

The four words on the back of the page—"Will you marry me?"—seemed to burn her eyes; she blinked hard. She looked back at the American she had been dating for eight months. "You know I will, Lute."

They clutched hands across the table. They stared into each other's eyes, and Lute's heart soared above the ancient city he had come to love over these past six years. Though the prior evening had *almost* convinced him she felt the same, now it was absolute. His beloved would be his bride. Ecstasy filled him. His heart raced; his arms were masses of goose bumps. *Yes*, he thought to himself, *even the little soldier is twitching with delight and anticipation*. The only woman he had ever truly desired wanted him as he wanted her. *I've never known what it was like to be absolutely filled until now*, he thought. *You are my everything. Thank You, Lord, for this incredible woman.*

"Who had the Roquefort?" asked their server, crashing into the idyllic moment.

Lute and Naomi looked at the aging waiter and back at each other. They burst into laughter simultaneously.

Lute recovered first, feeling bad for the befuddled waiter. "Salad? You expect me to eat *salad*, at a moment like *this*?" Naomi covered her mouth as she continued to laugh. The waiter straightened up. He looked at both salad plates with a quizzical expression, then around at the nearby tables to see if he had missed something important.

"The most beautiful woman in the world just said she'd marry me!" explained Lute, staring once again into Naomi's eyes.

She still ignored the man now standing forlornly beside them, except to say, "I'm not hungry now. Sorry."

"It's all right, leave them," Lute told the now grinning waiter.

For years afterward they bantered good-naturedly about whether either one had touched those salads, and whether Lute had thought to cancel their entrée orders. Whenever he told the story to others, he concluded with, "I'll never again get engaged right after ordering an expensive dinner at the King David Hotel."

* * *

November 1961

Lute drove their black Volkswagen under the carport, got out and stretched, and finally pulled his luggage out of the back seat. With another Dead Sea Scrolls conference behind him, Lute was glad to be back to his wife and his own bed. He was happy to see her standing behind the screen at the door to the apartment.

"Hi honey," she said with her winning smile. "I missed you."

"I missed you, too, babe." He hugged her a long time, then carried his two American Tourister cases inside, awaiting her inquiry about the conference. She was always so good about drawing him out. But there was silence this time as he pushed his luggage into their one small bedroom for later unpacking. He slumped into his favorite upholstered swivel rocker.

She approached him with two bowls and a pixie grin. "Any idea why I might have a craving for this?" She lowered one bowl into his hands. There was a scoop of vanilla ice cream with a slice of kosher dill pickle stuck into it where she usually tucked a little rolled waffle-stick.

"What?" he asked. Then he realized. "No! NO! Are you...?"

"Yes!" She danced in front of him, seductively highlighting her belly with her free hand. "YES!"

He stood and grabbed her. Their tight embrace culminated years of waiting. He laughed in joy at her typical Naomi playfulness: ice cream and pickles to announce pregnancy. Putting an end to their fertility anxieties, they would actually be parents. He was about to become a father!

I love you, babe. The words caromed through his head repeatedly. Not only to spend his life with her, but to share parenthood, to have a child together. *Praise God from Whom all blessings flow!* he sang inside. *You are my sunshine, my Holy Son-shine! And you, too, little one! I love you already!*

* * *

April 1962

Lute paced in the waiting room for what seemed like hours. Finally a doctor he had not met before came through the door and inquired of the half dozen men there, "Dr. Jonson?" Lute walked quickly to him. The man in surgical whites took Lute by the arm and led him back through the door into the quiet of the antiseptic hall beyond.

"I'm Dr. Schlosser. I assisted your obstetrician Dr. Samuels in the surgery. I'm sorry, Dr. Jonson. Your baby did not survive. Your wife is quite weak right now—Dr. Samuels is attending her—but her vital signs have improved in the past forty minutes, and I believe she will continue to full recovery. As he told you when you consented to the emergency C-section, the fetus had severe bradycardia—slow heart rate—and the only chance she had was immediate delivery. Even so we could not resuscitate. It was a girl. Her Apgar scores were all zeroes. I'm terribly sorry. You may see your wife soon. A nurse will come for you. I'll be in to see you both in an hour or so and answer any questions. Is there anything I can get for you?"

Lute shook his head absently and somehow soon found himself standing next to the window in the waiting room. *A daughter, Lord?* He fought a losing battle to control the tears welling up. *You brought a daughter to us, and took her away? A tiny girl, to carry the "we" of Naomi and me into the future? So close, God? And then You take her back? Why would You do that? What is "close" to You?*

What could you possibly lose by letting her live? I'll come through this, but Naomi, your dear Naomi—You'll break her heart! Why? Why would a good God torture His children? You have no right ... You have no fucking RIGHT!

Then, contrite and fearful that his Maker might take righteous umbrage, Lute retreated. *Nevertheless, not my will but Thine be done. It's Jesus' prayer. And mine. But please, PLEASE take care of my Naomi now. Lord, please give her back to me.*

CHAPTER 17

WINS AND LOSSES

Jerusalem
Wednesday, June 19, 1991
7:10 a.m.

Father Sean O'Derry pulled his maroon '84 Fiat into its assigned parking spot behind the Rockefeller Museum. Even as he uncharacteristically hurried his arthritic bones out of the small rusty car, he stopped briefly to read the reserved sign as he habitually did. Installed by Lute and colleagues two years earlier on the occasion of Sean's seventieth birthday, the 12" x 16" painted steel sign stood at eye level just ahead of the parking place to proclaim:

Parking Restricted
Fr. S. O'Derry
24 Hours
Violators Will Be Baptized

He did not grin today.

Inside, Morrie Staumper was waiting for him. The paraplegic nodded a greeting but both delayed speaking until they were behind the closed door of Sean's office.

"Have y'found him?"

"He's in Seattle."

"Seattle? He flew up the West Coast in the States yesterday?"

Staumper nodded assent.

"And you have agents, well, closing in?"

"Do we know precisely where he is in Seattle? No. Is the trail fresh? Yes."

The priest clenched his jaw. "You make it sound like Lute drops his boxer shorts every few hours." Their unsmiling eyes met.

"That's all I have, Father."

"No, it shan't be 'all I have.' Tell me about this fresh trail. Perhaps I can suggest an inquiry or two for your people."

Staumper recounted the meager facts unearthed: inquiries all over San Diego—including with employees at Lindbergh Field International Airport—had resulted in possible identification of Lute's picture by a United skycap. And that no destination was known—the skycap had only *seen* Lute, not carried his bags—but that lead had prompted personal and computer searches in the next widest circle of potential landing sites. An investigator in Seattle had traced what arrival times would have been probable if that Puget Sound city *had* been Lute's target, realized a late-night landing was likely, and had begun with visits to the nearby motels. A desk clerk remembered him because of a forgotten briefcase and a confusion over names. The scent, however, ended there, since Lute had signed in with a phony Minnesota address, paid cash, and not left any forwarding address or clue.

"I think our mailing list shows some contributors in the Seattle area; are you contacting them?" asked the old priest. "Have you checked Lute's address book for Seattle names?

Lutherans, relatives?" Sean thought a moment. "You might discreetly ask among the media. Religion reporters, you know. If anyone goes to church on the American West Coast any more, I think it's news." Neither man smiled at the sarcasm.

The security chief sat immobile but not tense in his wheelchair.

"Have you tried those ideas?" asked Sean anxiously.

"Yes."

"Any luck?"

"No."

Sean slumped. "Who can you go to now?"

Staumper's mobile motor whirred softly as he approached his superior's desk. "You."

Sean looked up with narrowed eyes, and stared unblinking at the enigmatic Staumper.

"You think I know where he is, Morrie?"

"If you wish me to find Dr. Jonson and bring him back, you must tell me the secrets he's carrying. Solving the puzzle without the basic clues is virtually impossible, Father. Sooner or later we'll lose his trail and he'll disappear. I must know what you know and what you suspect. Otherwise you handicap your own team." If Staumper recognized any personal irony in his statement, his face didn't show it.

Sean's eyes narrowed to tight, angry slits, then closed completely. As he opened them his entire face softened into resignation. "He's already won."

"Lute?" The priest nodded. "What has he won?"

"I believe he decided unilaterally to break a promise, Morrie. To reveal a secret we have repeatedly pledged not to tell anyone else. It's not just that you have to *find* him. You have to find him *fast*. And now you're telling me, if I want to bring him back—to reason with him, to remind him why we cannot tell that news to the world—I'll have to tell *you* the secret. So either he wins or I lose. Same-same."

"It will go no further than me," said Staumper in a flat voice.

"But if it goes to you, you'll use it—*as I would insist you should!*—to direct your people in Seattle. And your people are smart, Morrie. They'll put two and two together. They'll figure things out. Rumors start."

"Rumors are usually worse than the truth. Shall I call off the search?" Staumper backed his wheelchair up a few inches.

Sean's color drained as the horns of his dilemma became clear. He stood and began to pace toward the window overlooking the weedy, untended flower garden outside.

"No. No rumor can approach this truth, my friend. So I'll break silence. Share this news with you. Swear you to secrecy. Hope you're more successful than Lute and I, who swore the same oath to each other the first year we met—1947." He turned back to face Staumper.

"There are seven scroll fragments we've never reported, because we judged them too difficult for people to understand. All seven were nearly perfect. Quite readable. One was carbon-dated to almost exactly the beginning of the Common Era, as were others found near these seven."

Staring straight into Staumper's eyes, the scholar-priest continued with an eerie strength. "All seven have been kept in Lute's and my hidden fire-proof safe until now. They are missing. My Protestant co-director has stolen ancient parchments that describe Jesus of Nazareth, sketch incidents from His 'lost years' at Qumran, and explain that the community members there considered Him divine. It isn't all good news for us Christians, though. There are specifics. About His physical life. Stuff that could explode the Christian faith of millions and millions of people.

About His *sex* life, for God's sake. Now you know the urgency. Never has so much cat been stuffed into so loose a bag. You gotta find Lute, Morrie. Before he sets off a world-shaking explosion."

CHAPTER 18

FINALLY, HARALD'S KAIROS

On the road to Port Townsend, Washington
Wednesday, June 19, 1991
Noon

"I can't believe it, a 1970 Volvo! You bought it new then and you've owned it ever since?" Lute looked over at the old car's driver, and Harald returned the grin.

"Only a spendthrift buys a new car every year."

"But twenty-one years!" Lute feigned shock. "Nobody drives a car for twenty-one years!"

"At my Volvo dealer's there's a sign that says, 'Why celebrate St. Patrick's Day, when all he did was drive the snakes out of Ireland? Celebrate St. Olaf's Day! He drove the Volvos out of Sweden.'"

Lord, thought Lute as he grinned, *there's another sighting of a sense of humor.*

Aloud, he added, "My garage in Jerusalem has a sign that says, 'What's the use in having parts if you can't get service?'" Lute chuckled at his earthy joke, but noticed that Harald wasn't all that delighted with the double entendre.

Lute looked ahead, north up Route 16, through the endless column of firs lining both sides of this Olympic

Peninsula highway. The road was relatively flat, at least compared to the ones he imagined traversing the majestic Olympic Mountains a few miles to the west. Their snowy peaks occasionally came into view through breaks in the trees. It was all stunningly green beauty to one accustomed to the Middle East's barren desert lands. Lute watched as roadside patches of mustard-yellow Scotch Broom and gaudy, multi-hued Indian Paintbrush approached and passed. He took in the clean blue of the Pacific Northwest sky, punctuated with white cumulus clouds. It was a land that was easy to love, he guessed. Clearly worth the rain that made such verdure possible; Harald had said the region's precipitation was "worse by reputation than in actuality." Lute knew that characterization was true of stereotypes around the world, including his adopted Israel. Even in the worst days of the '80s, when every newspaper in the world carried a Minimum Daily Requirement of terrorism stories, the residents themselves went about their mundane lives for all but a few minutes a week, or a month. People everywhere seemed to need to hang their impressions of distant geographies on some kind of cliché hook.

"You're certainly pensive." Harald's words broke into Lute's stream of thought. "Are you trying to decide how to start telling me this news?"

Lute squeezed the briefcase between his heels again and thought about its incredible contents. Here, on a rural highway within a hundred miles of America's Pacific Coast, seven documents that were about to change the world rested in a black leather case. And he was about to begin the dress rehearsal for their world introduction.

"But no *pressure* on me!" Lute concluded aloud with an ironic grin.

"Pardon?"

"Sorry, Harald. Yes, I was thinking of that. And I was thinking how ironic that I should tell you—or anyone—my news in such a pacific environment. That's small 'p' pacific, although the capitalized version is clearly appropriate, too."

"Is it *devastating* news, Lute?"

"Oh, not so much *devastating* as, what, *monumental*? No, that's not right, either. Hmm. Maybe it is *devastating* to some. I . . . ."

Lute realized how pointless his present line of monologue was, and broke it off unfinished. It was time to begin the substance, and leave the reactions to the individual. No amount of prior manipulation, no quantity of intelligent setup, could possibly prepare every hearer to react as Lute might want. Maybe only four decades of quiet background thinking—as he'd had himself—would allow the world to accept God's newest *kairos*.

After locking his car door, Lute leaned a shoulder into it and began.

"I guess in a perfect world, I would have another couple of hours to do Q-and-A with you before laying it out. And we'll make time for that later, if you want. I *should* make sure that you remember what we learned in religion classes about the early Christian Gnostic heresy. I *should* do a little Socratic dialog with you about what an iconoclast our Jesus was, and ask whether you think He would piss off the religious authorities of *this* age if He were to return now. Mostly, I should go through the specific litany of Biblical stories of God's earlier *kairos* times. Let me just say this, old friend. Virtually *every one* of those begins . . . *begins!* . . . with God or His messenger actually saying the words, 'Fear not.' So I say it to you. Fear not the *kairos* you are about to experience."

Lute watched Harald for reaction, both to his laborious introduction and the awkwardly dramatic sound of the last sentence. Apparently intent on both driving and listening, Harald gave no hint of the impatience Lute suspected. *Maybe it is I who am impatient,* Lute thought. *Maybe only I need to get this out. Last chance, Lord! Stop me now, if this is not Your will.*

Harald said, "*Kairos?* What is 'a *kairos* time'? I'm not sure of the term."

"You know that 'chronos' is human time—the root word of 'chronology' and 'chronometer,' for instance. Well, '*kairos*' is 'God's time.' A Divine breakthrough into human events."

Harald nodded as if now remembering. He looked over at Lute and grimly asked, "Do the scrolls say Jesus was . . . ," he hesitated before finishing, "*mythic?*"

"Oh, no! No, no. Quite the opposite, and if my jerky start at telling you this story raised that fear, you can feel great relief!"

Almost on cue, Harald exhaled in relief. He removed his right hand from the steering wheel and flexed the fingers, then shook the tension out. He did the same with the other hand. A cautious driver, his eyes moved from the road to the mirrors to the speedometer and back to the road.

Lute took a deep breath and began. "There are seven scrolls which my colleague and I have never discussed with anyone until now. They actually name Jesus—'Yeshua ben Joseph,' a boy of Nazareth who had miraculous powers, and who was extraordinarily 'charismatic,' as we would say. They absolutely confirm the Jesus of history. And they tell of some in His own day who acknowledged Him the Christ of faith."

"But not everyone saw Him as the promised Messiah of Israel?" Harald asked.

"Not everyone."

"Carbon-dated gospels," whispered the professor. His eyes blazed wide open, and his grip tightened on the steering wheel.

"But the scrolls say more. They say he was fully human, Harald."

"He *was*! Of course He was. Did you ever doubt that?" Once again the driver stole a quick, safe glance sideways.

Lute stifled an urge to break in and instead allowed his old friend to continue.

"Lute, Jesus was fully *human*, and fully *divine*. It's two-thousand-year-old orthodoxy; it was true then and has withstood the heresies of time. If He had not been fully human, how could our redemption have been complete? If He had been a specter—God in 'apparent' human form—how could He have truly lived, or truly died, or truly risen to prove . . . ?" Harald's words were choked off in the emotion he apparently felt rising. He nodded to himself vigorously and finished, "That's the Gnostic heresy you mentioned: some thought He wasn't truly human. Now, proof. Lord God, Heavenly Father!" From Harald, it was a prayer.

Lute allowed the moment to settle. He noticed that the firs and flowers were passing slightly faster now; he leaned slightly to check the speedometer, and Harald noticed. They returned to a more stately Ericksenian speed.

"So," Lute finally said, "do you think Jesus peed?"

Harald frowned and darted a silent glance at his passenger.

"*Do* you?" Lute insisted.

"Yes, of course."

"Do you think his bowels filled, and that He moved them every day?"

Harald's dark face broke for a moment. "Are you trying to prove He was just a *regular* guy?"

Lute's hearty laugh filled the old Volvo, and even Harald joined him. But the driver soon turned quiet again, and Lute pushed on: "Answer me. Did Jesus defecate?"

"I fail to see where you're going with this," Harald said with renewed vexation. "It may not be sacrilegious but it's certainly self-evident and elementary. Frankly, it's uncomfortable. It's surely unnecessary to your point."

"Aren't some of those the words the scribes and Pharisees used to describe Jesus and His teachings?"

Harald glowered. "Thanks for including me in such company."

The two rode in silence for a couple of miles. Finally Harald spoke again. "Perhaps if I want to know what the Scrolls say I should maintain a scholarly curiosity, and not get defensive. I'm sorry. It's just . . . you're in hard territory. I don't know about *your* religious life, but mine hasn't included much thought about Jesus' bodily functions."

"It'll get much harder, Harald."

The driver sighed, "Please continue." Mild petulance was clear as he added, "And please, as they say, cut to the chase. I'm quite anxious to know if there is more to this *kairos*."

"Jesus—according to these parchments—was fully human. They mention His eating and drinking, His dung, and His sex life. He was, at the time of His residence at Qumran, sexually active."

"He was *married*?" Harald's eyes were exclamation points.

"No, not married. But He *was* monogamous, and it was with another major personage in the gospels."

Harald's gaze remained fixed on the road ahead and on the sign indicating that Port Townsend was 18 miles away.

"Are you saying the rumors through the ages are true? That He and Mary Magdalene were intimate?"

"Not Mary. Even more surprising, at least to us in this *enlightened* modern age. Although it has been suppressed for centuries, the Synod of Rome included four references to Jesus' lover when they confirmed the canon of official books of the Bible in 382 AD. His lover was John the Beloved Disciple, Harald. Jesus was gay."

John 13:21-23
. . . [Jesus] was troubled in spirit, and testi-fied, and said, "Verily, verily, I say unto you, that one of you shall betray me." Then the disciples looked one on another, doubting of whom he spake. Now there was leaning on Jesus' bosom one of his disciples, whom Jesus loved.

John 20:1-2
Early on the first day of the week, while it was still dark, Mary Magdalene went to the tomb and saw that the stone had been removed from the entrance. So she came running to Simon Peter and the other dis-ciple, the one Jesus loved, and said, "They have taken the Lord out of the tomb, and we don't know where they have put him!"

John 21:7
Therefore that disciple whom Jesus loved saith unto Peter, "It is the Lord . . . ."

John 21:20-23

Then Peter, turning about, seeth the disciple whom Jesus loved following; which also leaned on his breast at supper, and said "Lord, which is he that betrayeth thee?" Peter seeing him saith to Jesus, "Lord, and what shall this man do?" Jesus saith unto him, "If I will that he tarry till I come, what is that to thee? Follow thou me." Then went this saying abroad among the brethren, that that disciple should not die; yet Jesus said not unto him, "He shall not die;" but, "If I will that he tarry till I come, what is that to thee?"

CHAPTER 19

MANUSCRIPT 1Q-CETHER-3: YESHUA & JOHANAN

"From Cave 1 at Qumran. This is the scroll O'Derry brought me at 4:00 p.m. on Friday, December 9, 1948, the beginning of our '37-hour watch.' We didn't eat or sleep from Friday afternoon until the early hours Sunday morning. We discussed ad infinitum. Ended up postponing indefinitely a decision on what to do with it. Kept in my private file. Known only to the two of us. LJ 4-10-55"

YOUTH[S] PLAYFUL AS LAMBS. SPRINGTIME RAISES BLOOD FOR TH[   ]

NATHAN BEN SIMON PUNISHE[S] TRYING YOUTHS WITH BANISHMENT TO THE NIGHT. MORNING SUN RAISES DISCIPLINE

SONS OF LIGHT CLUSTER TO YESHUA. EVEN ELDERS FIND SPIRIT FULL [. . .] ALL QUESTION. YESHUA THINKS QUICKLY BUT WRI[TING] IN DIRT, DELAYS ANSWER UNTIL GROUP READY FOR LISTENING

HE [IS] 15 AND PURE OF HEART. HE VIOLATES COMMUNITY RULE[S] WITH INNOCENCE. BOYS TELL OF YESHUA DISCOVERING YOUNG PAARESH IN CAVE UNCOVERED. PAARESH SHAMED, BUT [YE]SHUA WAITED WITHOUT, UNSHAMED. OPENED CLOAK AND RUBBED AS HE WAITED FOR PAARESH TO SPILL

WHEN JOHANAN FIRST ARRIVED TWO PASSOVERS AGO, YESHUA MADE GREETING WITH OTHERS AND CARRIED FOR HIM. AS BEFORE, YESHUA HELPED NEW ONE TO KNOW THE WAY IN COMMUNITY, UP WADI AND DOWN [TO THE S]EA. JOHANAN FOLLOWS EVERYWHERE BUT YESHUA ALSO SEEKS HIM. INSEPARABLE, [BUT] YESHUA NEVER EXCLUDES OTHERS AROUND.

NATHAN BEN SIMON HID [AND] SPIED ONE NIGHT. HE REPORTED TO ONE ELDER, "YESHUA AND JOHANAN PULLED BEDROLLS [TOGETHER] AND LAY EMBRACING WITH NAKEDNESS. THEY TOUCHED WITH GENTLENESS AND WHISPERED. THEY LAUGHED AS ANGELS. TWO GAVE BODIES UNTO EACH [OTHER]."

ACTS ONLY OCCASIONAL AND NEITHER APPEARS OVERTAKEN BY NEED.

ELDER [indistinguishable].

NATHAN AGREED AND WILL NOT DISCUSS AGAIN. ELDER IS TROUBLED IN SPIRIT, NOT BY YESHUA'S ACTS BUT BY LAW BECAUSE OF YESHUA. EVIL SPIRITS DO NOT ABIDE IN THE YOUTH NOR IN THE LAW, BUT THE YOUTH WALKS BEYOND THE LAW.

[ELD]ER TROUBLED TODAY AND WASTING PARCHMENT WITH THOUGHTS, WATCHING OVER THE SONS OF LIGHT AT LESSONS. YESHUA DREAMING; JOHANAN CLOSE BY, DILIGENT AS OTHERS [ARE] IN COPYING. YESHUA [IS] AUTHOR, NOT SCRIBE.

CHAPTER 20

KAIROS DECLINED, REDUX

La Jolla, California
Wednesday evening

Christiana and Hjalmar Hansgaard walked the soft-sand beach uneasily, hand in hand, silent and unaware of the sun dropping below a cloud cover and toward the horizon. Its rays covered the beach with a pink glow that should have been calming, but Christiana clenched her teeth as they made slow progress toward the north. She wore designer blue jeans and a loose, stylish white top that revealed a modest décolletage and only hinted at how slender the figure beneath it was. Her husband, in stone-washed jeans, form-fitting tank top and sockless loafers, completed the matched-set of late middle-aged professionals. Both exuded California chic but with more moderate tans than the younger sun worshippers closer to the surf's edge.

"I haven't seen you this way before," said Hjalmar. "It's like walking into an old familiar painting and seeing the shadows behind objects. Not surprising, really, but unexpected."

"Thank God for you, my darling Hjalmar. Everything else in life seems totally unhinged. *Totally.*" She squeezed his hand. "I wish Paul would get here."

"I think I see him." Hjalmar pointed to a dune on the right a hundred yards ahead. Their 280-pound pastor was scanning the beach, hand shading his eyes. Hjalmar waved his free arm and the three were shortly united.

"Peace!" said Rev. Paul Larson, with a hearty handshake for Hjalmar and a light hug for Christiana. "How is life for my favorite married doctors?"

Christiana drew close to him and held on. Her shoulders shook briefly. Paul exchanged glances with Hjalmar, who clenched his jaw and extended his hands toward the pair as if to say, "Hold on; she needs you."

"Oh, Paul, thank you for coming."

A few moments passed while she regained control, and shortly the three took seats on a weathered public picnic table up a six-foot embankment. Side by side, the couple sat on the north looking across at their longtime Lutheran pastor, who straddled the bench to face the setting sun. His khakis and Hawaiian shirt suggested that he had not come directly from his office at the church, but had been home when the Hansgaards phoned an hour before.

"What's happening, love?" he asked Christiana. "How can I help?"

Her mouth formed first one word and then another, then still others, all without uttering a sound. She turned to her husband, her eyes pleading, "What can I say?"

Hjalmar began. "Christiana is torn up, Paul. She has some news that she feels the need to share, but she also feels like it is too ugly, too dirty to speak."

She shook her head as she spoke. "I shouldn't even have told *you*, dear. But I couldn't help it."

Paul nodded. "There is a pastoral privilege, you know, Christiana. Nothing you tell me in confidence will be passed on without your approval."

"Well," sighed Christiana, "I just don't know where to start. Talking about it—almost twenty-four hours straight with Hjalmar—hasn't helped. Sitting here silent isn't helping. If I tell you what I know, I may be violating a deep confidence; but if I don't, I feel like an accomplice to a crime."

Paul shook his head gently, and said, "Tell me where it hurts, doctor."

She looked up at him and laughed out loud.

The light spirit disappeared as quickly as it had arrived. She pursed her lips, shook her head, closed her eyes.

Paul spoke again. "Christiana, one of God's gifts to us is the release that talking provides. Whatever you tell me will be in confidence. Confession is good for the soul, you know, and there is nothing on earth He cannot forgive. Please tell me what hurts you so much today."

"Oh, I wish it were sin on my part that I *could* confess. No, I hurt because someone I love is, well, committing a blasphemy so evil that I fear for him, and for everyone who might hear him."

"Blasphemy?" asked the pastor, his brows raised.

"He's defaming the Lord. He's telling a story that he should know is false in the first place, and even if he believed it, he shouldn't repeat it."

Christiana stood up. She breathed in the salty Pacific air and squared her shoulders.

"All right, I'm going to tell you. But first, tell *me* something, Paul. Do you think I am incredibly old-fashioned? Am I the last educated Christian on Earth who believes the Bible literally? Correction—'who believes the *New Testament* literally?' I mean, it seems like during the space of our lifetime people have gone from believing the Old Testament stories were *literally* true to *mythically* true. My brother and I heard the Adam and Eve story from our mother's knee. That was probably in, oh, 1928 or '29. I'm sure that began when I was two or three years old, and neither she nor we questioned it. The Bible said it; it was true. God created the earth and the heavens in six days, and rested on the seventh."

"Six earthly days of twenty-four hours each," agreed Paul. His voice and face conveyed a sense of indulgence for naiveté and incomplete understandings.

"Right. Well, my college work in the sciences and the theory of evolution just about demolished that faith. But the professors at St. Olaf helped me understand that the *facts of evolution* didn't conflict with the *truth of the Creation story*. The truth of Genesis is that a loving God set all of creation in motion, regardless of the number of earth-days *or millennia*, it took. So I could accept some of the oldest stories in the Bible as mythological—you know, versus factual—so long as they conveyed the truth."

Both her companions nodded agreement.

"But no one has ever suggested—not seriously, not to me!—that the *New Testament* stories are the same kind of *mythological* truth." She came around to Paul's side of the bench and confronted him. "Don't you believe that Jesus Christ actually walked on the soil of Israel two thousand years ago?"

"Yes, I do."

"Lute didn't dispute that, dear." Hjalmar's comment was not a rebuke but an objective observation.

Paul's smile brightened. "So this is about your brother?"

Christiana slumped to the bench beside Paul. She rubbed her neck and shoulder. "Yes," she admitted. "But it's confidential?"

"Of course."

"Oh, Paul! Lute talked about Jesus, and His physical life on earth."

The pastor's eyes widened, his hefty frame straightened, his fingers stretched involuntarily as though an electric current had passed through him. "He has scrolls about Jesus?"

A flock of beach boys strutted a few feet away from where the three adults sat. Christiana allowed them to pass beyond earshot before resuming. Paul fidgeted as he watched her closely.

"Let me ask you one more question, Paul. Am I a shallow Christian if I prefer not to think about Jesus' *body*?"

"Why don't you want to?" countered Paul.

"Why do you answer a question with a question?"

"Fair enough. I don't think we have to *dwell* on His body. But we do need to accept Him as fully human or we fall into the Gnostic's heresy. Now what did Lute say?"

Both doctors looked at him curiously, and Christiana said, "I don't remember what the Gnostic heresy is."

"The Gnostics were people in the first century who believed that the body was evil. In fact, they said *all* physical matter was evil, and that God was purely spirit. They were *dualists*—people who saw the world as black-or-white, either-or, good-or-evil. They believed a man's body was a temporary prison for his soul, which yearned for its freedom. So the Gnostic Christians said Jesus wasn't truly human, because if He had been, He would have been part of the evil inherent in all flesh. They claimed he was a Holy apparition, the appearance of a human life but actually pure divine spirit."

Hjalmar spoke up. "And that was a heresy the early church drove out?"

"Yes. A heresy, of course, is what the winners in an ecclesiastical debate call the beliefs of the losers. All that aside, Gnosticism was declared heresy because—the early church fathers decided—if Jesus wasn't a flesh-and-blood man, he couldn't have truly lived and suffered and died, and then our salvation would be a sham. To this day we believe Jesus was true God and true man. That He was God *incarnate*." Paul pronounced the last word as two, then added, "God became flesh. He was *carnal*."

"I don't have to focus on His biological functions to believe that."

Hjalmar spoke up. "But you can't believe they were evil, either, Christiana." Her husband's argument surprised her, but he reached to hold her hand and she grasped his.

Paul shifted on the bench again. "Come on, now, what did Lute tell you? If this is from the Qumran scrolls, it's major news! Did he call from Jerusalem?"

"No," she answered. "He's here in town. Oh, Paul. Paul, it's such blasphemy. Lute claims there's a scroll that says Jesus was not a virgin."

A stunned silence surrounded the picnic table. Christiana's jaw tightened and her brows knit tight. Paul stared at her, eyes wide. Hjalmar stared off across the rolling Pacific Ocean.

"It's garbage," she said. "If it were true it would have been in the gospels. I have never known Lute to lie, but this is just monstrous! He's been taken in by a forgery. Or *something!*"

"Darling." Hjalmar's tone soothed his wife's feelings, but he also seemed prepared to engage her mind. "Sweetheart, what if it *were* true? Could we accept that?"

Christiana dropped his hand, sat bolt upright and raised her voice. *"I don't want to think about Jesus' penis!"* An awkward silence once again surrounded them. Hjalmar looked around to see if anyone heard this declaration. He saw no one.

Finally Paul asked, "Did Jesus eat? Did He drink? We're even told about those activities in scripture, of course.

Including an indication he was considered a wine-bibber, a drunk, by some of His critics."

The Hansgaards remained silent.

"So," continued Paul resolutely, "Jesus took a leak occasionally. And had a bowel movement every day. Healthy bodies take in nutrients and eliminate wastes."

Christiana was stone-faced.

"Is it blasphemy to say His body functioned normally?" their pastor asked. "Actually, if he had had *no* wet dreams, no intercourse, no sexual function at all, now *that* would have been a miracle!"

"And . . . Jesus . . . performed . . . *miracles*," intoned Christiana slowly and angrily. "He was *divine*. He didn't yield to earthly desires." Her tone conveyed frustration that her pastor hadn't quickly and emphatically shared her abhorrence of Lute's assertion.

Hjalmar almost spoke, but caught himself.

Paul did not hesitate, however, and as he spoke, Hjalmar nodded approvingly. "But you agree that Jesus ate and drank. Aren't those earthly desires?"

"Is it 'desire' or 'necessity' to breathe, Paul?"

"Necessity, of course."

"Is it 'desire' or 'necessity' to eat?" she continued.

"Necessity."

"Is it 'desire' or 'necessity' to have an *orgasm*?"

Both of her companions looked up curiously. Paul realized this was a word that she probably used easily in her medical practice, but which he could not recall hearing her say. He guessed that it was a subject she considered unfit for social conversation. Her clear skin reddened slightly and her jaws clenched tightly as she waited for his answer.

"Well, I've never been a woman, love, so this answer is only for a man. It's a necessity."

Since silence followed, Paul continued. "As a young teenager, I discovered the *terrible, awful, sinful joy* of solitary sex." His exaggerated inflection clearly conveyed his sarcasm. "And I thought my insides were pouring out every time I ejaculated. Remember, we had heard about *fornication* and other almost-unforgivable sins in Sunday School all those growing-up years, and I had finally discovered what they were talking about. I thought it was God's warning that I was going to die if I continued. So I fought the urge for weeks at a time. Poor little hormone-ravaged kid. At the end of every period of abstinence, I would wake up in the middle of the night lying in a pool of 'shame' my body had produced."

Paul shook his head as if saddened by the unnecessary guilt of his youth.

"Those who would answer your last question by saying *'desire'* want to control other people, Christiana. We have God-given systems, many of which function with kick-starters we *call* desire, but which will ultimately roar into *over-action* if they are not employed regularly. The sin is in letting any one of them assume too much importance, or get out of balance. Like I do with food."

Paul reflected a moment, then his shoulders slumped. "How impertinent of me! An 'M.Div.' lecturing an 'M.D.' on bodily systems!"

Christiana once again got up from the table and paced away from the men, lost in thought. She turned, approached again and asked, "Do you think He was married, then, Paul?"

"We can't know. That is, the gospels and all the ancient literature we have are silent on that. There *are* hints: Jesus clearly broke the traditional Jewish separations between men and women. His discussion with the Samaritan woman at the well, in John chapter 4, I think, was greeted with surprise by His disciples. It just wasn't done. And you remember the story of the prostitute who anointed His feet with perfume as He ate at the Pharisee's house?"

She shrugged as if to say, "Yes, so?"

"I certainly don't preach on this, but it's a very physical, carnal story. For one thing, she lets her hair down to wipe his feet. In Palestine in those times, letting the hair down had sexual overtones. It was a matter of self-exposure for a woman, and was an act associated with physical intimacy. And on top of that, Simon—that was the Pharisee, their host—Simon thinks to himself, 'If this guy were a prophet he would know what kind of woman is *touching* him.' A prostitute! In the original Greek, the word our translations show as 'touching' is the same as the word for 'fondling.' There are sexual intimations all over the story."

Christiana stared coldly.

The pastor drew in a deep breath. "It's in the Scriptures, friends. And for a reason, too. The end of the story is that Jesus scolds his self-righteous host *in public*. Well, not scolds, but forcefully tells the parable of canceled debts, and criticizes his host for failure to extend basic Middle Eastern hospitality. And He forgave the woman's sins."

"So prostitution *was* sinful in His eyes!" Christiana declared, clearly assured that she had proven her point.

"Sure. Did Lute say the scrolls contradict that? Did he say Jesus was paying for it?"

Hjalmar rolled his eyes and muttered, "Oh, jeez."

Christiana's jaw dropped.

Paul conciliated immediately. "I'm sorry. Forgive me. You deserve better." He stared at the fingers of his right hand drumming the rough tabletop, and finally explained, "It's my own devil—my own frustration with what I think our conservative Lutheran tradition fosters. Or festers, maybe. We love the Lord God dearly, but sometimes I worry that we get as 'stiff-necked' as He accused old Pharaoh of being."

"You think I'm *dogmatic?*"

Paul considered before answering. "Dogmatic is such a negative term. I wouldn't say that of someone I like as much as you."

"But you *think* it!"

"Christiana. 'Little Christ.' You have every bit as much insight—or blindness—as I do into God's love and will. How could I judge you?"

"Don't patronize me, Paul. Do you think I'm dogmatic?" When he opted not to answer, she pursued. "What's the difference between *dogmatic* and *faithful*, pastor?" She knew she had voiced a profound question, but the razor edge on it was unmistakable, and it had cut the warm skin of friendship.

The Pacific surf continued its ceaseless ebb and flow against the continent. One by one, the three turned away from each other and stared out over the ocean. Silence moved in like the dark clouds descending to the horizon.

John 4:7-10, 25-27

When a Samaritan woman came to draw water, Jesus said to her, "Will you give me a drink?" (His disciples had gone into the town to buy food.) The Samaritan woman said to him, "You are a Jew and I am a Samaritan woman. How can you ask me for a drink?" (For Jews do not associate with Samaritans.) Jesus answered her, "If you knew the gift of God and who it is that asks you for a drink, you would have asked him and he would have given you living water."

The woman said, "I know that Messiah" (called Christ) "is coming. When he comes, he will explain everything to us." Then Jesus declared, "I who speak to you am he." Just then his disciples returned and were surprised to find him talking with a woman. But no one asked, "What do you want?" or "Why are you talking with her?"

Luke 7:36-38

Now one of the Pharisees invited Jesus to have dinner with him, so he went to the Pharisee's house and reclined at the table. When a woman who had lived a sinful life in that town learned that Jesus was eating at the Pharisee's house, she brought an alabaster jar of perfume, and as she stood behind him at his feet weeping, she began to wet his feet with her tears. Then she wiped them with her hair, kissed them and poured perfume on them.

CHAPTER 21

A MIDNIGHT DECISION

La Jolla, California
Thursday, June 20
1:20 a.m.

Christiana kissed her sleeping husband lightly on the forehead, and quietly left the bedroom. Her tossing and turning were clearly not going to end. She would only awaken him if she stayed.

She began to turn a light on in the living room, then changed her mind and walked to the plate glass window to look out across her beloved Pacific. The surf was restless in the moonlight, too, she thought, and yet its constancy could hardly be called restless. If anything could calm her spirit, the eternal flow of its waters should. She sometimes felt the ocean was her life: deep, always rolling on, new each moment and yet unchanging over many years. Its proximate presence calmed and comforted her, and she loved their home above the waters so profoundly that it had been a factor in the early 1970's when she decided against divorcing Hjalmar. His admission of infidelity had almost driven her to a final separation, but her fear of losing that home was one of the considerations that brought her to the reconciliation he had begged for. Though she never admitted it to anyone, it shamed her that keeping her home was probably more important than her belief that divorce was religiously unacceptable.

She prayed silently.

Heavenly Father, Thy will be done. I beseech Your loving kindness for relief, Lord. As Your Son asked, let this cup pass from me. You are asking a decision too heavy for me to bear. I cannot betray my only brother, yet I cannot be an accomplice to his sin. What would You have of me, Lord? I am not Solomon. I don't know what You want.

Eyes moist, limbs trembling, the slender, sophisticated doctor slumped to the floor and sat leaning her back against the cool glass.

I feel like I'm being called to take action, Father, but I don't know if it's Your still small voice or the Devil's. The Evil One is so crafty; he uses my weakness. But which is the weakness, Lord? Is it love for my brother, or thinking that everything depends on me? Which is the sin? If I try to stop Lute from spreading his disgusting lie, is that the sin of pride swelling up in me? But if I do nothing, how am I different from those who have been tried and found wanting? What is Your will?

Now hugging her knees tight to her chest, Dr. Christiana Jonson Hansgaard finished her agonized prayer in a whisper to the universe. "There's no escape, no sidestepping a decision one way or the other. Please, Lord. Please show me."

She shivered as she looked up and down the moonlit beach. At last she stood up, started toward her bedroom, turned back toward the kitchen, peered listlessly into the refrigerator, closed it again, and finally sat on her favorite stool at the pass-through bar. She pulled the leather-bound Bible—lying there for daily devotions—close to her.

She straightened, looking intently at the old book in the darkened room. Turning on a reading light, she continued to stare at the book, so thoroughly used that its black cover and thin pages fell flexibly against her wrist. She closed her eyes, rifled the pages blindly, and opened at random to a page near the back.

Her eyes opened expectantly and peacefully. She looked at the chapter heading on the left-hand page: Matthew 10. She looked up at the ceiling and let her fingers trace the page Ouija-like. They stopped in the middle of verse 32, and she bent serenely to read. Thus engaged for sixty seconds or so—her fingers leading her eyes to the end of the chapter—Christiana tensed, but only briefly.

She bowed her head, closed her eyes, and folded her hands over the open scriptures. "Maranatha," she said softly. "Come, Lord Jesus."

She took the cordless phone out of its base on the counter near the wall, and pulled her lavender personal phone book over, too. Thumbing through its loose-leaf pages, she found a number and kept her finger on it. With her head cocked in mental rehearsal, she finally began to dial.

Stopping suddenly, she depressed the button and lay the phone down. She absently pounded the counter with a light fist, thinking. She looked at the kitchen clock, whose hands were sweeping past 1:35. She calculated with her fingers, and picked up the phone again. This time she dialed thirteen digits. The wait was short.

"Hello. I'm calling from America. I need to speak with the priest who is co-director with Dr. Lute Jonson of the Dead Sea Scrolls team there. I can't recall his name, sorry." She paused. "No, not Dr. Jonson; I know he's not there. Doesn't he have a co-director? Yes, yes, that's it. May I speak with Father O'Derry? Tell him it's Dr. Jonson's sister in the United States, please."

Christiana tried to smile as she waited to be connected.

Matthew 10:32-39 (quoting Micah 7:6)
"Whoever acknowledges me before men, I will also acknowledge him before my Father in heaven. But whoever disowns me before men, I will disown him before my Father in heaven. Do not suppose that I have come to bring peace to the earth. I did not come to bring peace, but a sword. For I have come to turn 'a man against his father, a daughter against her mother, a daughter-in-law against her mother-in-law. A man's enemies will be the members of his own household.' Anyone who loves his father or mother more than me is not worthy of me; anyone who loves his son or daughter more than me is not worthy of me; and anyone who does not take up his cross and follow me is not worthy of me. Whoever finds his life will lose it, and whoever loses his life for my sake will find it."

CHAPTER **22**

TELL YOUR TROUBLES
TO THE DOCK

Port Townsend, Washington
Thursday, June 20
5:00 a.m.

Harald sat on the edge of a short upright piling on the ferry dock. He gazed out into Admiralty Inlet, the water connection between the Strait of Juan de Fuca and Puget Sound. His eyes briefly surveyed the rising sun, the green-blue tide, and the large, green and white double-decker ferry moving in, but he soon de-focused. His lanky body clad in a Pendleton wool jacket and navy Docker slacks, the professor was lost in thought.

An odd pair of workers—a high school junior or senior with a remarkably handsome face and well-toned young body, and a black man in his 40's with a three-day beard and Seattle Seahawks knit cap—moved slowly onto the dock and began preparations for the incoming boat. They moved out to the jut of the pier, some thirty feet from his landward perch, and Harald found himself staring at them. He spoke quietly to himself.

"Nobody wants to hear this, Lute. Conservatives around the world will find this an incredible blasphemy. They won't believe you; they won't accept your faith; philosophically, you'll be beaten to death. And liberals! The few liberals left who claim any faith at all won't believe Jesus was God. Not even a Qumran-census Christ. Religious liberals are on a collision course with humanism. And the truth is, most Americans are totally beyond caring. Even if this is the *kairos* you claim, it's too late. Society has 'progressed' too far."

He shook his head sadly.

"It's a blip on the radar screen. It'll polarize the few who care one way or the other, and it'll just be a few days' media entertainment for the masses who don't."

As the upright log began to cut into his legs, Harald stood and stretched in the crisp morning air. He looked around; the odd couple at the front of the dock were still the only humans in sight, and he continued his moody monologue.

"Some of us single folks could stand some news to help take our minds *off* the subject of sex, my friend; we don't need another reminder of it. Galatians 5:13, you know. Still, if these are truly carbon-dated gospels…. But Jesus? A homosexual? It's antithesis to the beliefs of my whole lifetime."

Harald watched the younger of the dock workers. The professor's eyes traced the slim lines of the young man's legs, back and arms, and then again looked at the square jaw and clear, deep-set eyes on the boy's comely face. Harald wondered if the good-looking teenager was still a virgin.

"Good morning!"

Lute's greeting, called from the shore, startled Harald. His look snapped away from the dock workers and around to Lute.

"Mornin'." Harald walked the twenty feet back to the shoreline, nearly stumbling midway on a rotted-out section of plank.

Lute's mischievous grin framed a question. "Out with your pier group this early?"

It was one of those moments when Harald knew he might have smiled and acknowledged the pun, maybe even returned the little verbal gift, and the day would have gotten off to a good start. But he didn't feel like it. He felt small and tightly bound. And guilty, that he might have been caught watching the youth too intently. Harald faced Lute without expression, then continued his walk up the incline toward Water Street and whatever little activity there was to be found in the sleepy Victorian hamlet at that hour. Lute cocked his head quizzically, but followed.

As they approached The Admiralty restaurant just off the pier, Harald cleared his throat and said, "I'm hungry." He opened the door and the two entered. The walls were adorned with nautical relics, dominated by a wooden boathouse wheel five feet in diameter, with well-worn handholds among the top half of the dozen spokes. The wooden tables were neat but slightly rickety, each covered with a tall ships design on blue oilcloth. The two men were the only customers, and Harald picked a table next to the front window.

Taking menus from behind a napkin holder, Lute and Harald read in silence. A short, very heavy-set woman waddled through swinging half-doors that hid the galley, picked up a glass coffee pot from the Bunn-a-matic machine and continued her tanklike move fifteen feet to their table. As the two looked up and mumbled greetings, she raised her free hand—five chubby short fingers stuck like little potato sausages on a hammy palm. She pointed first to the pot and then to the inverted mugs on their table, raising her eyebrows questioningly.

The strange pantomime instantly caught both men's full attention. Harald nodded his head yes, feeling oddly guilty that the two of them had somehow violated a code of silence in the empty restaurant. When she turned to Lute he said, "Yes, please."

The woman poured, set the carafe on a nearby wooden ledge, and pulled an order pad out of her apron pocket. She fished a pencil out of the hair above her ear, poised to write, and cocked her head toward Harald.

Now believing that she was mute, the Washingtonian nonetheless considered the possibility they had stumbled into a peculiar local custom of silence. He pointed on his menu to order tomato juice and the #3 French toast plate.

As she faced Harald and attended to her pad, Lute said, "Miss?" She continued writing without acknowledging Lute, and he nodded gently to himself. Finished with Harald she turned expectantly toward Lute, who looked directly into her puffy eyes and silently mouthed, "Good morning!" She smiled and mouthed the same words back soundlessly. Lute pointed to the #2 Pigs in a Blanket option on the menu. After gesturing an offer of "anything else?" and seeing them shake their heads, the little woman turned and waddled toward the galley.

"When you bring those out," Lute said in her direction, "could you serve us in the nude?" Harald's eyes grew wide, but as the waitress proceeded without hesitation and finally pushed through the swinging doors, his solemnity was broken by a wide grin. He began to laugh, and it continued so heartily he finally cupped his head in his hands.

"I hope the Lord forgives a little innocent fun with a deaf-mute." Lute seemed honestly contrite. "You know I wouldn't hurt her. I'll leave a big tip and we'll call it a sin offering."

Harald's laughter slowed to an occasional chuckle, but it left a broad smile on his face. "I needed that."

"Tough night?" Lute asked.

"Very unsettled."

"I thought I heard you tossing and turning. Because of the translations I showed you?"

"Of course."

"Want to talk about it?"

"I don't know what to say."

"What are you *feeling*?"

Harald pushed away from the table enough to cross his long legs. He pulled a ballpoint pen from his shirt pocket and began to beat it lightly like a drumstick against his knee. Soon the move changed to a repetitive turning of the pen, absently running his thumb and two fingers down the length of it, turning it end for end. As he continued, lost in thought, his colleague watched his eyes. Twice Lute's mouth moved as if to begin speaking. Both times he held back.

Harald concluded his thinking. "That's a generous question but it's not important, is it? What *I feel* is irrelevant. If this is the truth, the only significant thing is that it be brought to light." His face muscles were tight again.

"It's important to *me* how it makes you feel, Harald."

"Thanks. This is one of those hard sayings. There are several in the Bible that I have yet to hear satisfactory explications on."

"Like?"

"Like Jesus essentially calling the Canaanite woman a dog."

Lute nodded knowingly. "Where she implores Him to heal her daughter and He answers, 'You must not take the children of Israel's bread and give it to dogs'?"

"Yes. Even though he relents, that's certainly one of 'The Hard Sayings' for me as a Gentile. And there's the apparent acceptance of slavery throughout both testaments. And the Apostle Paul's prohibition against women speaking or teaching in church." Harald shook his head. "So even *I* have to agree that the cultural milieu of Jesus' day was different. Still, if you open the door to wholesale re-interpretation, where does it all end? In 'relative ethics'?"

Moments passed.

"You're one of the brave ones," Lute said. Harald looked askance at his friend.

"You're willing to struggle. You haven't locked into simple dogma, or chucked it all as unfathomable."

The clunk and whoosh of swinging doors announced the arrival of their breakfasts. Each man nodded gratitude to the roly-poly waitress and waited until she looked directly at him to mouth the words "Thank you." When she turned and headed to the galley, this time it was Harald who spoke to her back.

"How about a lap dance for my friend here?"

Galatians 5:13
You, my friends, were called to be free; only beware of turning your freedom into license for your unspiritual nature. Instead, serve one another in love."

* * *

US Route 101
Northern Olympic Peninsula along the Strait of Juan de Fuca
9:30 a.m. Thursday

The two men were en route toward the coastal digs around Forks, near the northwest tip of Washington's massive Olympic Peninsula. Neither man seemed to have had his heart in it when Harald suggested the drive, but Lute sensed that both of them needed to complete the conversation which had so astounded Harald the day before. The Volvo carried their silence nearly twenty miles west of Port Townsend.

"I know a story about an old nun." Lute turned his gaze from the road ahead to see if his conversation starter would be accepted.

Harald didn't turn from driving but answered, "What's that?"

"She was a pious little woman. Loved the Lord with all her heart. One Sunday after mass a widow-lady from the parish was telling her about a visit to the doctor. Seems her doc had just diagnosed the widow as having a very serious problem with the semi-circular canals in her ear. She says, 'Sister, if I were to bend over real quick, I would die instantly!' And the nun says, 'However do you resist the temptation?'"

Harald nodded his appreciation.

"Is your faith that strong, Lute?"

"When the time comes, I'm ready to see Him face to face."

Harald hit the steering wheel with a fist. "That's what's so crazy! If you mean that, and I trust you, then you and I are true believers. We both have a fundamental faith (a) that God exists, (b) that He has prepared a life after death for us, and (c) that our sins are forgiven so we can be with Him."

Lute thought again how professorial his friend was, even in conversation. It made him wonder in turn if he himself had speech idiosyncrasies that others noticed.

Harald continued. "So you and I are conservative in theology. That Lutheran Church I gave up on had so many liberals the majority of them probably don't believe in God any longer. Sure, they may hold some intellectual philosophy about the importance of Christian ethics, but if you grabbed them and stared them down and asked if they believed a perfect man named Jesus died and was resurrected again, you'd get a lot of blanks."

"Then isn't this *kairos* fantastic news?" Lute glowed. "The liberals believe in science, don't they? How can they refute carbon-dated gospels? Eyewitness accounts, in the hand of a scribe who knew this Jesus in person! How can this not rekindle faith for some who have strayed off to a kind of empty humanism over the last fifty years?"

"The writer didn't witness the resurrection, did he?"

"No."

"So this Jesus could have just been a good man who was capable of miracles or magic." Harald's discouragement showed around his eyes.

"A youth whose spirit astounded his community, because he was so fresh and loving and playful and honest. Because he addressed God as 'Abba,' the Aramaic equivalent of calling him 'Daddy.' The first ever to do that. Don't forget those, my friend. Those are miracles, too."

They drove another mile in silence. Lute finally read a highway sign aloud, sounding out the town's name. "'Seekwim 2 miles'?"

"*Sequim*—it's pronounced 'Skwim'. It's a north coast Indian word. Means 'quiet waters'."

"Does Sequim have a claim to fame?"

"A 'rain shadow,' with a foot less annual precipitation than nearby areas. And the Dungeness Spit—the best crab you'll ever taste." Harald was courteous, but in no mood for small talk. "Lute, I don't know which I'm having more trouble with: the data from these fragments of yours, or the fact that they'll be absolutely counter-productive."

"Counter-productive?"

"This revelation can only backfire. It won't bring liberals back to the true faith; they'll just label you a fundamentalist. And we conservatives won't be any more receptive. This homosexuality thing is very difficult to swallow, Lute."

The metaphor seemed ironic, but Lute neither smiled nor checked to see if his companion did. He offered an answer.

"Saint Luke quotes the Master as saying 'Blessed are you who are reviled for my sake.' He was no stranger to the wrath of religious authorities back then. I don't expect to be now. But you yourself reminded me of the hymn Dr. Longaard at St. Olaf College loved to play: 'Once To Every Man And Nation, Comes The Moment To Decide.' I know a truth, Harald, one which may die with me if I don't release it. Truth-telling is a powerful deathbed force. I don't think I'm *that* near death, but who of us knows how long he has to live? A logging truck could come around that bend up there. If it crosses into this lane we're history. So what if the scribe had a fact wrong, but the truth is there? Shouldn't the story still be told?"

Harald mumbled, "John 8:32."

Lute missed that as he turned to face Harald. "And you seem so concerned with what the fragments say about Jesus' sex life. So was I when I first read them. To tell you the truth, I will never understand homosexuality. It is beyond me how a man could be interested in, you know, another man. Or how a woman could find any kind of pleasure with another woman. It's not natural; it's not productive in a, a procreation sense; it just doesn't seem to fit the Life Order. And frankly I'm damned if I understand how the mechanics of it work—it seems like whatever they do would be either painful or boring."

He wiped his hands on his jacket sleeves.

"I don't know if you've had this feeling too, Harald, but I've only known three homosexual men—at least, who admitted it—and every time I'm around one of them I have a queasiness in the pit of my stomach. You know what I mean? The fear that he's liable to reach over and touch me, or grab my crotch, or, well, you know. It's totally irrational, I admit it. It's like the feeling I get standing on a balcony several stories up. My gut says, 'Get away from the edge! A gust of wind is going to pull you over, or a crazy thought'll make you jump! Back up!'"

Lute shook his head at the inexplicable phenomenon.

"But then I ask myself, why is this so important to us? Why do we obsess about it? Why can't all of us, including both ends of the theological spectrum you described, realize that this is just a footnote to Jesus' ministry? A fraction of one percent of His life. Unimportant except in how it demonstrates, as the rest of His life did, that the old legalisms are fulfilled, the new life is here, purchased with His blood."

Harald's frown broke and he began to hum Handel's Hallelujah Chorus.

Lute laughed. "Right. Amen. End of sermon."

Harald drove onto the shoulder at a lookout point and the two men watched a freighter with Japanese and English markings steam eastward through the strait toward Seattle. A cloud cover grayed the day, but the water view held both men's attention. Gulls by the dozens glided above the shoreline on lazy wings. Others waddled the sands, and a few floated in the gentle surf.

"He did tend to embrace the outcasts, didn't He?" Harald's words came from high in the throat, and Lute looked over. The professor's emotion caught Lute by surprise. He shifted the priceless briefcase between his ankles and decided listening was better than answering.

Harald resumed. "The Jews considered the people of Samaria half-breeds. So when the Lord told a parable about neighborliness, and made the hero of it a person from there...the Good Samaritan...it was a slap in the face to the religious authorities. Jesus ate with tax-collectors, who everybody hated. He stood up for a woman who was about to be stoned by a crowd."

"Iconoclastic...?" Lute offered.

"Yeah. But always centered around one unchanging principle: love. The Son of Man loved God, and He loved God's children. Jesus didn't do much judging. Except of the 'holier-than-thou's'. Makes you wonder."

"How so?"

"It makes me wonder what outcasts we have in modern society that He would embrace."

"There's a wonderful Edwin Markham poem..." Lute began.

Harald's face lit up briefly. "I was thinking exactly the same thing! 'He drew a circle that shut me out...'."

"'Heretic, rebel, a thing to flout.'"

"'But love and I had the wit to win...'."

"'We drew a circle that took him in.'"

Instead of sharing Lute's broad smile, Harald seemed to grow very tense. His mouth contorted, his eyes squinted nearly shut, and he shuddered. Finally he cleared his throat and turned to face his passenger. Strained muscles around his eyes and along his jaws signaled a mighty internal battle. Still he could not seem to speak.

Lute reached across to feel Harald's forehead but his host jerked away, yanked the car door open, and got out fast. He slammed the door behind him and started down the little embankment as Lute quickly exited his side and came around to follow.

Lute caught up and grabbed Harald by the shoulder, pulling him around to face him. It looked like spray from the wind-whipped strait had splattered the old professor's face.

Harald stood ramrod straight, shivering, his jaw clenched and pointed away from Lute, to the north across the waves. Finally, words emerged as a kind of surrender.

"Lute, you said that whenever God or His angels come near us in the Bible, the first words are what?"

"Fear not." Lute searched Harald's face for some clue.

There was a long pause before Lute prompted, "What is it, my friend?"

"Then why am I so afraid? Why can I barely say the words?" His hands were clasped in front of his chest, shaking as if palsied. His eyes had narrowed to slits. Not one visible muscle on his body was at rest. "I am one of those who make you uncomfortable, Lute. I am a homosexual."

John 8:32

And ye shall know the truth, and the truth shall make you free.

CHAPTER 23

"ROME, WE HAVE A PROBLEM"

Jerusalem
Thursday
3:00 p.m.

Sean O'Derry exchanged nods with the uniformed guard in the Shrine of the Book and entered the cavernous, subterranean main room. There were, surprisingly, no tourists queued up at the stairs to the round exhibit dominating the axis of the circular space. The room's smooth flat floor extended almost a hundred feet in diameter to concrete walls which rose in concentric, ever-smaller rings to a central filtered skylight more than forty feet above.

Beautiful, he thought, as he always did. *Awe-inspiring simplicity.* From inside, the ceiling looked just like the top of one of the clay jars the Dead Sea Scrolls had been found in. *Perfect design. Why can't all of life follow the Heavenly Father's perfect designs?*

He eased up six slab steps and stepped onto the soft carpet surrounding the Isaiah Scroll in its massive circular case. He moved instinctively to the right, checking alternate columns of Hebrew characters until he found the words he sought.

When he began reading aloud, two high school boys on the platform turned to watch. Sean's fluency was so impressive that the shorter of the two boys traced Sean's gaze to the scrolls, then back again to the priest's now-closed eyes. The boy nudged his friend and pointed to Sean.

"Fear not; for thou shalt not be ashamed: neither be thou confounded; for thou shalt not be put to shame: for thou shalt forget the shame of thy youth, and shalt not remember the reproach of thy widowhood anymore."

He folded his hands for a few moments, then dropped them to his sides when he opened his eyes. Moving further around the scroll, he spoke to the young visitors.

"Isaiah fifty-four and four, my boys. A wonderful verse to remember when you are cast down. Are you Americans?" They shook their heads no. "Ah, too bad, for you could remember it from the rallyin' cry on settlin' the Canadian border: fifty-four four-(ty) or fight!" Their blank faces told him all he wanted to know about their knowledge of New World history. "All right, then, here's one all young folks like better," he continued, stopping a dozen columns to the right of his first reading. "Isaiah forty-three and eighteen, we've called it. 'Remember ye not the former things, neither consider the things of old. Behold, I will do a new thing; now it shall spring forth; shall ye not know it? I will even make a way in the wilderness, and rivers in the desert.' And then five or six stanzas further, I like the words of a modern translation: 'Review the past for me, let us argue the matter together; state the case for your innocence.' Ah, such an invitation from the Almighty! 'Tis a soft chair after a fifty-kilometer march."

Sean looked up to find the boys slack-jawed.

"Are ye surprised to find someone who can read these scribbles? Or that a stranger in a Catholic collar talks to ye like this?"

Both shrugged. Neither spoke.

"Well, forgive me. For either or both that might have offended you. Just remember to dig into The Good Book when you're looking for solutions to your problems, lads. No better answers on earth." He smiled as he moved on around the Scroll. His geniality would not last, however. Apparently unaware of the acoustics of the parabolic ceiling, the boys whispered together after the priest passed from their sight. Sean cringed to hear their British-accented evaluation of himself and Catholic clergy in general.

"Are they all faggots, then?"

"Yeah, weenie worshippers, every bloody one of 'em. The Pope can hardly pay off the altar boys' parents fast enough."

* * *

Sean's Office
4 p.m. Thursday

Sean pulled his center desk drawer out six inches and rummaged through the workaday flotsam and jetsam there: a box of staples, half a dozen dull pencils, innumerable paper clips which refused to stay tidy in their low wooden bin at the front of the drawer, a clipping or two and paper scraps galore. He pulled the drawer out further and stirred an arthritic finger through the back strata of modern-day business archaeology. To no avail.

He rose and walked back into his secretary's office. Coming around behind her better-organized desk, he opened the cover on her large circular Rolodex file and checked each card behind the R, V, and C tabs. Nothing. He absently flipped through the remainder of the letters.

"Ah!" He stood upright and returned to his office, where he unlocked the file drawer of his desk. Moments later he pulled a manila folder from the back of the collection there, and found a letter. Holding a finger on the phone number at the top of the stationery, he began to dial his telephone, but broke off and replaced the handset. He quickly returned to the outer office, locked his secretary's hall door, once more entered his own office, and locked that door.

He breathed deeply and dialed.

"Bonjour. Le Bureau de Cardinal Collins."

"Good afternoon. This is Father Sean O'Derry at the Rockefeller Museum in Jerusalem. Is the Cardinal available?"

"One moment, please."

Only a few seconds passed before another voice picked up. "Father O'Derry?"

"Yes?"

"This is Monsignor Connors. How may I help you?"

"Monsignor. Good to talk with you again. It has been some time."

"Indeed."

"I have a matter that needs the Cardinal's personal attention, I'm afraid, and actually, it's quite urgent. Could you put me through?"

"His Eminence is here in the Holy See today, Father, but preparing for a conference in Brazil next week. He asked not to be interrupted before dinner. But I know of his appreciation for your work, and if there's anything I can help with…?"

Sean drummed a clenched fist on his polished desktop. "Monsignor, this is a matter of great urgency. I'm afraid I cannot be clearer on the phone, and I should not speak with anyone but the Cardinal."

There was an awkward silence.

Sean cleared his throat. "I beg your forgiveness, Monsignor. Please tell the Cardinal I beg his pardon, too, but there is a, well, a major problem that has come up with some of our Scrolls."

"Has this to do with the temperature and humidity system improvements there which the Curia funded several years ago?"

Sean's nervous laugh sounded almost brittle. "No, no. Oh, I wish it were. It's a, a content problem. Can you just slip him a note with that while I wait? I'm sorry to be so insistent. Perhaps you know I have never called this way before."

The monsignor's voice took on a harder edge. "I'm sure Father realizes that the Cardinal receives many messages each day, most of which are considered urgent by the callers."

"Please tell him," intoned Sean in a carefully measured cadence, "that the Holy Father may want to receive my news through the Cardinal, not from his daily newspaper summary. We have a situation here which is spinning out of control. The Cardinal will want to hear of it immediately. Please trust me. And do not wait until his dinner hour to give him the message, Monsignor. The world may become a very different place for our church at any moment."

He paused. The line was open but there was no sound coming across the wire. "Have I made myself perfectly clear? This is an emergency, Monsignor. Will you take down my desk phone number so he can call back?"

"One moment, please, Father."

Sean waited. He checked his watch—4:15 p.m. He shifted in his chair, ran a finger under his clerical collar, rubbed his eyes hard, and shivered. He tried silent rehearsals of how to broach the subject, how to explain to the Cardinal his presumption in jumping several levels of Roman Catholic bureaucracy. He checked his watch again—4:19 in Jerusalem, an hour earlier in Rome, still 6 in the morning on the American West Coast.

"Grace and peace to you, Father."

Sean's blood ran cold. The benedictive words were not matched in the tone of voice which delivered them.

"Your Eminence, I am terribly sorry to interrupt."

"But you have, Father, so tell me why."

"We have a problem. There are some scroll fragments we have not discussed which have been under lock and key, and which are now at risk of disclosure. I had thought perhaps things were under control, but I've just had a phone call from America that indicates otherwise."

He waited for a response but heard only the sound of the Cardinal's quiet breathing.

"One reads so much these days about telephone interceptions, I hesitate to say much more on this line. And yet, we have the potential for a, well a kind of a worldwide problem. Possible. Sometime." Sean wondered how many senseless words he would have to fill time with before the prelate would respond.

The Cardinal's tone slipped from cold to icy. "'Fragments which we have not discussed,' you say?"

"Yes, Eminence."

"They deal with matters of our faith?"

"Intimately."

The silence seemed crushing to Sean. Over forty years of nagging concerns accumulated into one massive weight he currently felt in his chest.

"And what you have to tell me will cause you difficulty if it is revealed?"

"Cardinal Collins, its effect on me is infinitesimal compared to the effect it will have ...."

The Cardinal interrupted. "Enough. I accept your judgment for now and we shall tempt the telephone lines no further. I wish to see you in my office tonight. Are you at the Museum in Jerusalem?"

"Yes, sir."

"Leave immediately for Ben Gurion International. Call this office when you arrive at the airport and Monsignor Connors will give you instructions. Between now and then your transportation will be arranged. And you are to discuss this with no one until your arrival in my office tonight. Do you understand? Absolutely no one."

In the time it took Sean to swallow and say, "Yes," he had been hung up on.

Precious Savior, he prayed as he quickly locked his desk and moved to depart, *forgive me. I have failed you, Master, as I have failed those you put in authority over me. If it be Thy will, Lord, take me Home. May this pain in my chest be the beginning, and may I arrive safely in Your arms. Forgive me for my pride and stupidity, for trying to carry this burden myself, for trusting Lute, for worrying without taking action. Almighty Father, bless His Holiness and all the Princes of your Church, and lead them through the difficulties I am about to place before them. I pray in the powerful name of Jesus.*

CHAPTER 24

FULL-COURT PRESS-CONTACTS

Port Townsend
Thursday
2:00 p.m.

As they pulled back into the motel parking lot, Lute reached over to clap Harald's shoulder. "Well, I'm sorry we didn't make it to the digs, but maybe we can get back there in a few days after this calms down. Now that you know about Sean tracing me to San Diego, you can understand the urgency I'm feeling about getting a press conference called, or at least sitting down with a reporter of some stature. If you'll call the radio station manager you mentioned, maybe I can get this released tomorrow and life can get back to some kind of normalcy."

His friend's double-take was lost on Lute, who had turned to get out of the car. Harald shook his head and said to himself, "Life will never be normal again." As he, too, got out of the car, Harald nodded toward Lute's ever-present briefcase and spoke aloud. "I can't believe how light you travel."

"Toward the light, I hope," Lute offered.

"In the Elizabeth Kübler-Ross sense? Not for a few more years, Lute. We're too young." Harald headed the few steps toward the door of their motel room.

Lute stopped short. "Do you think it's possible we can see the woman today?"

Harald shrugged his shoulders. "No idea. It may take several calls to get through to her. Are you sure you don't want to call her yourself, so you can judge how much you need to tell her in order to get good coverage?"

"It's who you know, you know," Lute answered. "But if you get her on the line and she sounds receptive, sure, I'll talk." He checked his watch. "I'd better ask the manager for an extension since it's checkout time." He headed for the office, and Harald unlocked their room.

A hanging bell sounded as Lute entered the office, but the woman behind the counter had already been smiling through the window as he approached.

"Good afternoon," she said brightly. "How may I help you, sir?" She moved aside a small brushed aluminum sign which identified "Margaret White, Manager." In her early thirties, she stood five-foot-six in height, carried her hundred-thirty pounds gracefully, wore her silky black hair draped two inches below her shoulders, and had skin the color of barely-creamed coffee.

"Sheila!" The gruff semi-yell came through a door behind the counter area, which revealed a hallway leading right. As Lute's eyes adjusted to the dimmer inside light, he actually saw into an apartment by way of the mirror on the door which stood open at a 45-degree angle. Both Mrs. White and Lute turned to look in the direction of the aggravated voice.

"Sheila, you give up talkin' to the air, there. You be gettin' too old now for thinkin' they is any invisible animals in here."

The manager smiled almost conspiratorially toward Lute and raised one finger to ask for his indulgence a moment. She stepped to the door and spoke gently.

"Hon, please let little Punkin' play. No imaginary friend ever hurt a child as precious as our Sheila." She began to turn back to Lute but the gruff voice arrested her progress.

"'Tain't good for her."

"Sweetheart, every child grows up with an imaginary friend."

"And when they grows up they calls him God."

She sighed almost imperceptibly, and took the two steps back to her customer.

"I'm terribly sorry. What can I do to help?"

"Don't give it a thought. My friend and I need ..." The telephone operator's console buzzed loudly. The manager moved toward it while she continued listening.

"Well, we wondered ..." Lute broke off, deciding not to rush the request. "Go ahead," he said, gesturing toward the console.

In the half-minute it took her to answer and forward the incoming call, Lute was able to inconspicuously study her hands. The left one was withered, its fingers and structure smaller than her right hand, and the three middle digits appeared permanently extended. Lute noticed, curiously, that the left hand's cuticles were better cared for, and its skin appeared softer and smoother, than the otherwise normal right hand.

"Now," she said firmly as she came back to Lute. "No one else takes priority. You've been too patient."

"I'm always patient when I need a favor," he grinned. "I know it's checkout time, but my colleague and I need to make just a couple of quick phone calls. Would that be OK? Depending on how they come out, we may even need to stay a second night."

She stretched her good hand out and patted the counter near his own hand. "You're just fine," she said.

Lute expressed his gratitude and rejoined Harald in the room.

Harald was sitting on his bed, holding the telephone on his lap. The receiver was in his right hand and the index finger of his other hand held the switchhook down. His blank stare jerked up to Lute.

"What's wrong?" Lute was now alarmed.

"I just called home for my messages. I did remember to turn the answering machine on before we left, which I've been forgetting recently. Someone named Kathy Uglene from the St. Olaf alumni office called. She asked if I knew you, or how to reach you. She said she's calling classmates because the MacArthur Foundation—they give away the 'genius grants'—contacted them and need to get hold of you right away. She left a local number. Said she's on the road this week."

The two men's eyes met.

"Lute, this is either a solution..."

"... or, more likely, a problem." *Damn*, Lute thought, *now we're even finishing each others' sentences.*

"Do you know now why I asked you to keep my visit quiet when I first called you from the motel yesterday?"

"Yes. And I have told no one. Is there any way they could have traced you to Seattle?"

"I fell asleep last night worrying about that, and you know what? There is. I was so dead by the time I arrived at Sea-Tac, I left my briefcase at the front desk of the motel. As you've seen it has small locks on it, and nothing was missing. But the desk clerk saw my ID tag on it and I had to fib a little about who Dr. Lute Jonson was, since that's not the name I signed in under."

"Did you tell anyone at the motel you were going to see me?"

"No. Oh wait." Lute's face drained of color. "Phone records. Either at the motel, or the phone company. They know I called you. I'm sure they're waiting for us there. I can't go back to Seattle with you." He clenched his fists hard.

"Oh, Lord," said Harald. "How sophisticated are these people? Could they get my license plate number somehow? Do you suppose they have the police searching for that Volvo?" He motioned toward the door.

Lute nodded. "Our security chief—I guess I mean Sean's security chief—is a former Mossad agent. He's brilliant, and has intelligence-type connections all over the world. I should have known Sean would not sit back and let me do what I have to do. Somehow I thought our 45-year friendship would weigh more heavily with him. But of course he feels I'm the one who has betrayed him."

Lute walked to the window and awkwardly peeked through the drawn drapes. He blushed. "I guess you're not really paranoid if someone truly is after you. Right?"

Harald attempted to comfort his old classmate. "What did Jesus say in Matthew 18 about seeking for a lost sheep? If Father O'Derry is seeking you, Lute, it is a benign and loving search, no matter how misguided. If his people find us, you will not be harmed, and you'll have a chance someday soon to release this news."

Lute's brow furrowed. "Read Psalm 50, professor. Verse 9."

Matthew 18:12

"How think ye? If a man have an hundred sheep and one of them be gone astray, doth he not leave the ninety and nine, goeth into the mountains, and seeketh that which is gone astray?"

Psalm 50:9

I will take no bull from your house ...

CHAPTER 25

THE INQUISITION

Rome; The Vatican
Thursday, June 20, 1991
10:30 p.m. Central European Time

As Sean kissed Cardinal Collins' ring, he thought he
felt His Eminence's hand push slightly but angrily
against his face. The two walked in silence from the door
where the Cardinal had met him, through a high-ceilinged
library which appeared to function as an outer office, and
finally into the Cardinal's office. Hardwood floors gleamed
around the edges of an Oriental carpet. The Cardinal
motioned toward one of the hardback chairs facing his
gilded Louis Quinze desk. Sean used the unpadded arms
to ease himself down. The Cardinal stood beside his desk,
glowering at the priest.

"Tell me, concisely but completely, what you have con-
cealed from the Holy See."

Sean felt ice in his veins. "Your Eminence, in 1948, a
Bedouin named Abou..."

"Father O'Derry," interrupted the Cardinal as he con-
sulted an ornate desk clock near him, "it is 10:33. By 10:35,

I wish to know the core of the problem which you called 'an emergency' on the telephone."

The elderly priest breathed in deeply and began. "There are seven Qumran scrolls which mention the Lord." The Cardinal's eyes flared open and his rock-hard jowls softened. Sean continued, "Yeshua, son of Joseph of Nazareth, lived in the community and was considered divine by many there. Among other descriptions...." He hesitated under the stare of the wide-eyed man who was his ecclesiastical senior and chronological junior. "...Well, there's one that indicates He was, ah, physically intimate, with another resident. 'Johanan' by name. Probably the beloved disciple." Sean's speech paused, along with his heart. *It is finished. I am no longer carrying this alone*, he thought. Every cell in his body seemed to be jolted with an electric current.

The Cardinal, wearing a simple black cassock tonight—clearly demonstrating to his visitor that it was not scarlet robes which carried the authority he exuded—stared mutely at the priest. His jaw had tightened again. Finally he spoke.

"Carbon dated?"

"Only one of these seven, and two others found with them, yes. These seven have not seen the light of day in almost forty-five years. Until now."

"Yes," hissed the Cardinal as he seated himself behind the desk. "Yes, apparently it is not simply your willful failure to report such incredible findings to the Holy Father which you need to atone for tonight. They are now ... missing?"

Sean had known the conversation would not be comfortable, but had prayed repeatedly during the private jet flight to Rome that civility and Christian kindness would control the Cardinal's reactions. Now this Prince of the Church was livid, and his words cut like scalpels.

"Yes, Your Eminence. My co-director has stolen them. I believe he has flown to the United States to release them to the media. I have told my chief of security to bring him back. One way or another. If they can find him in time."

Cardinal Collins closed his eyes. Only the faint ticking of the desk clock and Sean's labored breathing kept the office from being totally silent for long moments.

The Cardinal began in low tones but built to a flaring fury. "Should I see your failure to share this information *for forty years, Father!...*" He paused to regain his composure, then finished his question. "Should I see that failure as something *other* than satanic pride? Is it not a sin of hubris so great it approaches the unforgivable? Did a parish priest who happened to be studying in the Holy Land in 1948— when an accident of history unearthed two-thousand-year-old parchments—did he think his judgment was better than those placed in authority over him regarding what to do with explosive news? Is it something *other* than pride that kept you from telling my predecessor, for twenty-nine years, and myself for the past fourteen?"

Sean's head drooped slowly to his chest.

"If we had time to waste, Father, I would ferret out the motives a man like you might have had for this unbelievable lack of discretion. But at the moment, we don't have time for that, do we? You have been good enough to wait until a millennium-level catastrophe is imminent for all Christendom to share this news. How thoughtful."

The Cardinal's stooping to sarcasm struck Sean briefly as a gift, a reaction so puerile that Sean could salvage a little dignity in comparison. He raised his head to look at this Cardinal Bishop, and was surprised to see his eyes were wet, even though full of fire.

"*How could you DO this?!*" he screamed at the priest. More moments of silence passed. Finally he stood and began to pace behind the desk, occasionally running a soft white finger along the cherrywood bookshelves which formed the wall behind him. "Well, clearly these seven scrolls are not authentic, and we'll need to be prepared to explain that, should this new Judas friend of yours—what's his name? Luther? How ironic—if Dr. Luther nails his ninety-five feces to some American library door."

"It's Lute," corrected Sean. Fear now began to rise in him that the Cardinal's predictably angry reaction was turning into juvenile irrationality. "Dr. Lute Jonson, Your Eminence. And with respect, we won't be able to claim the scrolls are fake. If need be, there are additional sections which could be sacrificed for carbon dating; we never did that for fear they would become public, except for the one blank square we submitted."

"And this Yeshua. You and I both know it was a common name in that era. There could have been many Jesuses, even with fathers named Joseph, even from Nazareth. Circumstantial evidence, that's all. The church will weather this. We can handle this."

"How many of those Yeshuas do you suppose performed miracles, Your Eminence?"

"There are miracles?"

"Crushed snakes inflated; water emergencies averted; His body glowing in the night."

Sean thought he heard the word *damn* escape the prelate's mouth, but it was too soft to be sure.

"This *intimacy* you alleged, Father. Clearly you must have mistranslated, or the language is ambiguous. If these are authentic scrolls, detailing pre-Galilean ministry events in the Lord's life, any sexual relationship you think you see in them is imagined. Matthew 5:17, 'Think not that I am come to destroy the law or the prophets; I am not come to destroy but to fulfill.' Yes, He healed and walked in the grain field on the Sabbath, but He did not break the holiness code. What you are suggesting is unthinkable. Clearly a misunderstanding on your part. Perhaps we *should* expose these fragments to the light of day, so that other scholars—no offense, Father, but scholars with perhaps a better grasp—can correct your misunderstandings."

Sean stood up. His stance was neither angry nor threatening, but he could no longer sit looking up at the Cardinal. "Haven't you ever wondered if the Lord would come back and rail at us as He did the religious authorities of His day? 'Oh ye stiff-necked people,' He said to them. How many times did He say to the disciples, 'Do ye still not understand?'"

"Ah. So now I am among the scribes and the Pharisees, am I?"

"I did not say that, Cardinal Collins. All I can say is, in the light of this revelation, much is clearer to me. It has taken many years to understand, but perhaps some questions are answered by this."

The Cardinal's head turned toward his guest, his eyes piercing, his jaw tight.

"At least they are questions *I* have had. About why John is called 'the beloved disciple' four times in the Gospel. About why Jesus is silent on the subject of same-sex affection and marriage. Frankly, even about why a crowd could turn from 'hosanna' to 'crucify him!' in one week."

Cardinal Collins approached the older cleric with steps as slow as the words he enunciated. "When this is over, Sean O'Derry, I ... will ... personally ... preside ... over ... your ... *heresy trial*. For even suggesting the possibility, let alone actively believing, that our Lord Jesus Christ was sexually active in *any* way, and especially *that way*. You may not burn in hell, pastor, but I assure you, you will never again wear that venerated Roman collar."

"Is it promiscuous priests that you fear, Cardinal?" Sean's voice raised in pitch and volume. "Or is it recanting all the papal bull put out for years which has fed the flames of homophobia in our pews long after scholars and theologians have debunked the sophistry about Sodom and Onan and all the other clobber passages used against the gays?" He was shouting now. *"Or does our beloved Church still trust the people less with truth than Jesus Himself did?"*

"Sit ... down." The steel in the Cardinal's voice served as a cold mirror of the histrionics Sean had fallen into. The two Irishmen looked deep into each other's eyes, and finally, a lifetime of obedience to authority regained its control. Sean backed into his chair and sat.

"Your opinions are noted, Father O'Derry. Now be very clear about this: if I decide that the souls given into our care on this earth are endangered, I will take whatever action God directs me to take. And you will wholeheartedly support it. If I continue to believe that the stories from seven ancient scroll fragments--which you *think* you understand—will create a salacious, carnal distraction from the transcendent truth of our Messiah's life and death and resurrection—and would therefore endanger the eternal life of the flock He gave us to shepherd—then you will follow the directives I give you without question to avoid such a distraction. Is there any lack of clarity in this, Father?"

Sean stared straight ahead, across the ornate desktop naked of papers and books. He unclenched his jaw to say, "I understand, Your Eminence."

Pressing a button on one of the shelves behind his desk, the Cardinal asked, "Then before Monsignor arrives to take down a full confidential statement from you, do you desire confession?"

Again Sean's head dropped in defeat. His words were soft. "Bless me, Your Eminence, for I have sinned. I have committed sins of pride, and failure to respect duly consti-tuted authority. I have not repented of these sins for many years. Furthermore, I have shown disrespect for your person and office this evening. For all these sins and many others, I am most heartily sorry."

The Cardinal was silent too long. His current lack of eye contact and a conspicuous withholding of absolution left Sean feeling black-hole empty. Only a knock at the closed office doors prompted the prelate to speak. "Since you had already issued a warrant for this apostate friend of yours, Father, even a death warrant, why did you feel it necessary now, after forty years of self-sufficiency, to involve Rome? As you wash your hands of this affair, the stagger-ing weight transfers to my shoulders, does it not? And on it would go to the Holy Father, if his heart could bear it."

A cold, heavy stillness reigned in the massive room as the monsignor entered.

CHAPTER 26

MANUSCRIPT 1Q-CETHER-4: COMMITMENT

"From Cave 1 at Qumran. Translated with others during 'our 37-hour watch.' In content, nothing surprising here; actually quite harmonious with gospel accounts. Still, it awes me to work with parchment contemporaneous to His life in Israel. LJ 4-27-55"

NOVITIATES STUDYING {IN PREPAR}ATION FOR RITE OF COMMITMENT TO COMMUNITY. YESHUA BEN JOSEPH LISTENS AND ASKS AS OTHERS {DO}, BUT HIS QUESTIONS BEGET UNDERSTANDING FOR ELDER AND CLASS.

ELDER ZAN-EL CHARGED, "YOU WILL COMMIT TO THE AUTHORITY AND DISCIPLINE OF THE SONS OF LIGHT." YESHUA TRACED FINGER IN DIRT THEN ASKED, "WOULD A SON SUBMIT TO THE SLAVE OF HIS FATHER, OR TO HIS FATHER DIRECTLY? WHICH IS WORTHY OF HIS FIRST COVENANT?" STUDENTS TURNED NOT TO ELDER FOR ANSWER.

"WE REWARD LOYALTY WITH COMMUNITY, AND PUNISH UNFAITHFULNESS WITH BANISHMENT," THE ELDER READ FROM THE BOOK OF DISCIPLINE. YESHUA QUESTIONED THE ELDER. "DOES THE LIGHT DRIVE AWAY DARKNESS IN WRATH, OR ENFOLD IT AND WARM IT AND CHANGE IT IN LOVE?"

THREE DAYS AGO, ELDER HOSHRAM REVEALED THE RULE ON MARRIAGE. "THE SONS OF LIGHT SHALL NOT COMMIT TO A PARTNER, NOR WIFE, NOR [A]SSOCIATE, BUT TO YAHWEH AND THIS COMMUNITY ONLY." AGAIN YESHUA SAID, "DID NOT FATHER MOSES SAY, 'THOU SHALT LOVE THE LORD THY GOD WITH ALL THINE HEART, AND WITH ALL THY SOUL, AND WITH ALL THY MIGHT' AND 'THE STRANGER THAT DWELLETH WITH YOU SHALL BE AS ONE BORN AMONG YOU, AND THOU SHALT LOVE HIM AS THYSELF'? DOES OUR HEAVENLY FATHER NOT REJOICE WHEN WE COMMIT TO ONE WE SHALL WALK WITH AND CLEAVE TO?"

CHAPTER 27

THE NEW CENTURIONS

The Vatican
Thursday, June 20
11:45 p.m.

Cardinal Collins and the monsignor walked Sean down the hall to a desk with a sleek black 12-line telephone on it.

"If you don't have the number with you," the Cardinal said, "the Vatican operator can get it."

Sean indicated Morrie Staumper had an unlisted number which would make that difficult, but he would find a way to get through to his security chief. The Cardinal nodded, gestured for his monsignor to take care of the scholar priest, and left abruptly, saying only, "You will be brought to me in the morning if I need you."

The monsignor was more gracious. "You may dial zero for the Vatican operator, Father."

"Thank you."

When the Vatican operator confirmed that Morrie's number was not available, Sean asked to be connected with Mrs. Naza. She sounded sleepy, of course, but not upset at being awakened. Following Sean's instructions, she retrieved his personal phone directory and dictated the security chief's residence number.

Staumper answered after two rings. "Yes?"

"Morrie, it's Sean. Sorry to wake you." Neither petulant grunt nor gracious demurring filled the silence, so Sean continued. "First, have you any news since we talked this afternoon? Did Lute's sister help?"

"She had no hard leads for us in Seattle. She has numerous professional contacts there herself but could think of no individuals Dr. Jonson might know. She suggested the obvious: archaeologists, biblical scholars, Scroll Project donors. She mentioned the media, as you had. I also have sources at Jerusalem Tel checking for long-distance calls he placed to America in the past year, also with his alma mater for any college classmates in that area, and of course with the skycaps in the Seattle airport. When I retired an hour ago, we had one possible connection but nothing firm. It's mid-afternoon there now."

Sean sighed. For once he had not had to pry open his "crippled clam," as his housekeeper had dubbed the paraplegic.

"OK, my friend. We have done as much as we can. We are 'standing down' as of this moment, you and I. We are under instructions to cease our efforts and call off anyone you have working for us."

"But..."

"Sorry, Morrie, I'm told it's as non-negotiable as a papal edict, even though it doesn't come directly from His Holiness. But I do have to ask one more favor, and I'm sorry that it's so late. You're about to have a visitor."

"There's someone knocking at the door right now."

Sean shook his head admiringly at the celerity of intelligence organizations. "Yes, Morrie, I'm sure it's a gentleman who has some questions for you. I'm not sure of his name or even who he works for. But if he says to you, "Is Father Jonson here tonight?" please admit him and tell him everything you know."

"Dr. Jonson," Staumper corrected absently.

"No, he'll say 'Father Jonson' so you'll know that he is the one the Cardinal has sent. Don't withhold anything, Morrie, even the names of your contacts. We really must submit now. Give him everything he asks for, then sleep peacefully tonight. You have fought the good fight."

"You're sure?"

"Yes, Morrie."

The security chief whispered into his phone, "If anyone is there with you, say, 'Father Jonson.'"

Sean knitted his brows. "Yes, Father Jonson."

Another whisper: "If they are forcing you to tell me these things, say, 'I'm tired now and need some sleep.'"

Sean laughed out loud. "Ah, I understand. No, my dear friend, I am not being coerced by the good monsignor who is with me, but he is preparing to show me to bed. They are not holding a Vatican knife to my throat. I am asking of my own volition. Please, go answer the door and do as I say."

Perhaps it was the lateness of the hour, Sean thought, or perhaps the fact that even highly-disciplined Teutons give up an interesting project only reluctantly. Whatever, it took several seconds before Staumper's answer came. "Yes sir." And he hung up.

"Do you know who it is he'll be talking to?" asked Sean as the monsignor led him down a corridor toward a series of dorm-like doors. The tall, brown-haired priest shrugged his shoulders noncommittally and showed the tired old Irish priest into a monk-modest sleeping room.

* * *

Langley, Virginia, USA
Thursday, June 20, 1991
5:45 p.m. Eastern Daylight Time

"Hey Mac."

"Hey Greg."

"Know why the owner closed the Roman Coliseum?"

"No, Greg, why did the owner close the Roman Coliseum?"

"Lions were eating up all his prophets."

"Is it God's revenge on you?" Mac was shaking his head in disbelief again. "He gave you a Phi Beta Kappa education, a movie star's face, a beautiful wife and three-point-four talented children, a cushy management job in the Central Intelligence Agency, and He decided to punish you for all that with an addiction to the worst puns known to civilized society? Is that it? Where I come from, they'd lynch anybody who inflicted that shit on other people. Tie a rope around your neck and kick your horse."

"No noose is good noose, straight man." Greg grinned and dropped a manila folder on his subordinate's desk. "Hey, bud, you just got lucky. Interesting case, even if it does look like the Christians are drawing up a circular firing squad. This stuff just came out of the code box; it's from a Company man in Jerusalem. I'm told it's a Number One. Lemme know, OK?"

The younger agent opened the file and quickly read the Summary Sheet. As he turned to the facsimile pictures and documents beneath that page, he reached up to use his computer's touch-screen to open a database. With two additional touches a modem began dialing a Seattle number, and the agent adjusted his headset telephone. As the number rang, he shook his head and muttered, "A circular firing squad it is."

CHAPTER 28

CLOSING IN

Port Townsend, Washington
Thursday
2:20 p.m.

L ute had thought about dressing in the tiny motel bathroom after his quick shower, but decided Harald's coming out to him demanded a reciprocal gesture of trust. He had hand-washed a pair of jockey shorts and an undershirt the night before and they were now dry; he pulled on the briefs but walked out to finish dressing in the room where Harald sat.

I hope he recognizes this as atonement for my saying I worry about homosexuals touching me, Lute thought. *Oh, jeez! I hope he sees it as a statement of trust on my part, not an attempt to tantalize him!*

Lute shrugged off such thoughts and spoke as he buttoned his shirt. "Hey, you know what I realized during my shower?"

"What?"

"If you keep your eyes open in life, God teaches the most amazing lessons. I didn't mention it to you, but the manager of the motel here has a left hand that's kind of withered; it's well-manicured and the skin seems soft, but it's disfigured. Her right hand seems to have perfectly normal functioning, but the nails were ragged and unpolished, and the skin isn't as smooth."

"And?"

"And you know what? I just got it." Lute used his own hands to demonstrate. "With her 'well' hand she's able to take care of her 'sick' hand--clip the nails, apply lotion and nail polish. You know? But not vice-versa; the dysfunctional hand can't do those things for the well hand. So God just told me the moral of the story! The 'well hands' of society can care for the 'crippled hands' of society—making them look as nice as possible—but they're still crippled. And conversely, society's crippled hands—the poor, the homeless, the despised classes— can't give back much to the rest of society, leaving the 'well hands' impoverished, too. We need to make each other well and whole. Otherwise we have some people who are painted up but crippled, and others who are whole but dirty."

Lute beamed from his eureka experience, but Harald did not. He began to frown, then asked in a bitter tone, "Are homosexuals painted-up cripples, Lute? Do we need to be cared for by whole men?"

"Oh, Lord, NO! I was thinking exactly the opposite, Harald! Heterosexuals like me who fear gays—we're the deformed hands of society! Whether it's homophobia or condescension or whatever, many of us put distance between ourselves and anyone different." Lute's shoulders slumped. "I'm so sorry the opposite connotation would even come to your mind!"

Harald's countenance softened. "Years of conditioning, Lute. Years and years. Besides, I've always believed it myself."

Lute still looked pained. "I'm embarrassed about what I said yesterday, about my discomfort with gay men. I told you how impressed I am that virtually all God's *kairos* events have begun—begun!—with God saying 'Fear Not.' And yet I fight fears and phobias all the time. Including homophobia. I'm so embarrassed now that I told you I worry about the same-sex orientation. I hope you'll forgive me."

"Forget it. Not sure I can forgive myself as easily, though. And I'm not sure which of us is more afraid of homosexuality."

The telephone rang on the bedside table. Harald answered and Lute listened intently, mentally filling the silences with the answers he hoped Harald was hearing.

"Hello? Oh, hello, Melinda. Thank you for returning my call so quickly. How is the radio station? ... Yes, it did sound like a successful pledge drive, but you know some of us tune out during that time... Well, thank you, I do what I can for you, and I do understand you have to run those campaigns to stay on the air. Listen, did your secretary convey my message ten minutes ago? I hope it wasn't too cryptic."

His eyes began to widen during the ensuing answer, and he motioned Lute to come close to listen. He held the handset away from his ear so both could hear.

"Melinda, I just switched the phone to the other ear. Would you repeat that?"

Her broadcaster's voice was clear and polished. "Yes, Dr. Ericksen, I just said that your message was quite intriguing. My intern said something about an important visitor with news regarding the Dead Sea Scrolls which he is willing to give us an exclusive on. Is that true?"

"It is. Would you be available if we drove down right away? There is a time pressure which will become evident when you talk with him. We're in Port Townsend and couldn't get to your campus for a couple of hours, but if you'll see him, I believe you will be breaking a, what do you call it, 'front page story'?"

"We broadcast journalists tend to shy away from those print expressions, but I know what you mean."

"I called you not only because we have met, but also because of your station's national reputation. You certainly have more than your share of stories on the NPR newscasts."

"Thank you, Dr. Ericksen. Yes. I might be able to arrange to have my news director available, but let me ask a couple of questions before transferring you. Is there any chance this has something to do with the wire reports just moving in the last half hour about the Vatican?"

Instantly, Lute and Harald's eyes locked.

"I haven't had the radio on this afternoon. What's happening?"

"Actually, I'm not sure we've had it on the air yet, but I did see an AP advisory to stations that several Roman Catholic Cardinals may have had emergency summonses to the Vatican. The reports are unconfirmed, but they say several Cardinals in major world capitals have canceled engagements, or otherwise sort of abruptly gone to their airports. The wire service advised stations to do some checking locally and contact them if we have similar situations. Do you know anything about that?"

Harald looked again at Lute, who shook his head no, but almost immediately raised one hand as if to say "wait." His eyes widened as the possible cause dawned on him, and Harald's train of thought seemed to follow.

Harald cleared his throat. His voice quieter than before, he answered, "It's possible, Melinda." There was silence on both ends of the line. "Listen, there could be a safety issue with this news source. I'm afraid this may sound a little melodramatic, but we might need to discuss meeting somewhere other than your studio."

"This is very weird, Dr. Ericksen. The AP also just moved an item asking for notice of any news leads having to do with archaeology, ancient literature, that sort of thing. Said they are doing a major piece and requested all stations' cooperation. Can I conference-call them in on this meeting? I mean, our station will break your news ourselves, but if your friend will allow it, I could make some points with the AP by letting them in on what you know. Can we do that?"

Lute was scribbling furiously on a pad. He showed it to Harald, who nodded and pressed the telephone handset back to his ear again.

"Melinda, I need to call you back in a few minutes. Are you at the number I dialed before? ... Good. Now one more thing. Promise me that you'll not call the AP or anyone about this until we talk again. That's very important to my friend. I'll get him there to meet you and your news director, but we need to talk seriously about the conditions and who knows in advance. ... I promise you'll understand why when we talk. OK? ... You're sure? I'm counting on that. ... Good, I'll call you back shortly."

The silence that followed Harald's hangup was as dark as the drawn-drape, dim-bulbed room. The two old classmates stared at each other. Harald finally broke the stillness.

"I think you should do a phone interview."

"Harald, the net is closing on me here. It feels like the whole game has gotten a lot more serious. I'll be embarrassed if it turns out they're not chasing me, but I'll risk that rather than having somebody show up at that door and take this briefcase away from me. I have to tell this story, Harald. I have to get these fragments into safe hands. I'm carrying a fifth gospel—a Good

News story—from God Himself. Only two people knew any of this two days ago. Now you and maybe some in the Vatican know. My sister heard a small part of it and couldn't even handle that. Far more people will be liberated by it, but not if its enemies steal it back. And silence me. Suddenly I have a big pit where my stomach was a little while ago. I wonder how desperate they are to keep this secret?"

Harald's eyes were lowered, but he said, "Fear not."

Lute slammed his fist on the briefcase spread across his lap. "I know that's what God says, but even if I try to take the advice for myself, I can't for you! Damn it! I'm struggling not to let my fantasies race ahead of reality here, but what if the Holy Roman Church decides that I'm carrying around the spiritual equivalent of AIDS? What if they decide that it has to be contained—or even destroyed? I've infected you, Harald! If they decide to quarantine this *kairos*, what happens to us? They'd lock you up with me, and bury these fragments. You said it yourself to the radio manager. We may not be entirely safe until the news is out, until these scroll fragments are seen and photographed and published."

"Lute, let's just drive down to Tacoma and see her. Let's just go."

"I can't! Let's talk worst case. They—whoever they are—think you and I might be together, if your answering machine message is a Trojan horse like I think it is. They can easily find your motor vehicle records, so they're on the watch for a 1970 Volvo. Your car doesn't just disappear in a sea of similar ones, Harald! Or maybe motels like this one use some kind of centralized computer-registration of their guests' automobile license numbers for safety's sake. Maybe 'they' already know we're here."

"Big Brother is watching us?"

Lute shrugged. He continued his hypothesis. "What if this woman tells somebody we're in Port Townsend? Or leaves the message lying around? Or what if this search for me—and Harald, at one level or another, they are searching for me—what if they've somehow put a trace on your home phone and are en route here right now?"

"I don't know how to put this gently, Lute. What if your mind has escalated this whole thing way beyond actual fact? Maybe people don't care about this as much as you think."

Lute stood and paced. He walked into the bathroom and splashed cold water on his face, then to the window and pulled the drapes open enough to peer outside.

"Then I'll be embarrassed. I'll feel foolish. Now, I don't know how to put this clearly enough for you: what if they do care that much? What if God's new *kairos* depends on me? On my staying out of anyone's grasp—real or imagined—until I can release this news and place these fragments into the hands of people who are not afraid of the truth?"

Harald nodded. "So you think you can't risk driving to Tacoma right now, even if the chances are minute that someone is trying to find you and stop you?"

"Bingo."

"And that giving them a phone interview wouldn't get the scroll fragments into safe hands?"

"Right again. It would just delay my disappearing. Give them more time to get here."

Harald tried once more. "You've said that God repeatedly invites us not to fear. If we run, isn't that fear?"

Lute walked to the bedside table and opened the drawer there. He pulled a Gideon Bible out and turned to the back, running his finger down lists of events and sayings in the concordance. Finally nodding in relief, he looked up

Matthew 10 and handed the book to Harald. Lute pointed to verses sixteen through twenty-three, and both read silently. Lute stabbed his lean index finger at the last verse.

Harald's shoulders slumped in defeat. "So how do we get out of here?"

"We don't." Lute picked up his briefcase from the bed opposite Harald. With jaw clenched, he said, "Go take a shower, will you?"

"Lute...?"

"Please, Harald. Don't they call it 'plausible deniability'? They might grill you but will leave you alone when you convince them you don't know where I am. Don't tell them what we've talked about; just give me a few hours. I'll get to Seattle somehow, and hide until I can go public. We'll both be safe again. I'll contact you as soon as possible. But for now..." Lute pointed to the bathroom.

Harald stood up and came face to face with his old friend. Lute set his briefcase on the floor and they hugged. Harald quickly broke away and moved toward the bathroom, but stopped and turned to ask a question.

"So your *kairos* means God doesn't hate me, even though I once broke the Leviticus laws about 'lying with a man'?"

Lute began to chuckle. Harald's scowl at the insensitivity quickly ended Lute's brief levity. "Sorry. I'm just remembering a statement I read recently, something like 'God's Word contains six prohibitions for homosexuals, and three hundred sixty-two for heterosexuals. It isn't that God loves heterosexuals less, it's just that He thought we needed more supervision.'" Both smiled and Lute continued.

"Back to your question. First, it's not my *kairos*. Second, there's much more for us to talk about in those laws, including terrible misunderstandings by translators and faulty interpretations of those verses. But finally and foremost, my friend—my dear gay friend—the answer to your question is, God not only doesn't hate you, He's wildly in love with you. And with me. And with my beloved Naomi." He squeezed his eyes closed a moment. *It hits me at the most unexpected times....* "And even with those who oppose this *kairos* of His. Maybe it's God's one fault: He's crazy in love with His children."

Harald smiled a little and his shoulders seemed to square slightly, but neither act of bravery lasted even the few seconds it took for him to raise an open hand of farewell to Lute, and to obediently disappear around the corner toward the bath.

Matthew 10:16-17, 21-23

I am sending you out like sheep among wolves. Therefore be as shrewd as snakes, and as innocent as doves. Be on your guard against men; they will hand you over to the local councils, and flog you in their synagogues ....

Brother will betray brother to death, and a father his child; children will rebel against their parents, and have them put to death. All men will hate you because of me, but he who stands firm to the end will be saved. When you are persecuted in one place, flee to another.

CHAPTER 29

FLEE, FIY, FLEW

Port Townsend
Thursday
2:45 p.m.

The woman in the front passenger seat of the Honda Civic turned to smile beatifically at the hitchhiker in the back seat. Lute had just closed the door and settled his briefcase between his ankles when the car pulled out onto the road again. There was no traffic in either direction.

"I'm Sharon Snyder, but everyone calls me Cherry," she said. "This is my husband, Stan." The driver nodded toward Lute's reflection in the rear view mirror.

"I'm Don. Don McKenna," Lute answered, hoping neither of them had seen the small billboard they'd just passed advertising McKenna Motors.

"We know Don McKenna!" said the woman. Lute froze. "But that one lives near us in Sitka." Lute breathed again.

"Well," began the driver, "what in the world is a distinguished gentleman like you doing hitchhiking?"

Lute thought a moment before responding, then spoke in exaggerated sonorous tones. "I'm proving something to my daughter and son-in-law. Do you have children?"

"Yes," answered the woman. "We have four boys. Peter, James, John and Andrew. Good strong Bible names."

Stan broke in. "If I'd've known they were gonna be four boys, I'd a named 'em Matthew, Mark, Luke and Ralph."

Lute laughed and he could see both his benefactors were grinning, too. "I needed that."

"Tough day?" asked Stan. He was in his 40's, Lute guessed. Male pattern balding left a monk's ring of nondescript brown hair. Expensive-looking sunglasses hid his eyes, but Lute could sense they had good strong laugh lines at the corners. Tan face, a little on the leathery side from many years of sun. He wore a khaki shirt with epaulet-like tabs across the shoulders. His wife was clearly a matched set: nearly 40, blouse of the same style as Stan's shirt but with narrower shoulder tabs, dark glasses wrapping around to the temples. But her skin was less weathered, and much more attractive with light makeup, blush and pale red lip gloss. Her hair, thought Lute, is what they call 'coiffed.'

"Yes," the old scholar answered, "a tough day. My daughter and her husband have started questioning my mental capabilities. Seems like I forget a couple of things once in awhile and they make a big deal out of it. Today they said the words 'rest home.' I don't like it."

"I'm almost forty," said the woman sympathetically; "I forget things all the time."

Her husband's shoulders shook gently and Lute could see his grin spread. "My sweetheart here is 'almost forty' like I'm 'almost fifty.'"

Lute knew better but the words were out before he could stop. "What are you? Forty-eight? Forty-nine?"

"Fifty-six on August 18th." He continued to chuckle while she discreetly slapped his arm.

"So what are you doin'? Runnin' away from home? I can't take you far since we're just headed a little way out of town. But Cherry here said I had to stop for you in case you had car trouble or something."

Lute's mind raced. "Well, I have to find a way to get away somewhere. Don't misunderstand, they're wonderful young people, but if they're starting to see senility where it doesn't exist, I have to challenge them. Have to clearly demonstrate that I am still capable of taking good care of myself. So I've decided to take a little trip. Let them know I have all my faculties."

"Good for you!" said Cherry.

"Damn straight," Stan chimed in.

"But you won't worry them, will you? You'll let them know you're all right?" Her maternal nature shined through.

"Of course. Don't we always correct our children lovingly?"

"Oh, always," the couple said in unison, and began laughing again.

Stan's laugh quieted to a grin, and he looked in the mirror again. "How far do you want to go? How strong a point do you want to make?"

Lute studied his hands silently a moment. *Holy One, bless me once more. Please help me get back to Seattle or Tacoma. If these are not your angels, Lord, send them soon.* He spoke up. "Well, you may not be able to take me far, but I want to get to some metropolitan center without using public transportation. And I don't drive. So the answer is, I haven't figured that out yet."

The couple in the front seat looked at each other and seemed to nod. Stan spoke for them. "You seem pretty straightforward, there, Mr. McKenna. I mean, you aren't some kind of ax murderer or anything, are you?"

Lute chuckled softly. He brought a mock-scholarly tone to his answer: "I am the quintessence of trustworthiness. And if you have even a scintilla of apprehension, please let me out along the roadside. I would not cause you concern."

There was stillness in the car. Finally Cherry said, "I think I understand about the quintessence of trustiness, but I don't think I have any scintillas...."

Stan said, "Hey Don, I'm goin' with my gut here, but a guy who uses quintessence and scintilla in the same sentence is probably not gonna do me or my wife much harm." He glanced at Lute in the rear-view mirror and grinned. "So here's the deal. If I got you to Sitka—free for nuthin'— could you get yourself back when your kids hear what you've accomplished?"

"Sitka? As in, Alaska?"

"That a little too far? Don't want to make quite that loud a statement?"

Lute whistled under his breath. "Is there anything there?"

"Sure," Don said. "Airport, fish canneries, Sheldon Jackson College. You can get out again when you're ready. But Cherry and I are about to take our little Cessna and GO THERE! And there's a free seat for ya if you want it. The extra weight'll probably cost me $30 more in aviation fuel, and I'd be glad to donate that to the cause of righteous upbringing of adult children."

"A college, eh?" Lute's mind was racing. "But only public transportation out?"

"Theoretically, yes, but you hang around the 'port and you always find private pilots headed somewhere, willing to take you along. Usually pretty reasonable, too, if some-body doesn't look like a gabby sort."

Lute tried to think.

"The airstrip's down here half a mile, Don. And we'd enjoy your company. But if you'd rather, I can leave you here at the little burger joint on the left."

Cherry turned around. "Why don't you come with us? I think those young folks would either have you committed afterward, or would have new respect for you."

"But I wouldn't want to get sick in your plane. Light planes are a lot choppier than commercial aircraft, aren't they?"

Again the couple acted as if in synchrony. Stan pointed toward Cherry's purse and she was already opening it. She retrieved a small vial and shook out two large, white, oblong pills.

"If that's all that's keeping you in the Lower 48, hon', these're the cure! If you can take them without liquid, do it right now and by the time Stan has the preflight done, you'll be good to go."

"Ever been up in a small plane, Don?" Stan asked.

"Never in all my years."

"'Bout time to try it, before you turn sixty, eh?"

"Thanks for the compliment. But yes, before I turn seventy, I think I should. I accept your generous offer. You are truly Good Samaritans. And I'll be trying not to think of Psalm 90 as we take off."

The Snyders' brows furrowed slightly, but they didn't ask.

Within 45 minutes the couple had turned in their rental car, completed a thorough checklist on their Cessna 210, stowed their suitcases—allowing Lute to keep his briefcase with him as requested—and taxied to the end of the runway.

Stan scanned the skies as he pressed a button on the control wheel and spoke into his radio mouthpiece. "This is Port Townsend, Cessna two-zero-three-six-six taking runway two-six for departure to the north. Port Townsend." He pressed the switch off again and spoke over his shoulder to Lute. "That's the CTAF—Common Traffic Advisory Frequency. We use it in airports like this that aren't radio controlled. Hope you're comfortable; I put long-range tanks on this rig so we could make this Sitka/Port Townsend run non-stop. It's 800 nautical miles. We should maintain an airspeed of 150, which will put us on the ground between 9:00 and 10:00 tonight Pacific time. Still daylight in the Land of the Midnight Sun." Lute nodded, though the noise level kept him from hearing every word clearly.

Stan pushed the throttle full forward and within seconds Lute was watching the ground fall away under their craft. Mesmerized as he always was by these aeronautical machines that defied the laws of gravity, he almost missed Stan's question. "So you think McKenna Motors can do without the head of the clan for a couple of days?" It took Lute a moment to understand, but he nodded to the back of his angels' heads and prayed thanks.

Three minutes after takeoff, at an altitude of 1500 feet, they crossed the Port Townsend waterfront. Lute searched for the motel from this unfamiliar vantage, and located it just before it passed under them. A black and white squad car was pulling into the lot, blocking Harald's '70 Volvo.

Psalm 90:10

The length of our days is seventy years – or eighty, if we have the strength, yet their span is but trouble and sorrow, for they quickly pass, and we fly away.

CHAPTER 30

A Rolling Flame Gathers No Moth

Port Townsend
4:00 p.m.

The police cruiser pulled into the parking lot and stopped behind Harald's vintage Volvo, parked at a curb facing the motel doors. A uniformed officer got out, closed the door, and stood facing Water Street. Within ten minutes a metallic green Chevy Impala pulled in and stopped beside him. The driver and passenger, both in dark business suits, got out to talk to the local officer.

The officer greeted the driver with a handshake. "Afternoon, Eddie."

"Hi, Jerry. This is Doug Winston from the Seattle bureau. He's been here on the Peninsula on another case today."

Agent Winston flashed the officer an FBI badge as he nodded toward the Volvo. "Well that's our vehicle, all right. Not many of those around anymore. Anyone come or go since you got here?"

"No," the officer answered. "How can I help, gentlemen? Dispatch only said to come intercept the Volvo if it was here."

He motioned discretely and both turned to see that the motel manager was walking toward them.

Eddie Cutler met her halfway, and showed his FBI credentials. They talked briefly and she pointed to room 127, almost directly in front of Harald's car. Cutler seemed to dismiss her, and with a worried glance over her shoulder, she returned to the office.

"We've got it," Cutler said to the cop as he rejoined the men. "Thanks for coming over; we were almost to Chimacum when the call came from an old pal of mine back east. This is one they don't want to lose." The uniformed officer shook hands with both agents and left. Cutler double-parked his car behind the Volvo and shortly knocked on the door of room 127. Harald opened it as far as the lock-chain allowed.

"Are you Dr. Harald Ericksen?" He nodded. Both agents held up their credentials. "FBI, sir. May we come in a moment?"

Harald stared at them a long minute, then closed the door to unlatch the chain and allow them inside. As the younger agent spoke, the older one walked to the back of the motel room and looked inside the bathroom.

"I'm Agent Eddie Cutler, Olympic Peninsula FBI office. This is a colleague of mine from Seattle, Agent Winston. I hope you can help. We're trying to locate someone named Luther Jonson, J-O-N-S-O-N, no H. Do you know him?"

Harald nodded and said, "Yes. Yes, I know Lute."

"Do you know where we can find him, Dr. Ericksen? It's a matter of some urgency."

"What's this about, Mr. Cutler?"

The agent's tight smile served as a response to Harald's question, but he pressed again on his own. "It really is quite important that we locate him as soon as possible. Have you seen him recently?"

Harald ran his hand over his still-wet hair, then fidgeted with his trim rust-colored cardigan sweater. "Well...." He turned and sat on the edge of the bed nearest him. The agents both stood watching him.

"Look, ah..." Harald rubbed his forehead and looked side to side.

Cutler's voice took on a slight edge. "Dr. Ericksen, the room is registered to you but the manager said there was another gentlemen here with you last night. Someone fitting Luther Jonson's description. Was he here?"

Harald stood again, then sat. He rubbed the pillow beside him absently, then his thigh. He looked at the telephone, then back to the immobile agents.

"How do you people know these things?" he stammered.

"He was here, then?" the Seattle agent asked.

Harald stood up decisively. "Listen, I think I should have some advice before we talk further. I mean like a lawyer or, uh, well, a lawyer."

"You're not under investigation, Dr. Ericksen. If you had been, I'd have read you Miranda. I'm just asking if you can help us with a very important task. We need to find Dr. Jonson. Did he stay here last night? Is he close by? We'll just stay until he returns, you know, so this can be a long visit or a short one. Where is he?"

Harald straightened his lanky six-foot-one frame and said, "I don't think I can help you, gentlemen, at least not until I have spoken with an attorney." He started toward the door, but his way was blocked by the younger agent. "Will you excuse me?"

The aging professor looked straight into the eyes of the FBI agent just half his age. The stare-down lasted half a minute or more. Finally, without moving out of Harald's way, Cutler spoke to his colleague.

"Mr. Winston, will you call in before we go? Dr. Ericksen, you don't have any outstanding warrants or anything, do you?"

Harald laughed out loud. "No, sir. No, indeed. But please satisfy yourself that I am not wanted in several states before you allow me to resume my constitutionally-protected right to privacy." Now the edge had moved to his voice, and his narrowed eyes showed a steeliness they had lacked over the past few minutes. Winston left the room and closed the door. Cutler backed up to lean against the triple dresser. Harald sat back on the bed and checked his watch.

"Do I understand you are both in archaeology?" asked the Peninsula agent.

Harald brightened. "Well I am, but Lute is the...." He broke off and looked closely at the visitor for a few moments. He shook his head. "Sir, I have to ask you to respect my decision not to discuss any of this. I really am sorry, but I have some concerns that I need to satisfy before I can answer any of these questions."

Cutler smiled and nodded briefly. The two spent several awkward minutes staring into neutral space. Harald examined his fingernails and wiped lint from his slacks.

There was a single knock at the door and Cutler moved to open it. Agent Winston came one step into the room, holding a sheet of curled paper in one hand.

"Dr. Ericksen, my office in Seattle just sent this picture through our car's fax machine. It may cause you to reconsider, sir. Please take a look. I think you may decide to help us."

CHAPTER 31

SHAME IN SHADOWS

Port Townsend
4:30 p.m.

Harald stared at the photo on the curled facsimile paper. His head shaking slowly from side to side, an attitude of disbelief surrounded him like an aura. He searched every corner of the image, returning his stare repeatedly to two figures in the right-center section. When he looked away, he did not meet the FBI agents' inquiring eyes, but instead peered down at his bare feet.

The agents waited in silence until Harald spoke.

"You people have surveillance cameras in men's rooms at truck stops?" When neither of the federal agents responded, Harald continued. "Is that even legal?"

Agent Winston said, "The activity you see in the picture is not legal. The camera was placed there by court order because of the number of indecent exposure and public sodomy violations reported at that rest stop. You may not remember it, but there was a sign posted on the building warning of surveillance 'For Public Protection.'"

"There is no question of your identity in the picture, is there?" Agent Cutler's sentence had the form of a question, but his inflection conveyed certainty that it was a statement of fact. Harald buried his face in his hands, his elbows propped heavily on his knees.

"Did you know the other man before meeting him there?" asked Winston. Harald was silent. "Was money exchanged? Did he pay you? Vice-versa?"

"So to speak," added Cutler, but Winston's scowl erased the local agent's brief smile.

Agent Winston moved between the beds and sat down opposite Harald. "Dr. Ericksen, we don't have to talk about this. It's not really why we're here. Matter of fact, you never heard about this at the time because the King County Sheriff's Office identified you from your license plate and declined to prosecute. Your age and career, your lack of any prior trouble with the law, the fact they didn't identify you up there again afterward—it just seemed preferable to let it go. Do you remember this incident?"

Harald nodded.

"Almost twenty years ago, was it? Indian John Rest Stop on Interstate 90, east of the Snoqualmie Pass summit?" Again Harald nodded.

The local agent spoke up from his position leaning against the bureau. "I'm getting the feeling that you remember the situation because it was not a frequent activity for you, sir. Anywhere, not just this one rest stop. Is that the case?"

Head still down, Harald answered in a soft voice. "It was the only time." He shook his head again slowly. "Once in a lifetime, and you have a picture of it."

"Once more," said Winston slowly and carefully, "do you understand that we're not here to talk about this, Dr. Ericksen? We will, if we hit a dead-end with our first priority. But if you'll just tell us when Dr. Jonson will return, or where he is, I don't think we'll have time for this." Winston held up the curled paper in his hand, then dropped it back into his lap dismissively.

Harald stood up, his shoulders seemingly weighted by extra gravity. He walked toward the bathroom but stopped before entering it. "I don't suppose you believe me, that I've never done that before or since . . . ?"

"If you say it, sir, I have no reason to doubt you," Winston said. "But if you want us to take your statement on this matter of your . . . well, this sexual situation, then Agent Cutler will do that while I go in search of Dr. Jonson. We can open a file on your case and proceed to discuss that with you now if you decline to help us on our more important search. Your choice, sir."

Harald turned angrily. "Does the Federal Bureau of Investigation have authority to blackmail U.S. citizens, Mr. Winston? This isn't even subtle. You're offering me Hobson's choice: turn in my friend, or you'll expose me."

Harald realized that his choice of words was unfortunate, and lowered his eyes again.

"I beg to differ, sir," countered Winston. "First, you're not 'turning in' Dr. Jonson since he's not charged with anything. We just need to talk with him for a little while. Second, we'll locate him with your help or without it, I assure you. Third, the decision to prosecute any individual on any allegation is based on many factors, not the least of which is how much time we have for investigations. If you refuse to help us with our priority, suddenly we have some time available to take your statement and look into this indelicate photograph. If, instead, you'll answer my questions about your friend right now, we'll be on our way."

"But I can't betray a friend!"

"Sir, help me with a little dilemma I have. Say, just hypothetically, that the FBI had information someone might be in danger. And say that we had been tasked with getting him safely out of that danger, but we had no authority to share the specifics of that situation with his friends or relatives to help them see how they would be helping him by cooperating. What would you suggest we tell those people?"

Harald searched the agent's eyes. He looked over at Cutler as well, then quickly back to Winston. He cleared his throat and began to ask, "Is that what...?" but Winston interrupted.

"Sorry, I've said more than I should have already. I need your decision."

"Give me a few minutes alone, will you?" Harald's request was ignored. Both agents stood staring at him. "To pray, gentlemen. Believe it or not."

"We don't have time, sir. If Dr. Jonson is not returning here, but is trying to escape from someone or something, we don't have five minutes to spare."

Cutler spoke up. "You're a man of faith, Dr. Ericksen?" Harald looked to see if there were an ugly irony in his question but the agent appeared to be asking a straightforward question.

"Yes. I am a Christian."

"So am I. And I know that sometimes when I've failed God, He seems to give me a chance to make it right in another way. Maybe that's what this is for you."

"And it has to happen quickly, Dr. Ericksen," repeated Winston. "At this moment, not deciding is a decision."

Harald drew in a long deep breath. "OK. I can't be much help so you'll probably prosecute me anyway. It doesn't matter. Nothing matters now." He slumped down on the foot of the bed and began to shake his head again.

"Tell me everything you know about where Dr. Jonson is," said Winston.

"He's on his way to Seattle. I have no idea if he's getting a bus or a cab or hitchhiking or what. He's running a little scared. He wouldn't tell me anything other than that he's got to get to Seattle to talk to the media. He left about an hour ago."

"What's he wearing?"

"Wearing? Oh, a blue blazer and light gray slacks. A white shirt, no tie; black loafers, I think. He has a full head of hair, white...."

"We have a physical on him," Cutler interrupted. "Carrying anything?"

"Black briefcase, fairly wide kind that you can put overnight things in."

"He's alone?" Harald answered with a nod.

"Are you telling us everything, Dr. Ericksen?" Now it was Winston's turn to look deep into Harald's eyes.

"Yes sir. He said it would be better if I didn't know specifics, for my own sake." The two agents moved for the door. Harald pointed at the facsimile photo still lying on the bed where Winston had sat. "You left something."

Winston shook his head. "Keep or toss. Original's in Seattle."

Harald's voice was strained as he picked up the curled paper. "Will you be . . . I mean . . . regardless of what you're going to do about me, you will help Lute, won't you?"

Cutler was already outside, but Winston paused and turned around to face the ashen professor. The agent smiled wordlessly, then walked out the door and closed it.

Harald stared at the door, at the fax paper, and then at a small smudge on his finger. He moved listlessly to the bathroom, drew water into the basin, and washed his hands for ten minutes.

CHAPTER 32

AN UNSCHEDULED FRIGHT

Airborne to Alaska
Thursday, June 20
7:50 p.m. Pacific Daylight Time

"You've been awful quiet back there, Don..." Cherry half-turned in her front seat and tried to raise her voice above the incessant drone of the Cessna's single engine. "That motion-sickness pill work for you?"

Lute nodded. "I'm fine. Just thinking."

Stan spoke up and Lute strained his best ear toward him. "We're just about to Prince Rupert, kinda the northern end of the British Columbia coast. Once we're over the panhandle, it's almost exactly two hours to touchdown in Sitka." He rapped on the control wheel and added, "Assuming this second-hand yoke doesn't break, and if our fuel lasts."

Lute jerked his face around to stare at the pilot. Seeing the younger man's grin, Lute breathed out and sensed his heart rate slow down again. "I may have soiled my linen."

The couple in front laughed heartily. "Stan, don't scare our first-timer like that!"

"Sorry, Don."

Lute nodded forgiveness.

"I'm a little concerned about the weather up front. It's been a hot day and now with these cumulus clouds moving in—which our weather briefer failed to mention to me—we're getting some variance in ground temperature. Causes down-drafts where it's cooler and up-drafts where it's still warm."

"So what happens in turbulence? Does it break up light planes?"

Stan chuckled. "Nah. Your kids aren't getting rid of you that easily. Mostly I worry about fuel. If I can't get above the bumps it just eats up fuel and we might have to make a pit stop somewhere instead of getting into Sitka nonstop."

Lute nodded and leaned back again. He watched the eastern horizon, with rugged snow-capped coastal mountain peaks passing continuously, each seemingly more majestic than the last. Under them a tiny town approached and passed, and then they crossed over open water. Unsure of geography in the Pacific Northwest, Lute guessed it was the Pacific itself. He remembered seeing folded maps in the wall-pocket to his left and retrieved one. Opening it proved difficult as the plane churned unexpectedly, then righted. He studied it a few moments.

"Is all of that down there the Inside Passage? We're not over the ocean, are we?"

"You're right," answered Cherry. "Way over there on the west you can just barely see some land mass of the Queen Charlotte Islands. That," she pointed straight down, "is Hecate Strait."

Suddenly the plane lost altitude; Lute felt thrust into his seat belt and harness as his body snapped upward toward the canopy. A whip of the plane wrenched his neck and he reached instinctively for the safety-holds on the wall beside him. His heart began to race. Looking forward to gauge his hosts' reactions to the plane's sudden misbehavior, he was not relieved to see their neck muscles tensing. The nose fell forward even though Stan had a tight grip on the yoke in front of him. He pulled it back, straining to correct the dive but clearly struggling to keep the nose from getting too high. Lute began to pray silently.

"Don't worry, Don."

Cherry's voice had a strained-calm timbre.

Just as suddenly as it had begun to plunge, the plane bottomed out with a shudder and began a rapid climb. Stan immediately reversed his pressure on the yoke and now pushed it in to bring the nose down. As the craft leveled momentarily he eased up, but the relief was short-lived and they rose again, apparently out of control.

Lute's stomach seemed to rise and fall more violently than the light airplane. Now he was pressed into his seat as the updraft continued, forcing the plane farther and farther above the Strait thousands of feet below.

Fighting panic, Lute shouted above the din, "Are we OK?" The question sounded stupid and childish to him, but it was mild compared to his sense of imminent death.

"We got caught in some turbulence," Stan answered. His face registered more annoyance than concern. "The weather briefer mentioned the possibility of a scattered cloud layer along our route, but he said nothing about this turbulence." He started to continue but held off to gauge another momentary change in the plane's bobbing. "All these scattered cumulus clouds we're flying under ... when we get in the shadow of one, the air can be much cooler so we start to descend pretty rapidly. But as soon as we fly back in the sun, the hotter air picks us up and lofts us higher."

Lute had a pang of realization that logic didn't govern emotions; the calm in Stan's voice did much more to ease the old researcher's mind than the actual aeronautical précis.

Still in the updraft, Stan pushed the throttle to the wall and maintained a steady rate of climb. "I'll get us above these clouds and then it should smooth out. Soon as we do, I'll call it in to save some other guy from the surprise. The briefer didn't have any pireps when I talked to him."

Cherry guessed that was an unfamiliar term for their guest and spoke up. "Pireps are pilot reports. The weather briefers have all kinds of fancy equipment for forecasting conditions, but the only way they really know what's going on up here is to hear it directly from a pilot who's in it. Especially when it comes to turbulence or icing or wind shears."

Under Stan's steady hand the Cessna continued to climb until Lute guessed they were a couple of thousand feet above the cloud level. Noticeably calmer there, both the plane and its oldest passenger settled into a welcome routine for the next two hours.

At first, Lute searched the horizon for a glimpse of the incredible Canadian mountains he had found so fascinating before, but the clouds obscured all the earth below. Lute admitted the tradeoff was worth it. He hadn't felt his heart pump like that in some time. *That's not true, I guess. I felt the adrenalin pump after Christy's phone call from Hjalmar. And I was starting to feel it in the motel at Port Townsend. Matter of fact, I definitely went through anxiety when I left Israel.*

He watched the cotton-like layers below and wondered how he could find a major media outlet from this Alaskan settlement where they were headed. He worried that he was running away from a solution rather than toward one, and that his escape from those who would steal his news would drop him into a safe but impotent isolation. He weighed again, as he had before, the possibility of mailing the news media photocopies of these astonishing scrolls between his feet. As usual, he foresaw only their dismissal as a hoax. Even if his claim were published, confirmation might not come before Sean's people could find him and steal away the precious *kairos*.

There is no other way. I can't escape this call. Only when I step before worldwide cameras will this news be safe. Only when I personally tell these scroll fragments' story and present them in evidence. I feel like the patriarch Jacob approaching Egypt—full of joyful anticipation before seeing his beloved son Joseph, and yet fearful of the unknown, afraid of dying in a strange land.

A verse came to his memory, and Lute spoke to himself words that were drowned out by engine noise. "Yes, Lord, Genesis 46. Down to Egypt. Up to Alaska."

Genesis 46:3

"I am God, the God of your Father," he said. "Do not be afraid to go down to Egypt, for I will make you into a great nation there. I will go down to Egypt with you, and I will surely bring you back again."

CHAPTER 33

SET MY PEOPLE FREE

Sitka, Alaska
9:15 p.m., Pacific Daylight Time

"Hey, Pastor," a smiling, long-haired coed called across the quad, "you were great tonight!"

The Alaskan Native stopped and turned toward her. "Of course," he grinned.

She waved goodbye and the Reverend Moses Tling resumed his unhurried stroll across the campus of Sheldon Jackson College. At five-foot-seven he would not have had a long stride even with a Type A personality, but his mellow nature and diminutive stature had produced a distinctively leisurely amble. Friends and family had long become accustomed to slowing their pace when they walked with him.

He reflected on his just-concluded speech to the student body. He was a reluctant public speaker anytime, but had struggled especially with this one. Invited by the student association shortly after his Fairbanks congregation's news-making decision late last year, he had declined twice before finally acceding to their persistent requests. "More

Light or More Heat?" he had answered when they asked for the title of his address.

Midnight Sun Presbyterian Church had called Moses to his first pastorate eight years ago. Little did that twenty-six-year-old know what lay in store as he began ministry there, and the only certainty he now felt about the future was how unpredictable it would be. Quietly conservative himself in most things theological and political, he had expected his Fairbanks church to be similar. They would be typically Alaskan: pulled like tightwires between environmental conservation and libertarian resistance to authority. They had no choice but to live with their cognitive dissonance, independent personalities in survival-dependent communities. Gregarious reclusives. There were eight Eskimo and Aleut families enrolled along with ninety Anglos. The young Reverend Tling had thought it a good match for him.

Still reflective, Moses approached The Rail, a traditional campus lookout over Sitka Sound, just a score of crow-fly miles from the Pacific Ocean. The blue of the midsummer evening sky calmed him. He scanned the humanless horizon, the rolling waves, the retreating tide on the rocky beach below. *Just like the soul,* he thought: *peaceful above, churning and murky below.* He turned right to feast his eyes on the mountains towering to the north around his alma mater, then continued his slow visual sweep until completing a 360-degree rotation back to The Rail. *God is an Artist,* he thought. *The Tongass Forest, Baranov Island, even pouring rains that turn into lush green surroundings. How can our souls be in turmoil in this good world You've given us? If we would only faith.*

"Faith is a verb," he had noted in his speech tonight. "We don't *have* faith, we don't *own* it. We either *are faithing* or we're *not.* Either we live like we know God is wildly in love with us, or we don't." He had paused then, grinning in anticipation of their laughter and groans after his next line. "Faith your future ... with confidenth."

It was an upbeat ending to a generally low-key but difficult presentation. He and his Fairbanks flock were not the only ones struggling to know God's will in the sticky matter of homosexuality. The predominantly conservative students at missionary-founded Sheldon Jackson came from religious and cultural backgrounds that did not approve, but they could hardly have missed the issue's rising tide within Christendom.

During the speech he had clearly seen which viewpoint individual students empathized with; most brightened during his presentation of the fundamentalist positions and darkened during the opposite.

He thought about how spare his opening gambit had been: he took a step from the lectern to the audience's right to role-play the conservative view, then eased to their left for a liberal rebuttal. Back and forth for several minutes. Although the dramatics were not typical of him, the lean language was, and it had been an effective way to begin.

* * *

"Well, how can we even be discussing this?" he had asked softly from the right. "Leviticus 18:22 says, 'Do not lie with a man as one lies with a woman.'"

Then he had smiled and moved left of the podium to answer. "Maybe God was speaking to lesbians...?" He realized from the students' puzzled reactions that any jokes during this simulated debate would be more confusing than tension-relieving. He returned to the right and re-phrased the fundamental question. "Why are we even talking here? God's Word clearly outlaws sex between two men. Or between two women. End of discussion."

From the other side: "Oh, there are many prohibitions listed in the Old Testament holiness code which we do not observe now. Leviticus prohibits eating pork, shellfish, and rare meat; women wearing pants; people wearing blends of fibers. It commands that we stone children who curse their parents and brides who are not virgins, but we don't do that anymore. We don't fire pastors whose eyesight is defective. We cut the hair of our heads and beards, but all of those things are prohibited in the Old Testament. How do you select which you will follow and which you won't? Remember, even Jesus and His disciples broke the ancient law when they picked grain to eat on the Sabbath."

The 33-year-old Eskimo pastor, wearing jeans and his old college sweatshirt with a proud whalebone cross hanging from his neck, crossed behind the podium to answer himself. He carefully measured out his "well's" on the audience's right and his "oh's" on their left.

"Well, there are timeless elements within those codes. They should still be obeyed. We still observe all the Ten Commandments, for instance."

"Oh, Christian gays and lesbians do, too. They don't condone lying or murder; they don't believe a married person should have sex with anyone other than their partner."

"Well, God destroyed Sodom and Gomorrah because of the abomination of homosexuality. Lot could barely protect the visiting angels against the men of Sodom who were determined to rape them!"

"Oh? Which is better: for us to interpret Scripture, or for Scripture to interpret Scripture? Every time the Bible itself mentions Sodom after that story in Genesis, sins like pride, idolatry, and inhospitality are named. Homosexuality—which some people claim is the whole point of the story—isn't mentioned even once. Check Ezekiel 16:49-50 and Matthew 10:14-15, for example."

Between opposing arguments, Moses' slow strolls gave the two hundred young listeners valuable moments to assimilate the debate points. He carefully monitored their eyes, pausing longer when their souls seemed busiest.

"Well, but some of those recountings also mention *abomination*, which refers to men lusting after men."

"Oh, but Isaiah 66:2-3 contrasts people whom God esteems—the humble and contrite— versus those who 'delight in their abominations.' Chapter six of Proverbs lists seven things that are detestable to the Lord. Being gay isn't one, but stirring up conflict in the community is. Is it possible that being judgmental of others is the greatest abomination to the Lord?"

"Well, if you won't consider the Old Testament, will you belittle the New?" Moses turned his Bible on the podium so he could read it from the audience's right side. "Saint Paul is crystal clear in Romans 1:26: 'Because of this, God gave men over to shameful lusts. Even their women exchanged natural relations for unnatural ones. In the same way the men also abandoned natural relations with women and were inflamed with lust for one another. Men committed indecent acts with other men, and received in themselves the due penalty for their perversion.' How clear does God have to make Himself? AIDS is the fulfillment of that prophecy!"

Moses stood there, picked up his Bible, held it close to his chest, and a moment later laid it back on the podium. Then, as his rapt audience had become accustomed, he moved several steps to the other side of the podium. He looked out over the darkened, hushed auditorium, then back at the podium. He walked back to that blond oak lectern, picked up the Bible, and hugged it again.

"Oh, so many accusations." He held up fingers to tick off answers. "First, unless you count the hint in Luke 17:34, Jesus Himself said nothing on the subject. But on several occasions He did denounce those who are quick to judge others. Second, if AIDS is the sentence, why are babies and hemophiliacs—but not lesbians—convicted Law-breakers along with gay men? Third, if a straight man abandoned his nature and had homosexual relations, that would indeed be unnatural and an abomination. But wouldn't it be just as unnatural for a homosexual man to abandon *his* nature by attempting heterosexual relations?"

Moses checked the eyes that he could see and paused. It was clear this was a little more complex argument, and the students' cranial CPUs were working overtime.

"Fourth, both Old and New Testament passages have been used throughout history to justify some practices that we no longer condone: slavery, the virtual servitude of women, even murderous anti-Semitism."

While the hall had been deathly still for most of the past few minutes, a bit of coughing and shuffling followed his extended counter-arguments from the left. Moses knew they were beginning to sense his bias. But he plodded on.

"Oh-kaaay," he finally said from the right, feigning surrender on one small debate point, "what's 'the hint' you mentioned in Luke 17?" He walked to the left to answer.

"Look up Luke 17:34 in the King James or Revised Standard Versions of the Bible. In His end-times prophesy, Jesus included the words, 'In that night there shall be two men in one bed; one shall be taken'—(up to Heaven)—'and the other left.'"

Moses ambled back to the 'conservative' side of the podium and thought a moment. Noting numerous students' expressions now bordering on disgust, he gave their reactions voice. "Aren't you ashamed of yourself for that?

For implying our Savior might have meant they were homosexuals and one might be saved?" Student heads throughout the auditorium nodded strong affirmation.

For the first time since he'd begun his presentation, the young Native pastor did not walk to the left to answer, but stopped behind the podium. His head hung low, his eyes downcast, he waited a long minute before continuing. Finally he looked up and across the Sheldon Jackson students and staff.

"I'm ashamed of myself for many things. Mostly for failing to love God with all my heart and soul and mind, and for failing to love His children with as much abandon as He does."

"Preach it brother! Love the sinner!" came an enthusiastic male voice from the center of the auditorium.

Moses turned toward the young man, smiling enigmatically. "Did you see that big sandwich board one of your classmates wore outside the entrance tonight, the one advertising the sock hop later in the gym? Imagine if I painted the word 'SINNER' on plywood boards like those and hung them on you. Then if I patted you on the back, would you feel it? What kind of hug could I give you with that between us? Could you give one back?"

* * *

Still immersed in the memory, Moses ran his fingers absently along The Rail and thought of the silence that ensued after that. He wondered what, if anything, the young college Christians would remember from this night. Whether it would be his mock debate, or the short history he had then detailed of his Fairbanks congregation's real-life conflict over the issue of homosexuality and the narrow decision to become a More Light—gay-affirming—church.

His stark narrative chronicled how one small group of university faculty families had proposed membership in that nationwide Presbyterian group, and how numerous study groups had discussed the issue from every conceivable point of view over the course of the following six months. Moses quoted the rallying words of the More Light movement, taken from a 17th century English pastor's sendoff sermon to the Pilgrims. As paraphrased in a later hymn, Rev. John Robinson's exhortation to them in 1620 concluded,

> "We limit not the truth of God to our poor reach of mind
>
> By notions of our day and sect—crude, partial and confined.
>
> No, let a new and better hope within our hearts be stirred,
>
> For God hath yet more light and truth to break forth from the Word."

Moses finished simply, noting that at a rancorous congregational meeting punctuated by a dozen or more uncomfortable—they would say "faithful"—members walking out, the vote to affiliate with More Light churches had passed on a vote of 43 to 38. The students—polite and attentive as ever—sat silently awaiting the Alaskan Native's own reflections after that. But having told the story he'd been invited to tell, and hearing no questions, he nodded shyly and walked off stage with Bible in hand.

He looked across the Sound and sky once more. Seeing a small plane approaching from the south reminded him of his early departure the next day, and he headed across campus toward the college's guest room.

CHAPTER **34**

AT SIXES AND SEVENS, AND ZERO

Port Townsend
9:20 p.m.

Harald hustled to the tiny motel bathroom to throw up again, but the dry heaves passed and he returned to lie on the bed. He stared at the ceiling for long minutes. He pulled the extra pillow over his eyes. He eased the downy form over his nose and mouth and pressed hard against it, but within a minute pulled it away and breathed in.

The professor rose on the window side of the bed and opened the double-lined drapes. It was almost as dark outside as in. He checked his watch. Almost five hours, and he'd been virtually catatonic for most of them. He looked across the parking lot and the street beyond but saw nothing. He drew the drapes again, flipped the light switch by the door, looked at the silent telephone, and then retrieved the curled paper from where he had stashed it under his overnight case. Before he could bring it up to his eyes he wretched. He dropped the paper and quickly went to kneel in front of the toilet.

There's nothing left, he thought. *Nothing.*

CHAPTER 35

TO KNOW WHICH WAY TO GO

Sitka, Alaska
9:50 p.m.

Once the Cessna was taxied in and shut down, Lute followed Stan and Cherry out of it, onto the tarmac, and into the general aviation office. As Stan completed paperwork at the desk, Cherry engaged Lute in conversation.

"We'd love to offer you a place to stay tonight, Don, but our handyman told me on the phone this morning that we have no running water. We had him come in to fix a problem in both the upstairs and downstairs bathrooms while we've been away, and—wouldn't you just know it—it was much worse than we realized. He said he had to tear out some drywall to get at the pipes in both rooms. So unless you want to share a thunder jug with us...."

Lute had begun politely shaking his head 'no' after the first sentence. The final phrase, however, was unfamiliar. "Thunder jug?"

"You know, honey bucket. Chamber pot."

Lute grinned and nodded. "Thanks anyway, Cherry, I'll find a room. You two have been incredibly kind. If you'll point me to a pay phone—and maybe suggest a hotel or motel—I'll call first and then get a cab from here."

"Of course not. I mean, of course you won't get a cab. Free drop-off service was included in your airfare."

"I think God sent you," Lute answered appreciatively. "Is it too late to buy you two dinner or a drink?" He was hoping she'd decline, but gratitude and a sense of reciprocity rose above his exhaustion.

She seemed to think about that as she grabbed his arm and led him around a corner to an open office area. She motioned toward the chair behind the closest desk, so Lute sat as she picked up a slender Sitka telephone book from a nearby workstation. She opened it, found a listing, and then placed it in front of him.

"The Sitka Sounder is run by a friend of ours. Matter of fact, he used to own a car dealership himself, so you two will have something to talk about during your stay here! It's a nice motel very close by. Moderate price. A little restaurant attached."

Lute's adrenaline glands started pumping. As he dialed, he began plotting how to avoid conversations about the profession his assumed name had placed him in.

Within minutes the Snyders had ushered him into their silver-grey Ford Explorer, and three minutes after that pulled under the portico entrance to a modern-looking two-story TraveLodge.

Stan spoke. "Thanks for the offer of a drink, but can we get a raincheck? Maybe next time we get to Port Townsend?"

Lute nodded and mumbled, "Of course."

The driver continued, "I'm going to wait until you give me the high sign. If there's any kind of problem, we don't want you stranded here."

Before he opened his backseat door, Lute extended a hand to his benefactors. "You two are wonderful," he said. "Someday I'll explain just *how* wonderful."

As Cherry turned to shake hands, Stan retrieved a business card from his wallet and handed it back. "If you're here more than a day or two, please give us a call. The number is both home and business; we operate informally up here. And I would like to hear how this turns out with your kids. I may need to use you as a model if 'Matthew, Mark, Luke and Ralph' ever act uppity with their mother and me." He smiled.

"Munga takk," Lute said as he opened the door, conscious of acting unconscious about not offering one of his own cards in return.

"Beg pardon?"

"Sorry—that's Norwegian for 'many thanks.' I *will* be in touch."

Cherry looked surprised. "I didn't think McKenna would be a Norwegian name."

Lute grinned but didn't answer. He walked into the lobby. As soon as the desk clerk made a check mark on her registration list, Lute turned to wave thanks. He watched until the Explorer had pulled out onto the street then completed the forms, feeling both guilty and anxious about re-using Don McKenna's name and a fictional Port Townsend address. As he collected his room key and picked up his briefcase, he noticed a small rack of paperbacks and magazines. He withdrew a copy of the new issue of *Time* and paid the clerk.

"The Sheldon Jackson College student newspapers are free, if you're interested," the twenty-something co-ed said, pointing to a stack by the door. "I'm co-editor," she added sweetly, "and we're very proud of our work." Lute couldn't refuse.

It wasn't long before he sank into an easy chair in the comfortable two-room mini-suite. His sigh seemed to reach the depths of his combined relief and fatigue.

Holy One. I love You. I'm so grateful that You have brought me safely to this place of rest. I will sleep soon, and trust You will let me know tomorrow which way to go in this new wilderness. If it's Your will that this kairos *be announced from this northern outpost, so be it. I will follow You as Joshua's troops followed Your ark. You fit me for battle, Lord. Lead on, for I ask it in the powerful name of Jesus.*

He opened his eyes and looked at his watch. Ten-twenty-five. He picked up the *Time* magazine and checked the date on the front cover: June 24, 1991. He looked back at his calendar watch, which showed the 21st. He shook his head. *I'll never understand news magazines, whose stock-in-trade is honest reporting, pre-dating their covers to the following Monday.*

Lute absently flipped through the magazine, but when his eyes strayed to the headline on the student newspaper nearby, he tossed *Time* aside.

For the moment, Lute focused on the skinny SJC newspaper, and its front-page picture and article titled "Fairbanks Pastor To Explain Why Gays Bring More Light." *Nuts!* he thought. *I wish I could have been there and met him. If only he knew how timely his topic was.*

Lute wouldn't notice until the next morning that the *Time* issue had fallen open to the Religion section and a major feature story. Under a two-column headline "What Does God Really Think About Sex?" was a summary sub-head: "Christians of all sorts are battling over the issues of homosexuality, infidelity and fornication."

The world waited. *Are You going to break into human time with this* kairos *today?* Lute asked again in prayer. *Show me how to do Your will. Lead on, Lord.*

Joshua 2:22 through 3:4

When they left, they went into the hills and stayed there three days, until the pursuers had searched all along the road and returned without finding them. Then the two men started back. They went down out of the hills, forded the river and came to Joshua son of Nun and told him everything that had happened to them. They said to Joshua, "The LORD has surely given the whole land into our hands; all the people are melting in fear because of us." Early in the morning Joshua and all the Israelites set out from Shittim and went to the Jordan, where they camped before crossing over. After three days the officers went throughout the camp, giving orders to the people: "When you see the ark of the covenant of the LORD your God, and the priests, who are Levites, carrying it, you are to move out from your positions and follow it. Then you will know which way to go, since you have never been this way before.

CHAPTER 36

HOLY SEE, HOLY DO

The Vatican
Friday, June 21
6:55 a.m.

"Father O'Derry." The voice was soft but insistent. Sean opened his eyes and saw the back of a short man in a monk's hooded brown robe. The interloper appeared not to be the monsignor who had led him to this room less than half a clock before, but instead a lowly initiate who was arranging something on the floor opposite Sean's cot.

"Yes?"

"You'll be leaving soon. There's a biscuit and tea here on a tray, and a lavatory across the hall. There's a cloth and towel laid out there. I'll come back for you in about twenty minutes."

"Where am I go...." Sean broke off the question as his wake-up cowl left and closed the lockless door behind him.

The scholar-priest had barely returned from the tiny restroom and a hurriedly completed spit bath when the young monk came back into the cell. To Sean's consternation, his visitor bent down to clear away the untouched tray.

"Wait, I'd like the biscuit and tea, if I may. And would it be possible to get a small rasher and an egg or two? I haven't eaten since lunch yesterday in Jerusalem. Been off my feed; bit of an upsetting day." Mentally he added, *to put it mildly!*

The monk stood up with the tray. "If you have a pocket, Father, keep the biscuit. But I've been told to bring you with me immediately. I'm sorry. Bring your things, please."

Sean did as he was told, grabbing the old black valise he had stuffed toiletries into before leaving for the airport twelve hours before. "May I ask where we're going?"

The hooded robe led him forward in silence. From the progressively darker hallway ahead, Sean sensed he was about to descend into the recesses of the Vatican.

CHAPTER 37

MORNING HAS BROKEN

Sitka, Alaska
Friday, June 21
5:00 a.m., Pacific Daylight Time

Lute awoke with a start. Even with the shades drawn there was sufficient light to see the unfamiliar walls and furniture. *Jerusalem*, he thought. *No. San Diego ... Seattle. Still no. Ah. From Port Townsend to Alaska yesterday. I'm in Sitka, Alaska. Unreal.* After confirming that his overnight case was still safely under the bed, he sank back into the pillow and closed his eyes again. He recognized the feeling; it was a sense of foreboding. Something didn't feel right.

"I'm just tired," he said to the empty room. "I've logged 10,000 air miles in the last four days, and this old body registers fright after that much flight." He chuckled at his wordplay, and tried to will the anxiety out of himself. He forced himself into the relax-and-release exercises he'd been taught in communications classes so many years before. Tensing his neck, then shoulders, then arms, then wrists, then fingers—straining mightily against nothing—then reversing the process, draining energy from the contracted muscle groups one after the other. *That helps.*

But when the exercises did not allay the internal gloom, he knew it was a tightened mind or spirit, not physique, that augured ill so early on this solstice day. He looked at the nightstand. The clock radio registered 5:09. He lifted himself on one elbow to look at the control knobs, pushed a promising one, and lay back when soft music began. It sounded like a Kenny G tune. Certainly a saxophone. *'An ill woodwind nobody blows good.' Wish I could remember who said that.* He recognized the song as the hymn "Morning Has Broken," made popular by Cat Stevens some years back. *I hope it's just morning that's broken, not me.*

By a quarter to six, Lute was up, showered, shaved and dressed. He gave his slacks and blazer a sniff test. Today he should try to acquire a second shirt and get his entire wardrobe cleaned somehow. Given his reliance on nightly hand washing of underwear and socks, he thought travel wrinkled not only the fabric but the nose.

He discovered and read the religion article in his *Time*, and expected inspiration. Nothing. He knew his task was to find a national or international news outlet—today, if humanly possible—but felt a great weight on his stranger-in-a-strange-land shoulders. He opened the drapes, looked out on a bright clear day, and prayed. It was one of his short ones, a "pithy prayer." *What now, Lord?*

He waited more, watching gulls swooping over the waves just fifty feet from the window. Hypnotic as the scene was, he felt impatient. As before, hearing no basso profundo voice cascading out of the cloudless sky, no *Ode to Joy* or *Hallelujah Chorus* welling up in his ears as overture to or background for a Divine Answer, Lute smoothed the bedspread tidily up to the headboard, put his room key in his blazer pocket, and carried his briefcase out the door.

A short walk through the ground floor hall took him into the lobby. He nodded good morning to a new desk clerk on duty, and left through the front doors. He strode through the portico area and out to the curb, where he looked first to the left, down the street the Snyders had driven him the evening before. Nothing stirred. He turned to the right. An interesting panoply of buildings fronted the two-lane street; it appeared that Sitka's Russian beginnings had been honored in each new era's architecture. A few onion-domes and a greater number of plain, eastern-looking grey clapboard structures with darker grey trim dotted the otherwise westernized small town street. There were half a dozen vehicles moving down the few blocks he could see, but not much pedestrian life. Not in view. Except for one lone soul. Lute shaded his eyes with his free hand and peered hard. A block away, a short darkish man seemed to be lolly-gagging along the sidewalk, making barely discernible progress in Lute's direction. It was an odd gait, Lute thought. Interesting in its nonchalant, unhurried pace. The fellow was carrying something about the size of Lute's briefcase, and in the interval it took him to reach the TraveLodge, Lute identified him as an Alaskan Native, somehow familiar. *He seems to be my Everyman of Eskimos or Aleuts or whatever*, the world-class archaeologist thought ironically. *It's like I've known him in an earlier life; he's a stranger I always knew I'd meet.*

Now with this sole visible human about to pass in front of the hotel, Lute faked scanning the majestic landscape around him but continued to steal glances at the walker. He caught the man's eye as the pedestrian crossed the motel's driveway, and both nodded silent greetings.

Lute realized.

It was the "Fairbanks Pastor" whose picture he had seen in the Sheldon Jackson College newspaper.

You are an awesome God, the old scholar exulted. The younger man had shyly walked past Lute and continued toward the airport. Uncertain of how to open a conversation but absolutely certain it was destined to happen, Lute knew he had to act. He'd narrowly escaped his international pursuers so far, but the safety he had bought with yesterday's flight wouldn't last long.

So am I in Exodus 17 now, Lord? Am I trying to lead Your people out of a fearsome bondage—an ironic term, since it is their modern preoccupation with sex which You seem to want to liberate them from—and are they resisting to the point of hating me? I remember Your answer to Moses in verses five and six.

His adrenalin pumping, the aging *Kairos*-bearer stepped toward the left to catch up to the young walker. Without a clue what he might say afterward, Lute cleared his throat. "Excuse me, sir?"

Exodus 17:4-6

Then Moses cried out to the LORD, "What am I to do with these people? They are almost ready to stone me." The LORD answered Moses, "Walk on ahead of the people. Take with you some of the elders of Israel and take in your hand the staff with which you struck the Nile, and go. I will stand there before you...."

CHAPTER 38

MANUSCRIPT 1Q-CETHER-5: BODY AND SOUL

"From Cave 1 at Qumran. Translated during our '37-hour watch.' We still wonder how many J-scrolls might surface. The seven in this lot are amazing and exhilarating— once we get past our profound fear of the likely universal rejection of their news. But practically speaking, both of us feel a gnawing worry that there may be so many additional fragments somewhere that we won't be able to contain the news. Perhaps it should not be controlled, but until we can think it through, it just has to be. LJ 4-27-55"

YESHUA ALREADY BELOVED AMONG COMMUNITY. ELDER TOUCHED [HIS] HEAD DURING LESSON AND SENSED STRENGTH FLOW. ELDER ASKED "WHENCE COMES YOUR POWER?" [YESHUA] ANSWERED, "MY FATHER WILL FILL YOU WI[TH IT], AS WELL. ONLY PRAY AND WA[LK] WITH HIM."

ELDER QUESTIONED, "ART THOU GOD'S OWN CHILD?" Y[ESHUA] REPLIED, "THOU SEEST."

OTHER YOUTH JOIN JOHANAN IN CALLING HIM THE ANOINTED. ONLY BEN-DAVID REFRAINS, WITH TAUNT THAT YESHUA'S FATHER IS LAID IN THE TOMB. YESHUA SAID, "VERILY, THE SON OF THE LIVING FATHER PASSES HIS LOVE THROUGH TO THEE." THE ENMITY BEN-DAVID WOULD PLANT CANNOT ROOT IN YESHUA'S KINDNESS.

YESH[UA] ....

...SUNSH[INE] ... ... REFINED GOLD AS ...

... SITTING WITH OUTCAST, LAUGHING. OTHERS THEN WANDERED [BA]CK TO JOIN THE TWO.

APPETITES ALL RISE IN SPRING. COMMUNITY RULE EASES FOR GAMES. MANY REMOVE CONSIDERATION OF OTHERS WITH THEIR CLOAKS BEFORE EXERCISE. MOST TROUBLE [INDECIPHERABLE] AT THESE TIMES. BUT GOD'S-OWN-CHILD RADIATES CARE FOR OT[HERS].

ELDERS ALL AGREE THAT NONE BEFORE HAD THIS GENTLENESS, ABSENCE OF FEAR, LOVE OF CREATION A[ND] EACH SPIRIT.

CHAPTER **39**

MESSAGES

Seattle
Harald's home answering machine

"Dr. Ericksen? If you're there, would you pick up? This is Melinda Patrick, at KPLU-FM... OK, you must not be there. Listen, if you hear this sometime soon, would you give me another call? After our conversation an hour ago which was ah, most intriguing, I really want to follow up. The AP wire continues to register some strange goings-on, and you sounded like you might be able to shed light on them. One thing I want to emphasize, because of how you ended that conversation, is that if you need us to go off the record, you have my word: whatever you tell me will remain off the record until such time as you release it. You can trust that. I have a reporter friend who accepted jail time rather than violating his pledge of confidentiality, and I would, too, if it ever came to that. OK, I've rambled on long enough. My number again is area code 206—in Tacoma—555-8200. I'll wait here until you call. Thanks, Dr. Ericksen. Bye-bye."

* * *

"Hello? Dr. Ericksen? Hmmm. I'll call back."

* * *

"Yes, Dr. Ericksen, this is Melinda Patrick once more. Sorry to bother you again, but it's gotten late and I'm going to call it a day. If you return in the next couple of hours—before, oh, about 11:00 tonight—please call me at home, 206-555-9026. I'm taking a couple of wire service stories with me so I can read them to you when you call. I think you'll find them interesting; the search for archaeologists seems to be intensifying. Well, good-night. I hope you'll call. You're important to us here at the station, Dr. Ericksen."

CHAPTER 40

Moses, Meet Luther

Sitka Airport
Friday, June 21, 1991
6:30 a.m.

"Thank you for the coffee, Dr. Ericksen."

Lute nodded acknowledgement and set his own Styrofoam cup down on a table in the coffee shop, mentally questioning the advisability of his adopting yet one more persona. Harald wouldn't mind. With any luck and God's leading, the whole affair would be over today or tomorrow, and he could come clean with the whole world. He didn't like all this phony stuff, but he couldn't shake the sense of being chased. Using his own name was too risky for now.

"Call me Harald," Lute insisted. The two fell quiet as they took first sips of the tepid vending machine brew.

"You didn't miss much last night," Moses said.

Lute cocked his eye at the young pastor. "Somehow I'm guessing that's modesty talking, not truth. I kicked myself when I realized I had just missed your lecture. So you described to the college crowd your congregation's struggle with the homosexuality issue?"

Moses nodded. With gentle prodding from Lute, the Reverend Tling recapped what he had told the student audience. His taciturnity soon left the two of them in silence again.

Lute looked at the clock on the wall. Set in the center of a miniature totem pole with Tlingit-Haida-like carvings and colors, its digital face registered almost 6:40. He pointed to it. "The clock seems anachronistic, doesn't it? That's probably an ironic term for a clock, but nonetheless fitting for a 1990's face in a ...what? ... 1800's setting?"

Moses grinned and nodded. "You do sound like a professor."

Lute changed the subject. "How long before your pilot arrives?"

"Should be soon. Maybe around seven. Native time." Moses clearly enjoyed using and thereby dulling the slang that was too often used cuttingly. "Alaskan natives use a casual clock. Helps us keep our Bering Strait."

Lute laughed, then caught himself and ended with an appropriate groan. He decided he had to plunge in. There wasn't time to explore the ramifications of the seven secret Dead Sea Scroll fragments with this kindly soul, at least not at the moment. Besides, something about him made Lute wonder if this Alaskan Native would welcome such a conversation, even if time were unlimited. But at least they could discuss Lute's most pressing issue at the moment--a media outlet.

"Reverend Tling," he began.

"Moses."

"Thanks. What can you tell me about national media in your state? As I told you, I find myself here quite unexpectedly, and need to make contact with someone in broadcasting, preferably. I'm just taking a wild guess here, but I suspect there are no CNN correspondents based in Sitka. Right?"

"Yup. No local TV station, let alone national reporters."

"Do they have a journalism department out at the college?"

"Yes. He also teaches English and marketing, and coaches basketball. At least when I was here."

Lute's spirits sank. *Whatever possessed me to come here?* he berated himself. They were silent as the older man racked his brain for a next step.

"There's a video originating in Fairbanks tomorrow."

Listlessly, Lute asked, "Some kind of local production?"

"Nope, international hookup."

"What?"

"From the PBS station at the University. One of my church members is a TV director there. Told me last Sunday they're hosting a teleconference with live participants in London, Tokyo, Rome, some other capitals."

"From Fairbanks?"

Moses nodded yes.

"How'd that happen?"

"The university at Fairbanks specializes in geology and earth sciences, naturally. They've got some kind of breakthrough they're announcing, and Exxon-Mobil is funding this worldwide interactive video thing."

"So it's a news event?"

"Guess so. I told you everything I know, plus a little more." Moses had irregular teeth, but his smile had a perfect shine. The combination of sparse speech and an irascible humor that poked up through the few words he did speak was very attractive.

Lute began to see light. "There will be reporters in a studio in Fairbanks, and a kind of news conference that will be seen around the world?"

"In a few countries. All their videos will come in to the Fairbanks control room. This guy from my church picks who's on the worldwide feed and when."

Lute fell silent. He looked at the clock again, surreptitiously felt his wallet in the inside breast pocket of his blazer, and let his mind churn. Moses seemed quite comfortable with the stillness, but did look down at his watch and back up at the door.

"Do you think your friend would allow a visiting professor from the University of Washington archaeology department to observe tomorrow?"

Moses shrugged. "Might."

"I always wanted to see a live production from inside a TV studio but never have."

Moses' half-smile reminded Lute of the Mona Lisa.

"Do you have any interest in the Dead Sea Scrolls?" asked Lute.

The abrupt turn in the conversation seemed to surprise Moses. Despite the momentary delay while he assimilated the sudden shift in topic, his eventual assent was firm. "A lot," he said simply.

"Then why don't you invite me to accompany you home, to the heart of Alaska, for a day or two? I could share some news about the scrolls—I know someone who has worked on them since they were discovered. You could get me in to see that TV news conference, I could hear you preach on Sunday, and then I'll disappear. I'll get out of your life."

Lute felt his heart rate climb. He watched Moses' face for some sign of the considerations going on inside. Finally the young pastor spoke.

"We don't have a very big home. My wife ..."

"Oh, my!" Lute interjected. "I didn't mean to invite myself to *stay* with you. I'm so sorry. I just meant, may I accompany you on this flight, book a hotel room, spend a little time with you tomorrow, and see the television station."

"So you don't like my wife? You don't want to meet her and eat her cooking?"

"No, no, of course that's not...." Lute realized the young pastor was enjoying watching him squirm. They both laughed.

"It would be a pleasure, Dr. Ericksen." He seemed to insist on addressing the older gentleman with the honorific. "I wish I could offer you free passage, but I'm poor. If you have the airfare to join the flight, you'd be welcome to the guest room in our parsonage."

"And you'd try to see if I could get in to watch the teleconference from the studio?" Lute looked closely to see if his gentle insistence on that point would be met with suspicion or resistance.

"OK."

Eureka! Praise God! "That's great, Moses. If you'll point the way to the men's room, I'll be ready when your pilot arrives."

Lute followed Moses' directions and was shortly locked in a stall with his ancient-cargo briefcase. He frantically sanitized his wallet of all foreign traces, stuffing his Israeli driver's license, two credit cards on Jerusalem banks, and the half dozen business cards he carried, into his calf-length stockings. He fitted Harald's business card—given him when they had first reunited two nights before in Seattle—into the driver's license pocket of his wallet. *It might pass*, he thought. If I have to show ID to anyone, I'll just tell them I don't drive and I pay cash because .... *Damn it. I'll just have to cross those bridges if they come up.*

Lute returned to the sink area and splashed water on his face. When he searched his own eyes in the mirror, he saw more desperation than he should have. More anxiety. More deceit. He knew in his head that this charade was necessary to the success of his mission, but his stomach grumbled at the newfound lack of candor in his life. *Someday*, he laughed unconvincingly to himself, *someday Harald and I will enjoy the story of the day I stole his identity.*

As Lute walked out of the men's room and down the short privacy hall leading to it, he heard a voice that froze his viscera. He carefully peeked around the corner toward the restaurant, and confirmed what he hoped he would not have seen.

Cherry Snyder was talking to a patron at the table behind Moses. Don McKenna/Harald Ericksen/Lute Jonson returned to the lavatory, sick to his stomach.

CHAPTER 41

HOLY SEE, HOLY DO (2)

The Vatican
Friday, June 21
4:00 p.m.

Cardinal Collins thanked his messenger and excused himself. He left the eight other Princes of the Church in the well-appointed conference room. He stepped across the hall and through his suite's outer office, closing the door to his private office behind him. He took a calming breath before picking up the phone and punching the blinking line awaiting him. He crossed himself absently.

"Bonjour. Grâce et paix."

"Cardinal Collins?"

"Yes?"

"Your Eminence, this is Mac Evans, in the United States—Langley, Virginia. I was asked to call you with a status report."

"Thank you, Mr. Evans. I've been waiting to hear. I assume you're from the Company?"

"Well, let's just say I'm acquainted with an order that you put in through a mutual friend. That sufficient identification?"

"Certainly. And your news?"

"I'm afraid the item you ordered isn't available at the moment."

The Cardinal waited without answering.

"A number of our people have been searching, but it seems to be missing from inventory."

Still the black-suited ecclesiastic waited.

"Thought we had located it way up in the Northwest corner of our country—a little Victorian hamlet called Port Townsend, Washington—but it turned up missing."

"Is this 'code' necessary?"

Now it was his caller's turn to pause, and the silence was all the answer the Cardinal needed. But words finally came to reinforce it, anyway. "Not sure what you mean by that. Perhaps I have the wrong party."

"No, no, I'm the one who asked for … the item."

He clenched his free fist and hammered his desktop lightly in frustration. "What now, Mr. Evans? You'll keep searching for it for me?"

"Yes, sir. I understand my boss owes you a favor of sorts, so we're continuing to see if we can't locate the exact copy for you. It sometimes takes us a few days, but we don't often fail." He paused a moment before continuing. "I do understand that it's a fairly high priority item for you. True?"

"It is."

"May I ask exactly *how* high, Your Eminence? Have you identified the maximum you want to pay in order to retrieve this item?"

"Forgive me. I'm not used to dealing with your Company, so I need to make sure I understand. Are you asking about our reimbursement for your expenses in finding this for me?"

"Oh, no," soothed the American voice on the other end of a crystal-clear line. "No, my boss says your expenses have already been covered. He's grateful to you for your help on a little project a year ago in the Balkans."

"Then what..."

The voice interrupted. "Well, I just meant have you identified what *condition* you would accept this item in? Do you want us to acquire it only if it's in pristine condition? Or slightly damaged? What if it were totaled? If that's the only way we could acquire this particular item, is that acceptable? These are things we have to know, Your Eminence." A long silence followed, which he broke himself. "I know it sounds like the movies, but it's the marketplace that we have to operate in. Our buyers have to know what to do if they find it. You know?"

The Cardinal breathed in deeply and asked, "Do you know your Bible well, Mr. Evans?"

"I think we have one on computer here. I can search it for a particular section, if you'd like to refer me."

"Then find the words of the Lord in Ezekiel 28, beginning at verse 7. And know that this item you seek for us considers itself as wise as a god. So my answer to you is exactly what God's answer was through the prophet Ezekiel about such items. It is not my decision, but God's. Is that clear enough?"

"Can you hold a moment, please?"

"Can I *hold*?" asked the Cardinal, incredulously. But since the line had fallen silent, he held. He continued doing so for two and a half minutes, until the incorporeal Mr. Evans returned.

"I am to understand that my people are the 'foreigners'?"

"If it is impossible to bring this item to me in good condition, yes. And I assure you again that this item holds itself out to be 'wise as a god,' which is abhorrent to the Lord."

"Whatever."

Mr. Evans' dismissive word and tone infuriated the Cardinal Bishop, but he held his peace.

"You fully understand the order you're giving?"

"I can give you no orders, Mr. Evans. You are not in my employ."

"I beg your pardon. Let me re-phrase. Do you fully understand the request you're making?"

"It is not my judgment. It is God's. He's made it clear He does not countenance such attitudes."

"Father," said the crisp long-distance voice, oddly demoting the church official, "all I need to know is that, if we cannot bring the unit in, wasting it is the preferred alternative. Given the price—at least to the unit itself—I like to make sure I understand. So is this your preference?"

"I confirm that this is the preference of the Eminent One."

The Cardinal thought he heard the mouthpiece covered and the name Jesus Christ uttered in disgust at the other end of the line. Regardless, Mr. Evans' audible sign-off was a simple, "So be it," followed by a click.

Robert Cardinal Collins breathed in and out slowly to release the tension in his shoulders. He closed his eyes and whispered the initial words of Extreme Unction, and shortly rose to rejoin his colleagues in the conference room. He mentally rehearsed words to tell them only that the fugitive was still at large.

Ezekiel 28:6-10

Because you think you are wise, as wise as a god, I am going to bring foreigners against you, the most ruthless of nations; they will draw their swords against your beauty and wisdom and pierce your shining splendor. They will bring you down to the pit, and you will die a violent death in the heart of the seas. Will you then say, "I am a god," in the presence of those who kill you? You will be but a man, not a god, in the hands of those who slay you. You will die the death of the uncircumcised at the hands of foreigners.

CHAPTER 42

REFORMATION ON DECK

San Diego
Friday
10:00 a.m.

Christy Hansgaard relaxed in her favorite deck chair. The white swivel rocker and brightly colored cushions comforted her spirit as they had not for most of the prior week. True, her mind still endlessly replayed the scenes of the last four days—of her beloved brother's surprise arrival at the door on Monday, their all-too-brief and deeply disturbing conversation, the wild ride downtown, his mysterious disappearance in the parking lot of the San Diego Zoo, her despair at his claim that the Savior had been sexually active, the numerous conversations she'd had with her husband and their pastor over this painful revelation, and ultimately her call to Lute's Jerusalem colleague to report his presence in Southern California.

"And his failure to call me since," she said quietly. But today it wasn't bitterness in her voice, though there was concern for his safety. She very much wished she knew where he was and that he was OK. She hadn't tried calling hotels or motels; Lute's obvious fear of being found would have precluded his registering in his own name. She knew the cash she had given him would buy whatever freedom and anonymity he thought he needed for some time. Regardless of all that, today she felt a lightening of the load.

Hjalmar opened the sliding glass door behind her and walked onto the deck. His tennis whites were sweat-stained; his tan face was still flushed after an invigorating set.

"Hi, sleepy." He kissed her head and lightly rubbed her neck.

"Hi, hon. Thanks for not waking me when you left. I finally nodded off sometime after 3:30 this morning. If this tossing and turning doesn't end, I'm going to have to medicate it; I can't meet early morning patients next week in this groggy condition."

He sat on the matching love seat next to her rocker. "I knew we should have gotten out of here this week—at least after my consult on Monday. Time off doesn't really work for us if we stay here, does it?"

"But I love this place. If Lute hadn't just appeared out of nowhere...."

"If Luther hadn't had his Diet of Worms, he wouldn't have been constipated...."

She chimed in to finish his favorite phrase with him. "'And we wouldn't have had a Reformation.' I know. I still haven't looked that up. You sure the Diet of Worms was pre-Reformation?"

He shook his head and shrugged as if to say, "Don't know...or care." "Speaking of diet, I'm worried about yours. This thing seems to have affected your appetite." She didn't respond by word or gesture, so he pursued. "You didn't touch your chicken last night. An asparagus stalk a day won't keep you going, love."

"I had part of a banana and milk when I got up about 2:00."

A long moment passed as Dr. Hansgaard, husband, studied the drawn face of Dr. Hansgaard, wife. He settled back in the outdoor settee. "Where are you today? Whatcha thinkin'?"

She arose and walked a few steps to the wooden railing, staring out over the ocean beach and tide that usually pacified her so profoundly, but which had utterly failed in that function of late.

"Well, you'll be surprised. Something's different today."

She couldn't see it, but his raised brows and cocked head proved her prediction right.

"Something's changing, Hjalmar. I feel some joy starting to mix with the terrible ache, the grief I've been full of. It's like a great day ended, and I hated to see its sunset. I've mourned its passing all week. But this morning I feel like, well, like it's a new day. Corny as it is, I feel like Reagan's vision—it's the dawning of a new day in America. Except this isn't for America. It's just for me."

Hjalmar whistled. "Wow."

She faced him and continued. "I've felt so rigid since seeing Lute. I've felt so stiff and unbending, and the winds of his news are so strong, I knew they were going to break me. So when your Pastor dropped off that book..." They both smiled at her use of the pronoun 'your' instead of 'our.' "OK, I'm over my aggravation at him. So when Paul left that *Was Jesus Married?* book here—despite my wishes—it sort of haunted me until I leafed through it."

"And?"

"And I'm so full of conflicting feelings now that, well, I don't *know* what. It doesn't feel like I can go back to my old beliefs about His virginity. Actually, I never even considered any other possibility. But that book of Paul's claims the gospels' *silence* about Jesus' marital status actually supports the possibility He *had* a wife. It says that teachers of the Torah had to be married. Tradition required it. Since He was called 'rabbi'—teacher—it would have been extraordinary if He *was* single. The gospels didn't hesitate to tell stories of all the ways He challenged old rules, so they probably would have mentioned it if He broke this ancient tradition, too. Still...."

She stopped, shaking her head in wonder, then rambled on, full of her new knowledge. "First Corinthians 9 confirms that the apostles and Jesus' brothers had wives; they even accompanied them on their missions. It doesn't say the Lord Himself did—the book suggests He might have been a widower—but since He was an obedient Jewish son, would He have refused if his father Joseph had done his paternal duty and found Him a wife? And Luke 7...."

She stopped in mid-thought and turned to him. "I'm sorry. You didn't ask for all this. I'm just so consumed by these ideas...."

He leaned forward and reached out a hand. "You can't know how much I want to hear you tell me this. I love you, hon."

She smiled lovingly and touched his fingertips. "You, too, my love."

Christy sat next to her husband and he put his arm around her as she continued. "I just can't stop thinking about this 'new thing,' as Isaiah says... Luke 7 quotes Jesus, directly *contrasting* His own lifestyle with the asceticism of John the Baptist. Like He was a radical. There's so much more. All of it challenging me to think. I grew up believing what society taught: sex is dirty, ugly, and shameful, and you should save it for someone you love."

Hjalmar threw his head back and laughed. She chuckled too, then returned to both intellectual and physical meandering. She got up and walked to the rail.

"This is hard, hon. I remember feeling mentally slapped around this way when I first struggled with evolution and creation; what I had naively thought was a contradiction—a threat to my childlike faith in the Adam and Eve story—didn't turn out that way at all. But spiritual journeys can give you soul blisters."

He joined her and pulled her into his arms. She felt peace there. She felt their combined strengths doubled, their combined weaknesses halved. *Thank You for this helpmate*, she prayed. *I need him so much. How did You live without such intimate physical touch, Lord? Or didn't You? Were You holy, or physical? Could You have been both?*

Genesis 2:18
The LORD God said, "It is not good for the man to be alone. I will make a helper suitable for him."

Isaiah 43:19
See, I am doing a new thing! Now it springs up; do you not perceive it? I am making a way in the desert and streams in the wasteland.

1 Corinthians 9:5
Don't we have the right to take a believing wife along with us, as do the other apostles and the Lord's brothers and Cephas?

Luke 7:33-35

[Jesus said,] "For John the Baptist came neither eating bread nor drinking wine, and you say, 'He has a demon.' The Son of Man came eating and drinking, and you say, 'Here is a glutton and a drunkard, a friend of tax collectors and "sinners."' But wisdom is proved right by all her children."

CHAPTER 43

TOILET-STALLING FOR TIME

Sitka, Alaska
Friday, June 21
6:45 a.m.

L ute returned to the privacy of the men's room stall to hide and think. *I have to get on that plane with Tling, but I can't let Cherry and him see me together. If one calls me Don and one calls me Harald, this thing is going to come apart. How in hell is this happening to a boring old scholar like me in a fishing village halfway around the world from home?*

He prayed that Moses would come looking for him but didn't know what he'd say if it happened. Minutes passed. His anxiety grew as he conjured mental images of Moses' pilot arriving and their leaving the terminal without him.

He left the stall, pulled the restroom door open a crack, and peeked out. The little hallway was empty, but Lute realized that the window in the wall at the end of those few steps looked out over the airfield. He took a few steps into the hall and pressed back in the public phone alcove just at the corner to the dining room. Cherry's recognizable voice still alternated with others in the small room. The window's excellent view allowed him to scan the tarmac abutting the terminal. A Piper six-seater sat thirty-five or forty feet from the building. The apparent pilot, a slightly built thirty-something fellow in blue jeans and windbreaker, climbed out and approached the passenger-loading door at the far corner of the dining room. In a few moments, Lute realized, he would either have to walk through that room and try to avoid Cherry's eyes—impossible, since his sociable hostess of the prior day was standing with her back to the wall, talking to one of the few people in the room—or he would have to wait her out and try to find another flight to Fairbanks. The only other alternative, and he cringed at the idea, was abandoning his current plan and plotting an entirely different search for a worldwide media outlet.

* * *

Moses looked up toward the rest rooms, and wondered whether his new acquaintance was too indisposed to make the flight. He had seen his pilot's plane arrive, finished his coffee, and pulled his small overnight case into his lap.

"Hi, pastor." The approaching pilot's greeting was warm, his grin wide.

"Hilary. You didn't forget." Moses grinned, too.

"Forget what?"

"That you're flying me back to Fairbanks."

"Oh! Is it *you* I'm here for?"

Moses nodded, playing along with his light-hearted friend despite the early hour.

"So where are you headed?"

Moses deadpanned, "Fairbanks."

"Hot damn!" the pilot exclaimed, then corrected himself: "...darn! That's where I'm going. Wanna come along?"

Moses stifled a laugh, so the pilot tried again. "Did you read the news out of Jerusalem this week? They think they found the real tomb of Jesus!" Moses shook his head and grinned as he waited for the punch line. "Yeah, they're pretty sure of it because on the floor of the little room they found a bracelet that read, 'What Would I Do?'"

Now Moses did have to laugh. As he stood, he started to excuse himself to check on Lute, but the public address system broke in at a volume that trumped all private conversations.

"Your attention, please. This is Gaylord out in the maintenance shed. I've just taken a call from someone on a cell phone passing the terminal. He says there's a gray Ford Explorer in the parking lot with the lights on, and they seem to be dimming. I asked him to just stop and turn them off. He said, 'Just tell her to get back here.'" The speaker buzzed off, but shortly came back to add, "Cherry, if that's you, tell Stan his attempt to disguise his voice in a raspy whisper didn't work. I recognized him. If he's waiting in the lot, tell him he owes me coffee. If he's at home, I'll come there and get it, with pie."

The handful of early risers joined Cherry in hoots of laughter. She quickly said her goodbyes and headed through the anteroom toward the front entrance on the opposite side of the building from the airfield.

Before Moses could make it over to the restrooms, Lute rounded the corner. "I was afraid you might have left," Lute said. "Sorry to be so long."

"We're ready to go," answered Moses, "and the pilot says there's a seat available for you. You're a lucky man."

Except for having that American quarter in my pocket for the pay phone, 'lucky' isn't the word, grinned Lute. *'Blessed,' maybe. OK, OK: 'crafty.'* His thinking turned to praying. *But Lord, remember Psalm 119 and forgive Your servant.*

Lute quickly climbed into the Piper, wondering if the sense of foreboding he awoke to would transform into one of safety.

Psalm 119:109-111

Though I constantly take my life in my hands, I will not forget your law. The wicked have set a snare for me, but I have not strayed from your precepts. Your statutes are my heritage forever; they are the joy of my heart.

CHAPTER 44

FLAPS UP

Sitka
7:00 a.m.

From his passenger seat, Lute observed Hilary Shoemaker complete a preflight walk-around and then climb into the cabin of this well-worn plane. The pilot asked his passengers to sign a manifest and waiver sheet, and by the time it got to Lute he could see all three signatures: Sarah Kashwitna, Moses Tling, and his own "Harald Ericksen." To fill in the required telephone number, Lute nonchalantly checked Harald's card in his wallet. Moses was preoccupied with the mountainous vista and didn't seem to notice. Hilary retrieved the document, removed a carbonless copy, got out to poke it into a safety box nearby, and was soon back in the Piper, ready to go. He checked each of his passengers' seatbelts manually, having to ask just Lute to cinch up tighter. "We hit turbulence occasionally," he explained over the engine noise. "A tight belt keeps you from hitting your head on the ceiling."

"Been there," Lute called back as he complied. He was glad that the rather dowdy late-middle-aged Native woman took the front seat next to Hilary. Moses and he occupied the twin seats behind. It would be difficult to converse up top, but his new friend might be willing to point out some landmarks. The only concern nagging at Lute was having his briefcase stowed in the luggage compartment behind the passenger cabin wall. He knew it was a groundless worry—no one could run off with it en route, and if the plane went down, it didn't much matter whether the case was between his ankles or behind a bulkhead. Still, he worried its invisibility like a tongue worries a newly-chipped tooth.

Before taxiing onto the runway, Hilary stopped to check items off on a clipboard. He brought a hand mike to his face, pressed a switch on the side, and, with his three passengers as the only certain audience, spoke to any planes that might be approaching this small uncontrolled airport. "Sitka traffic, Piper niner niner six eight hotel, entering runway two niner for takeoff. Sitka."

He simultaneously scanned the skies. Lute caught himself and the other passengers aping their pilot's actions. There was no radio response, so the plane taxied onto the runway and then toward the north end to prepare for takeoff.

"Make sure your seatbacks and tray tables are in their full upright and locked position," Hilary called out over the din. Both Moses and Lute laughed.

Suddenly, as their small craft approached the giant numbers painted on the north end of the runway, Lute sensed trouble. Hilary's hands and head began jerking nervously. Following the pilot's line of sight, Lute saw the sickening emergency about to befall them: a high-wing single-engine aircraft was landing headlong toward them, rapidly closing the scant quarter mile distance between them. Hilary immediately hit the throttle and pressed hard on the right rudder pedal, turning the Piper off the runway onto the grass. Its tail barely cleared the concrete before the incoming plane settled onto the same runway fifty feet away. Its speed looked almost leisurely, and the craft gave no hint of recognizing the multiple fatalities that would have resulted had Hilary not averted a fiery collision.

Despite his own adrenalin, Lute winced for the sensitivity of Moses' ears and the woman's, as Hilary shouted into his mike, "Goddammit, what the hell are you doing, asshole? You almost hit me!" The Piper had slowed substantially in the soft grass, but Hilary kept his prop turning and pushed his plane to keep moving. Once the offending plane was down, Hilary turned and was able to taxi back onto the runway. Hearing no answer on the radio, he angrily taxied the Piper all the way back to the Maul two-seater, now dead-stopped almost halfway down the mile-long runway. It was very clear: their pilot's prior playfulness was history. His moment of near-death terror was now concentrated into a fury that clearly was going to be vented at the other pilot.

As the Piper approached, the Maul's pilot jumped out and ran recklessly toward the moving plane. He was shaking his head, raising his hands palm up, nearly bowing down to the Piper's pilot. When Hilary was close he quarter-turned his Piper on the deck and shut down. He barreled out the cabin door, verbally bullying the other pilot. "What the fuck?!"

Lute winced again. He looked at Moses and the woman—both appeared pale. All three strained to listen through the open door.

The Maul pilot—appearing closer to eighteen than twenty-eight—could not get apologies out fast enough. "Thank God!" he called as the two pilots approached each other. "I am *so* sorry! You're a hell of a wing-jockey, dude. I can't believe it; you saved us both."

"Why the hell didn't you respond to my takeoff call?" countered Hilary, unwilling to accept the younger man's obeisance without some serious explaining.

"I lost all power, man. Total electrical failure about twenty minutes ago. No radio, no lights, no instruments, nothing. I took off from Wrangell for Anchorage, got forty minutes into the flight, and then, zap! I've been praying ever since losing power that I could make it this far. About four miles out," he pointed skyward, "oh God, the engine started misfiring. It was 'get this baby on the ground' from that second on. When I throttled back on final approach, the engine quit entirely and I had to glide in. I had no flaps, dude. I barely made it to the numbers before touchdown. I saw you there, hoped you saw me, realized you hadn't, and started to bank toward the grass but you made the move first. I am really sorry. We're both lucky to be alive."

Hilary turned from Code-Four-Pissed to full sympathy. Lute thought he could read, "There but for the grace of God…" on their pilot's face.

Hilary shook his head and took a deep breath. "Unreal. Under those circumstances, you did a great job getting down safely without bendin' metal." He gestured toward the Piper. "We're OK. I got three passengers who mighta crapped their chaps, but we're OK."

"Jeez, I guess the sun kept you from seeing me until the last minute. Shit, man, you veered off but kept control the whole time. I can't believe it. Any less experienced pilot and all of us would be ashes right now."

Gaylord, the airfield's one employee, was by now tearing down the runway toward the two parked planes in his '86 Dodge pickup. As he arrived, the Chevron agent came racing up, too. It took ten minutes for Hilary to extricate himself from the gaggle of aviators and get back into his Piper.

"I think the field is cleared for takeoff now," he announced, his sense of humor returning. He apologized to his passengers, confirmed that all three had been able to hear the other pilot's explanations, and re-started his engines. Taxiing back north and turning to face the long runway again, Hilary pushed the thumb-switch on his mike and tried once more. "Sitka traffic, Piper niner niner six eight hotel, departing the pattern to the north. Sitka." He released it before asking rhetorically, "Anybody in here know how to pray?"

Lute answered silently. *I don't think I've stopped since we first got onto this runway.*

CHAPTER 45

PEAKS AND VALLEYS:
THE OLYMPICS AND THE
SHADOW OF DEATH

Friday, June 21
10 a.m.
Hurricane Ridge in the Olympic Mountains
Washington State's Olympic Peninsula

Harald parked his Volvo in the Visitor Center lot and sat silently for several minutes. The ninety-minute drive from Port Townsend had been aimless at first, a forlorn attempt to pull out of the emotional quicksand whose trap he had feared all his life. And which he had avoided until now.

When he reached the turnoff to the Olympic National Park entrance just east of the Port Angeles city limits, he turned south and headed up the mountain. Lost in thought, he drove the fifteen switchback miles to this viewpoint at the mile-high elevation.

He walked down to the Center's lower level, through the door and out onto the concrete deck. He took a solitary place at the west end, stepped over the short stone wall, sat on the ground, and leaned back against the cold stones. He looked out over the majestic peaks of the Olympics, crown jewels of all Pacific Northwest mountains. Today no exhilaration from the view rose in his soul. Long still minutes passed, then Harald began reciting to himself the dirge of deathbeds and funerals from time immemorial.

"The LORD is my shepherd; I shall not want. He maketh me to lie down in green pastures: he leadeth me beside the still waters."

The aging professor gazed half-heartedly over the midsummer high meadow cascading downward in front of him. Even the white explosion-top avalanche lilies that had so often delighted his eye seemed monochromatic. The purple scalloped onions near his outstretched feet seemed not so much bold as old.

"He restoreth my soul: He leadeth me in the paths of righteousness for His name's sake."

His expressionless voice could barely be heard beyond the hands he crossed on his chest. He felt neither restoration nor righteousness, only shame and dishonor. Not only had the most private and depraved moment of his life been exposed to others' eyes, he had betrayed Lute. No, they weren't blood brothers—they barely knew each other in college, let alone over the forty-six years since graduation—but Lute was a human being, a fellow Christian. Harald's heart sank below aching to empty hopelessness.

Out of the seamless blue sky behind the craggy ridges to the south, one cloud floated slowly up behind towering Mt. Olympus. It billowed white around the edges, but condensed threateningly in the center. Harald's empty eyes followed it. As it tracked eastward, its dense heart cast a moving darkness on the meadow lying so dramatically, so colorfully, below this ridge.

"'Yea, though I walk through the valley of the shadow of death, I will fear no evil: for thou art with me; Thy rod and Thy staff they comfort me.'" *And so with me, Lord. No matter what, You'll welcome me home. It's the one dogma Your faithful church has wrong: nothing, not life, nor death, nor any means of death, can separate me from Your love. I know You'll catch me in Your mighty arms.*

He drew his eyes away from the floating, murky shade on the ground, up to the precipice hidden at the end of the trail to the east. Obstruction Point—a panoramic lookout from a stomach-churning flat ledge above a two-hundred-foot drop.

"Thou preparest a table before me in the presence of mine enemies."

Mindless of time and yet sensing its fullness, he rose from his nearly prone position and sat on the thirty-inch-high stone wall. He massaged his knee joints a moment.

"'Thou anointest my head with oil; my cup runneth over.' My cup is dry today, Lord, but it has run over in the past. Once or twice."

Harald stood and set his face toward the Obstruction Point trail. Despite the clear weather there were few visitors at this hour. He saw no one on the trail ahead. He envisioned the end of it—a small concrete crow's nest with a sturdy four-foot safety wall. From that isolated point, he could see forever.

"Surely goodness and mercy shall follow me all the days of my life..."

"Dr. Ericksen?"

Harald stopped, turned, frowned. "What do you want?" he asked with resignation.

"Just to walk with you a bit. Shall we take the Obstruction Point trail?"

Harald stared into the deep-set dark eyes, turned again, and continued on the path.

"...And I will dwell in the house of the LORD forever."

CHAPTER 46

LUTHER IN THE SKY
WITH DIAMONDS

En route to Fairbanks, Alaska
Friday
8:15 a.m.

Moses pointed to a small town on a peninsula below them and leaned close so Lute could hear his soft voice above the constant roar of the Piper's engine. "That's Haines down there. Look on your side—twenty or thirty miles over there to the east, see the little clearing?—that's Skagway. Jumpin' off point for the Gold Rush. Chilkoot Pass's up that mountain. White Horse over the peaks another 60-70 miles."

Lute shook his head in wonder. "Never thought I'd see that."

Moses' head cocked in surprise. "How long you live in Seattle? Never been up the Inside Passage?"

Sighing shallowly in frustration at his seemingly endless charade, Lute just shook his head to answer the second question. He stared intently at the rugged beauty of the snow-covered peaks and darkly variegated mountain slopes. He turned to ask what he'd forgotten to ask before, "When do we get into Fairbanks?"

Hilary turned to answer before Moses could. "Another three and a half hours or so. Alaska Airlines coulda also got you there in five hours, at twice the cost and a stop in Anchorage, but you'da had to wait til tonight for the privilege."

"That's a big airline. What do they fly into Sitka?"

"Seven-thirty-sevens, the workhorse jet."

"But there's no tower. And from our experience a little while ago, it sounds like air traffic has to control itself there. How do the jets avoid what we went through?" Lute wasn't over the experience, and doubted his flightmates would soon forget it, either.

Hilary grinned. "When the ninety-ton gorilla wants to take off or land, nobody ever argues."

Lute nodded and turned to watch the land pass under them four miles below. He realized as they continued past Haines that the strait or canal they had flown above since shortly after takeoff was gone. Apparently now inland, the route's scenery flattened out somewhat from the earlier craggy terrain, but it still fascinated the curious world traveler. He noticed a road heading off into the wilderness to the northwest; the Piper had begun to track its course 20,000 feet below.

"What's the highway?"

"Still 'the Haines' until Haines Junction up here, where it merges into the Alcan."

"Alcan?"

Moses looked over. "Alaska-Canada Highway. Two lanes from Dawson Creek, BC, twelve hundred miles to Fairbanks. Open year 'round with rest stops and gasoline available every two hundred miles, whether you need 'em or not."

Hilary turned so he could be heard. "D'you know the terms VFR and IFR?"

Lute guessed, "Visual Flight Regulations and Instrument Flight Reg…"

Hilary interrupted, "Yeah, but 'Rules.' We're flying the poor man's IFR today: 'I Follow Roads.' Luckily, we've got great weather all the way. Anybody who needs a nap can get one, because the next three hours look pretty much the same down there."

Lute did settle back into a corner and pulled one leg up under him, but he had too much to think about to sleep. How to make sure he got into the teleconference studio. How to get on camera. What to say immediately, to keep security from removing this geriatric guerilla from their set, or the director from fading to black. Despite all the uncertainties, he felt peace coming. The chase was almost over, the running and hiding were nearly complete, the end was close. But he knew those were selfish reactions. The real news was the *kairos* he would soon unveil for the entire world. God's Time was at hand. Not an end, then, but another beginning. *Thank God I'm in the homestretch! I love You, Lord.*

CHAPTER 47

NEWSROOM

Tacoma, Washington
Friday
11:45 a.m.

"Newsroom, Rosedahl." The khaki-and-T-shirt-clad reporter continued keying a story into the computer in front of him after punching the blinking button and adjusting his telephone headset. "Nope, no Lynn here." He stopped typing long enough to roll his right hand in a silent 'hurry up, willya?' gesture. "Well, that's not this number, but I know it dumps into this line when our manager doesn't answer. Wait, did you say Lynn or *Melinda*?" He looked around the large reporter's bay and then semistood to peer into the raised audio booth at the end of the long room. "Yeah, you probably mean *Melinda* and I see her in the studio. I think she's recording a spot; wanna hold on or call back?" He caught her eye and pointed first at her and then at the phone. She shrugged and shook her head, continuing to read into a microphone. "What?" The caller now had his full attention. "Hang on, let me see if I can't get her."

The young man took his headset off and approached
the soundproof glass separating him from his station manager. He waited until she looked up again, then beckoned
her fairly urgently with hand and eyes. She frowned, but
adjusted a control or two and came around the back hall
into the newsroom.

"What's up, Matt?"

"Some woman wants to talk to you. Sounds important.
Line three."

She took a seat at the closest desk, picked the handset
off the phone and answered, "This is Melinda Patrick."

The reporter returned to his story, glancing several
times at the wall clock moving closer and closer toward a
12:05 local newscast.

"You're serious?" Melinda asked incredulously. "What's
he look like?" She began taking notes. "Doesn't sound
familiar. No ID on him?" She listened another minute,
then broke in. "Can I put you on hold while I go to my
office? It'll only take a second. Thanks." She punched hold
and laid the receiver in its cradle.

"Sounds mysterious," the reporter said without looking
up.

"More'n a little. She's a police detective in Port Angeles.
My name and phone number were on a piece of motel note-
paper—the *only* thing, actually—found in the pockets of a
guy who died up on Hurricane Ridge this morning. They
just reached his body at the bottom of a two-hundred foot
cliff."

She walked a couple of steps toward the exit, then
breathed in sharply and exhaled the words, "Oh, my God!"

CHAPTER 48

MANUSCRIPT 1Q-CETHER-6:
LOVE NOT FEAR

"From Cave 1 at Qumran. We love this. LJ 4-27-55"

THE ANOINTED ONE W[AITED IN LINE F]OR RITUAL PURIFYING {BATH} TODAY FULL OF WISE PLAYFULNESS. BUT JOHANAN NEARBY COWERED FROM LARGE LIZARD. YESHUA WROTE IN DIRT תידא ["FEAR"]. JOHANAN CAME CLOSE FOR SAFETY. WITH FINGER YESHUA SMOOTHED AWAY FIRST [LETTERS] AND ADDED NEW STROKES TO REVEAL אהבה ["LOVE"]. HE JOINED JOHANAN TO RUB CHEST OVER HEART WITH SAME MOTION. YOUTHS WHISPERED LOVE NOT FEAR, LOVE NOT FEAR.

COUNCIL CALLED TO DECIDE ABOUT YESHUA. SOME ADORE, BUT HIS QUESTIONING OF COMMUNITY RULE CONTINUES. UNSE[…]

CHAPTER 49

VISTAS AT THE END
OF THE WORLD

Fairbanks, Alaska
Friday
11:30 a.m. Alaska Daylight Time

The Piper rolled to a stop in a tie-down line just a hundred yards from the modern, main passenger terminal. The small concrete block building they would soon be entering instead was more like what Lute had expected to see in Alaska's interior. When Hilary shut the engine down, Lute felt a mix of emotions. He was profoundly grateful for the silence after their proximity to that seemingly endless mechanical roar. But he could feel a headache coming on, one that could be a crippler if he didn't get some strong aspirin soon.

Hilary crawled out and came around to help his passengers deplane on the right side. All four of them stretched and then contracted sore muscles, then Hilary pulled luggage out for them and led them toward the door under the sign "General Aviation."

Lute gripped his briefcase tightly and visually surveyed the landscape in awe. The low rolling hills of the Tanana Valley north of Mt. McKinley were filled with slender stalks of brown-and-white-barked, green-topped spruce and birch trees. Clearly, central Alaska in midsummer was a glorious place. The sky was baby-blanket blue, and the handful of wispy clouds randomly scattered across it seemed embarrassed to be marring the perfect bowl of color above them. Lute realized again how homebound humans attach stereotypes to the world geographies they've heard about but never seen. How his longtime home of Israel was often viewed unfairly as totally barren and its people universally bellicose. How the American Midwest was considered by coastal sophisticates as flat and uninteresting—geographically and humanly. And how he himself had unconsciously thought of Alaska as one long snowbound winter, regardless of calendar. Here he stood in a bright, balmy, 60-degree Fahrenheit Fairbanks morning in late June, and he could not have told the difference between this atmosphere and San Diego's just four days before. "Perfect. Mild," he said aloud, glad the others had continued walking ahead. "What a place for God to stick His almighty finger into Earth's history again!"

He turned to look south toward the rugged range of peaks which Moses had pointed out on their approach, including Mt. McKinley, North America's highest point. Snow-mantled majesties they were. He had come so far. From the ancient rocky ground of Israel, through cosmopolitan bustles, first in San Diego and then in Seattle. Now, into this heart of lightness. A reverse of Joseph Conrad's infamous journey almost a century—and half a world—away. Lute felt a sneak of gooseflesh, knowing he brought a great light to this land of the Midnight Sun. Yes, he thought, it will be scary at first to the most frightened of God's children, but in time His *kairos* events always raise His children up. God's messengers always greeted the people they surprised with open arms and the same mantra: "Fear not." Every time He broke physically into human's lives, He left them better equipped for agape—selfless love.

"Harald?"

Lute turned to see who was calling his friend but checked himself before blowing his cover. "Coming!" he called back. *Blessed is he who comes in the name of the Lord,* he thought. *And I do. I do!*

"What are you preaching on Sunday?" asked Lute as Moses led him to the parking lot.

"It's Layman's Sunday so I don't have to do anything. I'm attending the Little Chapel Between the Sheets." Something about Moses' grin assured Lute his leg was being pulled. But he played along.

"Really? You'll take the day off?"

Moses shook his head. "I trust 'em—the elders who do it are fine, Christ-centered folks. But I like to sit in back and pretend to fall asleep."

"Ah-ha. Turnabout's fair play."

Moses nodded. "Show 'em how hard it is to satisfy everybody. You know, when we do contemporary praise songs, the older folks call me and suggest we cut back on 'the camp songs.' When we do regular hymns, there are some teenagers who love to catch my eye and poke their fingers down their throats."

Lute laughed out loud. "So we put our pastors in the middle of our circular firing squads, eh?"

Moses nodded as he unlocked the driver's door on a ten-year-old Jeep Cherokee. He got in and reached over to open Lute's door. "I prefer a car with a little maturity," he explained with a straight face.

During the drive Lute's eyes were riveted on their surroundings. It was as if he would only have one chance in life to see Fairbanks, Alaska, and he was determined to memorize every sight. *Paved roads*, he thought. *I'm so naïve to be surprised by that.* He was struck by the normalcy of it all; passing drivers didn't seem to be properly amazed at finding themselves in this northern outpost. And the place itself had all the earmarks of civilization. Hadn't they read the lore? Didn't they realize they should look like characters in "The Cremation of Sam McGee" or some other Robert Service poem? That in place of all this asphalt and urban sprawl, there should be just one log building—the Malamute Saloon—on one dirt road? That all the men should be whiskered, and huskies should outnumber humans ten to one? *Such fantasies I live*, Lute thought. *Such cardboard cutout lives I think others live. So childish. Why do I still think that way?*

"You're frowning."

Lute felt caught. "Oh, just a little self recrimination. But I just realized: the answer is in Corinthians 13."

"The love chapter."

"But after its famous *is's* and *doesn'ts*...?"

"Remind me," prompted Moses.

"...Now we see but as a poor reflection."

Moses nodded, "Ah yeah." They were silent a few moments, and as the young Native pastor slowed down and turned onto a residential street, he said, "I have a sense you're carrying a great weight, Dr. Ericksen. And that you're only letting people see *you* 'through a glass darkly'."

Lute turned and studied his driver's eyes, his white but crooked teeth, his calm. The old scholar felt torn: whether to trust this pastoral young man, or to avoid any revelations that might interfere with his guerilla plan. *Lord, which of Your voices do I listen to? "Fear not" or "Be still and know that*

I am God"? Can I tell Moses Your news? Or would that endanger it? I keep asking for signs, Lord. But without Your Word I don't know what to do.

Moses spoke again. "Well, I'm here for you this weekend if you need a willing ear. But I'm into truth, not stories. I'm curious about things like why a Seattle professor doesn't know what the Alcan is. You know what I mean?"

Lute took a deep breath and, with fear rising, listened for divine guidance.

---

1 Corinthians 13:8-12

Love never fails. But where there are prophecies, they will cease; where there are tongues, they will be stilled; where there is knowledge, it will pass away. For we know in part and we prophesy in part, but when perfection comes, the imperfect disappears. When I was a child, I talked like a child, I thought like a child, I reasoned like a child. When I became a man, I put childish ways behind me. Now we see but a poor reflection as in a mirror; then we shall see face to face. Now I know in part; then I shall know fully, even as I am fully known.

CHAPTER 50

The Parsonage

Fairbanks
11:45 a.m.

They pulled into the driveway of a white ranch-style home and parked. As he pulled his key out of the ignition, Moses said matter-of-factly, "You used God's name."

Lute looked over in surprise.

"You just sighed. That's God's name, isn't it?" Moses got out of the Jeep, so Lute did. As they approached the front door, Moses acknowledged his new friend's confusion with a shy smile. "The four letters—the tetragrammaton—that the Hebrews used for God can be pronounced 'Yahweh,' of course. I read that we speak that name, His name, with our first breath and our last. It's the sound of breathing in..." he demonstrated, forming an unvocalized 'yah' as he drew air in, "and out." He finished with a whispered 'way' in his exhale. "Yah....wey. Yah...wey. So we speak our Creator's name moment by moment, awake and asleep. Like a baby says 'mama' over and over, rejoicing in its first word, naming its all-in-all. Yahwey. A newborn's first word, and a dying man's last."

Lute felt goosebumps crawl up his arms. He copied Moses' mantra softly himself: Yah…wey. Yah…wey. "That's incredible! Wonderful. Never heard it." He tried it again. "You probably know that the other Old Testament name, 'Jehovah,' takes the consonants of the tetragrammaton, and the vowels of 'Adonai—My Lord.'"

Moses nodded and chuckled. "This is a pretty intellectual conversation for a Friday noon, isn't it?"

"Auspicious way to enter the solstice, eh?"

Moses looked skyward. "That's right; I forgot. If you want to stay up you'll get to see the Midnight Sun at its brightest tonight. Most visitors find that kinda cool." He thought a moment. "So do I, actually."

Unlocking his residence, Moses ushered Lute through the double-doored arctic entry and into his home. Lute was instantly intrigued both by the ordinariness of the living room—quietly chagrined with himself for having thought a Tling household might have had more primitive, village-style furniture than these middle-class chairs, sofa and end tables—and by the splendid Native artwork hanging on walls and adorning so many surfaces. As Moses murmured an excuse and checked his answering machine, Lute examined pieces of Eskimo beadwork, a drum, elegant feathered dancing fans, baskets, and bright watercolors of summer and winter village scenes displayed around the comfortable room.

Moses returned to his guest. "My wife Tana is at the grocery store. Let me show you your room and the facilities."

"Thank you, Moses. This is extremely gracious of you."

The younger man just nodded and led the way down the hall.

Within a few minutes, Lute rejoined his host who had taken a seat at the table in the dining area adjacent to the living room. Lute sat, too, and when Moses looked up from a small stack of mail, Lute said, "Listen, I'm sure you're busy, so I'll stay out of your way this afternoon. I just wondered if you might want to call your friend and make sure we can get in to see that television studio during the worldwide conference tomorrow. The more I think about it, the more I'd like to see that."

Moses nodded and reached to the sideboard for the telephone and the thin Fairbanks phone book. He searched for a name and dialed. It apparently rang only a couple of times before being picked up.

"H'lo. Randy Savage, please?" Moses nodded silent acknowledgement to the answerer and waited, his eyes straying back to the mail. "Randy. This is your beloved pastor." The Alaskan Native grinned at Lute. "It was fine. Musta been three or four hundred students. I told them all your secrets."

Lute admired the young man's wry insouciance.

"Hey, listen, I have a houseguest who's never seen a TV studio during a production. Can we come watch that thing you're doing tomorrow? He's an old guy but very distinguished-looking, and people will think you know important people." Moses winked at Lute, but soon lost his smile. "I know. Yup, you said it was kinda high security." Moses shook his head apologetically at Lute.

Fear rising, Lute thought frantically. He grabbed a pen from the table and checked his pockets quickly for paper. Moses turned an envelope over and pushed it across the table as he listened to his parishioner talk. Lute wrote, "Archaeology? Dead Sea Scrolls?" and pushed it back. Moses looked and then raised a quizzical eyebrow. Lute added, "—big news."

"Well," said the pastor, "he'll understand." He paused, then finished, "I just thought you'd want to meet a Dead Sea Scrolls expert."

For Lute, eternity arrived in all its unhurried leisure, passed through the room, and finally took leave before Moses spoke once more. "Yup. He's in the archaeology department at the University of Washington. We met in Sitka and when he mentioned the Scrolls, I invited him up for the weekend. You know I'm not interested in 'em, but I thought you'd want to meet him." Moses grinned again at Lute. He nodded silently at whatever he was hearing, then summarized the unheard conversation for Lute by hooking a little finger in his mouth and jerking as if to say 'this fish is caught.'

Thank You, Lord! Lute's tight muscles began to relax.

Moses cocked his head. "Really? When?" He eyed Lute. "What was his name? Well, my visitor would probably want to know. Sure, I'll wait."

Lute's curiosity burst through. "Wha'd he say?"

Moses looked at him but didn't answer. A few seconds later he began nodding, then asked, "Where'd you see it?" Again he nodded. "Standard spellings?" He listened. Finally he straightened up from his slouch. "OK, thanks. I will. Now just tell me where we should come tomorrow and when."

Moses retrieved his pen from Lute and made notes on the back of another envelope. "Thanks a lot, Randy. We'll, ah," he paused a moment, "we'll probably see you tomorrow." He hung up the receiver. Lute waited for what seemed like minutes while Moses traced circles on the polished white ash tabletop. Finally he looked up, but not at Lute.

"Dr. Ericksen?"

Lute nodded, but reminded his host, "Just Harald."

"*Are* you Dr. Ericksen?"

Lute sucked in air. He turned to stare at the same invisible speck in the air that held Moses' attention.

Moses pressed, "Is there another Harald Ericksen on the archaeology faculty?"

"Moses, let me explain."

"...Because if you're the only Harald Ericksen, the news reports are wrong."

Lute looked back toward him. "What news?"

"Is Harald Ericksen a friend of yours?"

Lute nodded.

"Then the news is sad. He was found dead this morning."

Lute's eyes widened. "Wha... How? Are you sure? Harald Ericksen—Harald with two a's, Ericksen, '...S E N'?"

Moses nodded. His face registered a little sympathy for this man across the table, but mostly his eyes narrowed in suspicion and concern. Even through the grief that was flooding through his head and heart, Lute could see that his host had become tight, even fearful.

"The man on the telephone told you? How did he know?"

"It's on the Associated Press." Moses relayed the report's sketchy details of authorities finding Harald's body, and how, despite the lack of a wallet, they traced his identity through a single phone number in his pocket. "There's more," Moses said. "But first, you need to tell me who you are, and why you told me you were him."

Lute could barely control himself. *Harald ... dead. Why?*

"Did they say, was it an accident? Do they think it was suicide?"

Moses said, "Perhaps he was pushed." He edged imperceptibly back from the table Lute was leaning over. Moses' voice sounded icy. "What is your name, sir?"

Lute was shaking. "I'm Lute—Dr. Luther Jonson. Co-Director, International Scrolls Study Team, Jerusalem.

I'll get you my card." He started to rise, but Moses stood more quickly and spoke firmly.

"Please stay right here. Please don't move, sir."

For the first time in his life, Lute saw fear in the face of someone he was conversing with. A fear approaching terror that he, mild and bookish Lute Jonson, might endanger the life or safety of that other person. Even his grief was set aside at this astounding realization. He had known a sense of personal peril himself on occasion—three times in recent years, outings in strife-torn Jerusalem had put him arm's length away from desperate-looking Palestinians with covered faces and menacing handguns. But never had he knowingly instilled the high alert of caution he now saw straining Moses' face and eyes.

"I'm so sorry," Lute babbled. "So sorry...." He sat compliantly, dropping his face into his hands. "Forgive me." When he raised his eyes again, he could see that his words—meant as bridge-builders—had had the opposite effect; Moses stiffened. "I mean, forgive me for lying to you. I can tell that you're worried that I'm a threat to you, your wife.... I had nothing to do with Harald's death. I'm shocked by it. And scared, myself. If I caused it—NO! no, I had no part in it directly, but maybe by something I said, or the attention I drew to him—then I'll never forgive myself. I'll tell you the whole story. Everything. I'll show you some things from my briefcase—you can open it yourself if you like; *please* know you don't need to fear me—that will prove to you I am who I'm telling you I am now. It will make sense. And while I urgently need your help, I'll understand if you can no longer trust me. Oh Lord, what has happened to Harald?"

Lute's blathering reassurances had temporarily dammed up the pain of Harald's loss, but the moment Moses softened a little and sat again, Lute plunged his face into the crook of his arm on the table. He felt something break inside. He'd been strung too tight, too long. Now events loaded one more crushing burden—the life of a friend—onto his aging shoulders. Now the Midas turned to a Minus Touch--anyone he talked to, he put at risk.

Moses observed Lute for a spell. Finally he rose and stood beside the old scholar, resting his hand on Lute's shoulder. "I told you there's more, Dr. Jonson. The news said the FBI wants anyone who saw Dr. Ericksen in the last three days to contact them. They're offering 'protection'—that's the word he read me, 'protection'—for friends and associates of Dr. Ericksen's. There is some concern for their safety."

"Oh Lord." Lute didn't raise his head for that soft ejaculation nor for his plaintive coda. "Is *God* dead, too?"

CHAPTER 51

THE SECOND BIRTH OF MOSES

Moses Tling's freshman journal
Sheldon Jackson College
Sitka, Alaska

February 14, 1976
Dear Journal,

I'm floating on air!!! It's over!! GOD IS NOT DEAD!!
Oh, man, I was near suicide. It was awfull. I haven't even been able to write in this thing for three weeks. Heck, I haven't even been to even one class for a week, and I think my two roommates were this close to committing me to the Looney Bin.

OK, start from the start, Eskimoses. (That's what Janey has been calling me. I should probly be offended, but I like it.) Here's what happened.

During Christmas vacation, I got in this huge bull session with Pete Susulatna and George Shublik back in the village. Pete has never been a Christian and George and I were telling him he's going to go to Hell if he doesn't, you know, accept Jesus. And he wasn't listening. All's he did was ask questions like why should he believe, and did we believe in all the myths of our People, and that stuff.

Granny Ooliika had died during fall semester, and they were telling me how peaceful she slipped away. We started talking about where she was now. Not her body, natch. But where was whatever was in her that made her laugh like she did, laugh so hard that everybody around her did too. Pete said "If that's a soul, I belive in that. But does that *go* somewhere and live after her heart stops pumping? Naa." George said "Pete, God took her up with Him." And Pete said, "What *is* God?" It got dead silent. So Pete said, "Is it an old man in the sky with a white beard?" Well, we said of course not. He said, "is it a spirit in human hearts?" I said I thought that was closer. I said "God is love, the love that is in us when we're really unselfish." Then Pete said (I'll never forget this because it stumped me), "So if Moscow shoots missles over here, and America retaliates, and every single human being is killed in a nucular war, then does God die?"

George started BS'ing about that's not gonna happen and stuff. But I kept thinking, if God's a spirit, and a spirit can only be inside us humans, is He trapped in us? What *would* happen if a war or TB or something wiped out the whole darn race? It really started to bug me. I quit talking to them, just sat thinking. Pretty soon I got my parka on and went home. I went to bed, and said my prayers, same as always. But I felt kinda guilty when I said "Dear God" to start, because I wasn't sure who I was talking to. You know?

Well, trying to keep dad sober and all our Christmas presents kept me busy the rest of the vacation, but when I got back here to school last month, the thoughts came back a couple times. In philosophy, Professor Hubaugh talked about existentialism, which sounded kinda bleak. I don't understand it very well—guess I better hit the book hard before the mid-sem exam next week!—but what

I remember is that individuals set the standards. There are no absolute laws. (I don't know what that makes the Ten Commandments, but the people who believe in existentialism don't seem too worried about fitting them in!) Anyway, long and short, it was something else that kinda chipped away at everything I'd been taught by Mom and Granny and the minister who used to fly in each month.

Then the capper. Last month I found a *Time* magazine article from 10 yrs ago. Mrs. Jordan let me look in the archives in the college library for some Easter stories. I was just browsing and this one from 1966 jumped out at me. the cover had huge letters that said IS GOD DEAD? Wow. Blew me away. It said a lot of scholars have been discovering that the Bible is full of myths. Or that's their opinion, but they can explain it in real logical ways, big words, etc. etc. etc.

Long and short, all this stuff started replaying over and over in my head. "Is God an old man in a long white robe and beard? No? Then a spirit? What happens to the spirit if every*body* dies? If an *external* spirit, then isn't that a myth? A great story to explain the world to primitive peoples, but "insufficient for mankind whose understanding has grown beyond its nascent ignorance." (I copied that out of another article.) It had to be the last one! We had evolved beyond telling stories around the campfire—we weren't cavemen anymore, or just talking animals who made up deities to explain everything that their little minds couldn't understand.

But Holy Smokes! The more that made sense, the more uneasy I felt. It was like I had walked off winter's frozen tundra and somehow, magical, onto summer's marshy ground. I felt like I was sinking in. Like my foundation I had built my whole life on had evaporated. It reminded me that Mom says two days after I was born, Sputnik went up.

She used to tell me she thought the missles were going to come across the Bering and we were all gonna die. But we didn't. When I was a kid I wanted to be an astronaut, and get out of my space capsule and float in space. Cool, right? I'd be perfectly free up there—no gravity to hold me down, no traffic laws saying where I could go and when I had to stop. You know?

I kept thinking about this stuff. About three weeks ago it started to get really intense. Nobody here at school wanted to talk about it, or if they did, they just laughed and wouldn't take it serious. So I kinda withdrew a little, and spent more time up at the Lib, sitting in that one lone carrel hidden back of the state lawbook stacks. Just thinking. Feeling more and more alone in the universe. I knew how corny that sounded, but I absolutely and totally couldn't get back to the solid floor my whole life had had under it: my faith in God and His Son Jesus. (and the Holy Ghost.)

I'm so embarrassed about it now, but I got kinda snappy with my friends. (I need to find Janey and The Oookman and apologize heavy duty.) And when I was so distracted that I cut classes last week, I knew I had to do something.

Then came the Worst Time Ever last night. (I wonder if I'll cry when I read this someday; even if I do it won't be as hard as that night.) Yesterday, I had kinda shut down with everybody. Janey asked if I was ok after dinner, and Oook did the same a couple hours later. I didn't even answer them, I just walked away! Jeez. Anyway, long and short, I was feeling pretty desperate (or desolate) about midnight—laying in bed, couldn't get to sleep. I got up and went into the dorm lounge and sat there in the dark. Totally alone. Even God had deserted me. So I did what I had done all my "good little Mo" life—I took it to the Lord in prayer. And immediately started crying when I realized

I couldn't even start, "Dear God." It was like, "Dear To Who It May Concern." My "faith," (if you can dignify it with such a title) was completely gone. And there was nothing there to replace it with. I didn't give a beaver's butt if others found some kind of high-falutin' intellectual comfort in being masters of their own universe, the One True Eternal Presence had just moved out of mine and left no forwarding address. I never cried that hard, even when Debby broke up with me our junior year.

And I thought about how to get out of life, if it was going to be like this. It was scary. Too many have done that in the village over the years. The adults don't like to talk about it, but when they say, "Life was just too hard for him," we know the guy had blew his brains out. Now I was starting to think about that. Except mine wasn't because of booze, like all of theirs. Mine was because I didn't believe in God anymore. Because I had peeked behind the curtain and saw that the wizard of oz was just a myth.

When I woke up this morning, I called Pastor Jim. Thank God for Campus Pastors!!!!! I said I needed to talk to somebody and he said come on over.

He had a cup of coffee and offered me one. I WAS SO GOONED, I DIDN'T EVEN WANT COFFEE!!! (Now you know how upset I was, ha-ha.)

He listened to me spill it all. All this. I tried to write down the same words I told him here so I could remember someday, except I can't imagine it won't always stay one of my most alive memories of all my life. I kept trying to stop since it must be really boring for him. He's so great, he kept asking, "then?" and "how'd that make you feel?" and like that. Finally I really did wind down. There was nothing left to say. I even ended all my jabbering with terrible words. I said, "I'd say that God's dead, except I guess he never existed in the first place."

I was crying in his study. It just felt like the world was all over.

Then he said, "Mo, I know this will be hard to believe right now, maybe even for some time to come. But you're one of the luckiest young men on this campus. Youre faith is being born."

Then he said, "If you were a fetus, inside your mother's womb, and you were offered a chance to come out, would you? No! Of course not! You'd have a cozy waterbed there, your food and drink would be brought to you, wastes carried away, temperature's perfect. If we could *choose*, we wouldn't choose the inconvenience and the disruption and the pain of getting pushed through that birth canal. Right?" I nodded. He was right, and he was making it so clear, where I was right now. I mean, *then*. Now is totally different.

Then he said, "But if a fetus WASN'T born, it would die, right? It can't live forever in its mother. And it wouldn't want to, because all the joys of life begin when we become separate individuals. Well, that's what's happening to your faith, Mo. Right now. You're coming out of your parents' faith. Your own faith is being born. You're making your own decision, not just accepting what others have told you."

Then he said, "So what about all these questions people raise about God? They sound pretty smart. And I'm not too smart, but just smart enough to know it's true... all this God stuff could be a myth." (He says he's "simple" sometimes in sermons and chapel talks. But he's soooo smart.) "It could be that human beings have made up all this stuff about God, Creation, miracles, God's Son, all that. To me, it seems much wiser than anything people could make up. But I have to admit it: even though <u>they</u> can't prove God is a myth, <u>I</u> can't prove He does exist."

Holy Smokes. I never waited for a "next sentence" in my whole life as much as I waited for his next one. I was on the edge of my chair. It was like he had led me out to a giant hole in the river ice, with water so cold you knew you'd die in a second if you stepped off into it. Whatever he said next might just push me in. Instead, looking back, I realize now he showed me how some of us lucky ones get to walk up to the edge, then step out ... and fly!

What he said was, "Nevertheless, I do believe. I believe that a power beyond all human imagination created the world and everything in it. I believe that power came down to this planet almost 2000 years ago and walked and talked, and ate, and died. And that that power rose out of death to prove to me there is something beyond, something magnificent waiting for me. Nevertheless, I do believe."

THAT'S ALL HE SAID! And it reached so deep inside me I felt like I floated out of his office a few minutes later. I honestly haven't touched ground yet. I *am* the luckiest guy on campus. I was born again today. God never moved, but I did, and now, because of His grace, I'm back.

I want to shout! I'm on solid ground. Total freedom (like that free floating astronaut) is no freedom at all. I'm grounded in God, not adrift in existentlism or whatever. I will never forget this day as long as I live.

Is this COOL?!!!!

* * *

May 2, 1976

Dear Journal,

It's been so busy, I never write here anymore. But last week another cool thing happened and I don't want to forget it. So here goes.

First, the Valentines Day spiritual birth wasn't a still-born event! (Ha-ha.) I didn't realize it til afterward, but it was Valentines day when I walked out of Pastor Jim's office a brand new Christian, having made my own decision and not just wearing my parents' faith. So I was born again on the day of Love.

Anyway, long and short, Pastor Jim came up alongside my mentor and me on Thursday or Friday. We were going to the CUB for coffee and he asked if we could stand a little company. (He's so cool.) On the way, he asked Prof. Stuart a riddle: "what have you got if you have a green ball in this hand and a green ball in this hand?" (he gestured.) Prof said he gave up, he didn't know. Pastor Jim said, "Complete control of the Jolly Green Giant!"

I bet my jaw dropped a yard. Heres this great preacher, a loving and gentle soul who loves the Lord like I do, an intellectual. And he tells a joke like that! I've been thinking about it ever since, and you know what I realized? He's right. I mean, what that joke showed me is, "Hey, God made some funny body parts and we put funny names on 'em, and for some reason we all laugh when they're in jokes. And *we don't dishonor God with a joke like that that doesn't hurt anybody*! It wasn't filthy, it wasn't nasty, it didn't hurt anybody, and little old Eskimoses who sucked in air when he heard it can just jolly well relax. Our beloved Jesus came to earth and loved life; he ate and drank and was even accused of being a wine-bibber. (That word always gets me this picture of someone whose Mogen David is dribbling on his shirt front.) So Pastor Jim not only helped me see God as real, and almighty, and holy two months ago. He's now also helped me see that God's not a tightass little Pharisee.

"God saw all that he had made, and it was very good!" (Genesis?) YAY, GOD!

CHAPTER 52

THE GATEKEEPER

Fairbanks
Friday, June 21, 1991
Just after noon

Lute looked up again, into Moses' eyes. The kindness of his pastoral office had been entirely replaced with a steely alert, distrust, even fear. It was clear to Lute that this was a make-or-break moment. Moses had huge hurdles to run before Lute himself—not to speak of God's new *kairos*—was safe. The long-haired pastor had to be convinced not only that Lute was a kindly, non-threatening scholar, but also that the scrolls he brought carried verifiable turn-of-history reporting. *Oh yeah,* Lute thought, *and one more little thing. Regardless of how he accepts the message, I need to convince Moses not to kill the messenger.* He gritted his teeth, catching himself in his own overblown sense of importance. Still, Harald's death—*death!*—might not have been either accidental or self-inflicted. If Sean told the wrong people, this thing could be spinning out of control. *Out of my control, anyway. Lord, please don't let it spin out of Yours.*

"Perhaps we should take advantage of the FBI's offer, Dr. Jonson, and get some protection for you?"

Lute sprang into mental action. "No. That could be disastrous, ahh, pastor. I feel like I've forfeited the right you gave me to use your first name, but I wish you'd call me Lute." Moses' gaze didn't waver. *At least I have his total attention.*

"May we both retrieve my briefcase?" Lute asked, sensitive to Moses' need to guard him. "I'd like to open it up—or rather, for *you* to open it—so you can see the seven parchment pieces that are about to strip away whole layers of misunderstanding about our God. A revelation. Not just for you, but for the whole world. For all the years remaining before His return."

He watched for an answer, but his host stood eerily immobile. Thirty seconds passed as the two stared at each other. The sound of a car pulling into the driveway ended the impasse. Lute thoughtlessly began to stand up for what he assumed was Mrs. Tling's arrival. Apparently expecting the same, Moses spun to the wall behind him and grabbed an aboriginal hand-ax off its display brackets. He whipped around and held the ax up with the curved sharp edge toward Lute. Lute eased back down to his chair.

The old scholar's peripheral vision took in the sinewy thong strapping the dull gray iron head to its aged wood handle; his eyes, however, locked onto Moses' eyes. His every muscle taut, Lute sensed Moses' condition to be identical. Once again he was locked in a threat-and-retreat episode. It felt to Lute like he was a metal duck in a carnival's midway shooting gallery; the only moments he was safe were when he was upside down and approaching the next vulnerable exposure.

They heard the car in the driveway back out and drive off. A lost driver would never know the adrenalin rushes he had caused.

Suddenly, Moses lowered the blade. His tension seemed to melt into some kind of submission. Lute thought he could hear words in Moses' mind: "Let go, let God." Moses laid the ax on a woven cloth place mat at his end of the table. He pushed it a few inches toward Lute and took a step back. "Are you a killer?" he asked.

Lute exhaled. "I'm so sorry you feel you have to ask that. And I'm astounded at your faith, to offer me this." He dismissed the ax with a small wave. "Moses, I lied to you about my name because there are people who don't want my news to be released. There are authorities—religious and perhaps even secular—who seem to know by now that I'm determined to tell the world about these secret scrolls. They believe I'm carrying a kind of spiritual AIDS virus. An extraordinary conflict is in progress—in some ways it mirrors the battle other Scrolls describe: the sons of darkness being joined in combat with the sons of light. Whether I'm a hero or a villain, the instrument of God or a tool of the devil, I'm all alone against them. I only have one hope. If I unveil these incredible 'memos' from two millennia ago to one or two local reporters, my adversaries could 'take care of' them afterward. As they may have taken care of Harald. But if I can announce them to a wide audience, in an international forum, then I'm safe again. And far more importantly, God's new *kairos* will begin. His presence will break into this selfish, smutty, vacuous age in a fresh new way. It's as if He waited for this moment, knowing we would soon need a Third Millennium tune-up, a reminder of what's central in life and what's incidental. If you'll look at these scroll pieces, you'll understand."

Moses stood transfixed. His face, normally unreadable except for that frequent mischievous grin, seemed to billboard internal conflict. Finally he spoke again. "You did not kill Dr. Ericksen?"

Lute shook his head sadly. "No. No. I knew nothing about my friend's death until you told me. Because of that shock it is a struggle to keep my sights on what I must do. No, I couldn't kill, Moses. Not for anything."

"I could. For family. For faith. 'Only he who raises his knife gets his Isaac.' Kierkegaard, I think."

Lute awaited Moses' verdict. They avoided each other's eyes.

"Who else knows about these scrolls?"

Lute swallowed hard. "Only two of us—myself and my study team co-director, a Jesuit priest—knew until this week. I told my sister a little bit about them in San Diego on Monday before learning that somebody was coming for me. I told Harald everything and showed them to him. You'll be the fourth to know the full secret that two of us hoarded for over forty years."

"Why would you trust me with such news?" Moses asked.

"I have to. You're the door." Lute studied Moses' reaction while he heard his deity's mantra repeating in his head: *Fear not. Fear not. Fear not....*

The pastor seemed to be praying with open eyes. Without warning, he walked behind Lute and through the living room. Gone for only a few seconds, he returned with Lute's briefcase which he deposited on the table in front of the old scholar. He stood back and spoke.

"Open Sesame."

CHAPTER 53

CHEROKEE'S AFIRE

The parsonage in Fairbanks
Friday, June 21, 1991
1:10 p.m.

Moses hung up the phone. "It was our pilot Hilary," he said. "He asked if you were any relation to the guy who died in Washington State. He heard about Dr. Ericksen on the radio—we get a lot of Washington news up here—and since the name sounded familiar, he checked his passenger manifest. Now he's even more curious, after confirming your signature as the same name."

Lute shook his head slowly, dispiritedly.

"As you could hear, I played dumb. Not too hard for me. You probably won't be too happy to hear that Hilary's brother is an FBI agent."

Damn! Are you sending me a message, Lord? Is it "Stop!"? Lute walked to the living room window. He stared out over a forest of skinny white birch trunks topped by their minimum daily requirement of photosynthesizing greenery. He was fearful now, despite the greetings God repeated as each of His *kairos* events began.

Still in the dining room, Moses spoke. "Lute, I believe you. I'm in awe of these parchment fragments. My Hebrew was shaky even back in seminary, and it's hard to read these tiny faded characters. But I believe you about this, even though my gut is wrenching at the thought of it all."

Lute nodded thanks, but then his chin sank to his chest.

"Do you have a plan for releasing the news?"

Lute turned around and faced his host. "Yeah, Moses, I *did*. I was going to betray you—just one last time—by highjacking the teleconference tomorrow. It was my only hope. As I said before, until this box is wide open, whoever's looking for me can silence everybody I tell, one by one." He paused, watching in vain for the pastor's revulsion at the admission. "I'm sorry. I was at the end of my rope."

"And now," Moses volunteered, "you feel it's around your neck."

Lute nodded.

Moses re-examined the plastic-sleeved scroll fragments spread out on the table before him. He turned the one labeled 1Q-Cether-7 over, looked at the back, and returned it to its place at the right end of the line. His eyes were open but seemed only to be looking inward. At last he spoke. "Well, we better get you out of here."

Lute looked up again, eyes narrowing.

"I mean we need to get you to safety. I have to figure out how to deflect anybody from guessing your plan, so when I deliver you to the studio tomorrow, God can 'break through into human time' as you called it."

"Where...?" Lute began, visibly shedding tension from his face, shoulders, and hands.

Moses answered first with his habitual impish grin. "Did you ever know an Eskimo who didn't know remote places in the interior of Alaska?"

Ten minutes later, the two of them were once more seated in the Tling Jeep Cherokee, buckling in and snapping door locks. Lute settled his briefcase between his feet again, wondering if there were ankle indentations in its two sides by now. Moses opened his yellow windbreaker, emblazoned with the words "Iditarod Sled Dog Race 1990," and revealed a holstered black handgun. It appeared to have the kind of squared off handle that contained a magazine clip.

"I'm leaving Tana defenseless. We're apt to see some wildlife up close, and if it thinks you look tasty, I'll have to argue with it. This has a more convincing voice than I do."

"Only me? Wouldn't you look tasty, too?" countered Lute.

"When I'm alone, I'm quieter and sneakier than any of them."

Moses backed the four-wheel-drive sport vehicle out onto the street and began to retrace their earlier route. Lute scanned the streets for prying eyes. He half turned toward Moses, mostly so he could glance at cars behind them—anxious when any failed to turn after a block or two, relieved when they finally did. He had no idea where they were headed, and with the sun still almost fully overhead, it was difficult to gauge a direction. But shortly he noticed a floating compass mounted on the dash and began to keep track of their general northbound progress. The two were silent all the way through the city streets and outskirts, but once they turned onto a carless stretch of highway, Moses broke the silence.

"I keep a couple of sleeping bags and a camp stove in the back during the summer. Canned goods, too. Sometimes Tana and I just take off. A couple of months of this summer mildness makes the other months bearable. But ya gotta get out while the gettin's good."

Lute nodded, and both returned to private thoughts.

"I think most people just look at one frame at a time," Lute finally said.

Moses' head cocked and his eyes asked, "Whatchoo say, white man?"

Lute smiled. "Sorry, I was thinking about watching my old super-8 movies of Naomi—my wife. She died four and a half years ago. I used to edit them on a little mickey-mouse film editor, so I got used to examining individual frames to find the right picture to start a scene, or end it. One day I was looking at a frame of her on the editing screen. She was modeling her 'fat pants'—those maternity slacks with the expanding-fronts that look like kangaroo pouches. Since I had seen the whole reel, I knew that in a second or two she was going to pull the front of those pants way down, revealing that beach-ball belly she had by the end of her pregnancy. It was surprising and funny—the veiny, stretched-out skin covering an undulating glob inside, and her normally being so petite and ladylike in public. I always think of that frame when someone asks about 'my theology.'" Lute enunciated the two words as a rigid pedagogue might, then grinned to underscore his view of such pomposity.

"Why?" prompted his driver.

"Because it reminds me how God reveals Himself over time; not in single moments or events, but in the sweep of history. Anybody who only saw the one frame of Naomi, or even all the reels of film I had taken of her up to that moment, might have known just one side of her—they might never have known that she had impetuous moments that were so endearing. But a few frames later, that whole other side became evident. It seems to me my conservative friends tend to concentrate on the minute details of individual scenes in the Bible. Single verses or words, even. Single frames."

"So they miss the flow, the action," Moses summarized. "The direction."

"Yeah. And the grace of movement. Always the Grace of His movement through His children's history. Always the agape love—the undeserved, selfless, other-directed love. And what do we do? We try to take His place on the Judge's bench."

They rode on in silence, the sun now two hours into its descent from the west, arcing down toward the northern horizon. Lute felt at peace, but he suspected it was the calm before tomorrow's storm.

"What's happened to your colleague the priest?" Moses asked.

"Don't know. I'm sure he must have called Rome; I doubt our own security chief, as good as he is, could be directing this search for me. Sean's probably the hero in the Vatican's eyes now, despite our mutual lack of candor for so long. Maybe he'll be elevated to bishop as a reward. Or cardinal, to ensure that he 'contains' this dirty little secret."

"Or maybe he's with Dr. Ericksen now."

The thought caught Lute off guard; he couldn't believe two fatalities might have resulted from his decision. He wondered again what had happened to Harald. If the reports of his death were true—and at this point Lute didn't know *what* was true in this hall of mirrors he had created—then what had caused it? Sure, Harald had seemed depressed, but could such a solid Christian commit suicide? Perhaps, if he felt his lifelong faith had been shaken, especially if that news collided with his evident discomfort about his own sexual orientation. Or had he had a heart attack? Or—and once again Lute struggled to overcome what he suspected was paranoia—were there truly murderous people coming after him, mopping up the dirty little messes they thought he was leaving on his trail? If *that* were true, then Sean would be at risk, as well. Lute's chest seemed to empty. Despite all they were going through half a world apart— and their diametrically-opposite decisions about releasing this news—he loved his colleague of four decades. Which hell could he wish for Sean: forgiveness and promotion in the Church as payment for his silence? Or castigation and punishment, even death, for either having remained silent so long or for breaking that silence now? *Holy One, protect your son Sean. Save us all, Lord.*

Lute's shoulders sagged, and he turned his face away.

CHAPTER 54

STONEWALLED

Somewhere in Italy
Friday, June 21, 1991

Sean woke up on a cot in a monk's cell enclosed by walls of ancient stone. He felt groggy, and his head ached when he tried to raise himself. It felt like a hangover, but he couldn't remember drinking anything the night before. Come to think of it, he couldn't remember anything at all after that foul-tasting stew they'd given him when his stomach had begun rumbling. He'd tried to loosen up the monk who had been guarding him, complaining, "Faith, man, I'm giving organ recitals in here." When was that? Yesterday afternoon? Had they moved him now to a new area in the Holy See?

He lay back and settled for exploring this eight-foot-square room by sight only. The cold gray flat stones extended up a dozen feet or so to a slate-colored ceiling with a single rough timber beam across the middle. Near the joint of the wall and ceiling above his head was a two-foot-square window, latticed with four iron bars. Turning his head, he could see the floor was a well-swept slate.

A crucifix hung on the wall to his left, with a black leather-covered Bible lying on a small shelf underneath. Even lifting his head slightly, Sean couldn't see his valise anywhere. The only familiar sight in the ascetic space was the pair of plain black shoes of a poor religious, poked halfway under the cot at the foot.

Sean spoke softly in the direction of the heavy wooden door in the wall close to his feet. "Hello?" Hearing no answer, he raised his voice to conversation level. "Hello? Anyone there?"

A rustle of robes outside preceded the sliding open of a small view port in the door. Sean looked into an unfamiliar eye. The port closed and the door was opened by an unremarkable monk in a brown robe just like that of Sean's keeper the day before. The new man carried a heavy porcelain lidded jug into the cell and set it in the corner by the door. He pulled a small roll of bathroom tissue from his pocket and balanced it on the lid. He made the faintest gesture—the sign of the cross?—and began to leave.

"Wait," Sean begged anxiously. "Please, tell me when I'll be returning home. I'm here from Jerusalem."

The monk turned and looked at Sean for the first time. He shrugged dumbly.

"Would you ask Cardinal Collins if I could talk with him? Is he still here in Rome?"

The monk tilted his shaved head curiously, and shrugged again. He briefly crossed his closed mouth with his right index finger; it was not a gesture requiring Sean's silence, but a sign that his own lips were sealed. The men looked at one another from the two ends of a short, mute space. Suddenly Sean was aware of bird calls through the high window. Not the sleepless urban traffic sounds he had heard even at his late arrival at the Vatican, but the idyllic aurals of nature.

"We *are* in Rome, aren't we?" he asked. The monk's wordless stoicism gave no hint of answer. "Can you just nod your head?"

The monk looked up at the window a moment, then turned and left, closing and locking the door behind him.

* * *

An hour later, the monk returned. Sean feigned re-smoothing the blanket on his cot, blushing in embarrassment as the poor wretch did his duty retrieving the used chamber pot. Sean attempted to follow him through the door, but the monk was clearly having none of that. His deep scowl was a shout of silent communication. He did bring back a large tray holding a bowl of warm water, a face cloth, hand towel, plate of fresh country biscuits, cup of steaming water, teabag, and spoon.

"Are you permitted to speak?" asked Sean. The monk laid the tray on the cot.

"Can you nod an answer?" The old scholar-priest's voice sounded a bit more desperate with each unanswered question. He looked into the sad eyes of his server. As the mute turned toward the door, Sean said, "You're under a vow of silence, aren't you? Is it difficult?"

The monk stopped short. He stood still a long moment, then turned to the small altar in the cell and knelt before it. He reached for the old Douay-Rheims Bible there, opened it to the middle, and turned back a few pages. Sean could see that he was reading from the left page. Without a glance or a sound, the monk set the open book back on the personal altar, rose, and left.

Oh, God, thought Sean as he approached the scriptures. *Psalm 38.*

Again the door's lock punctuated the silence like the period on a sentence.

Psalm 38 (Douay-Rheims)

I said: I will take heed to my ways: that I sin not with my tongue. I have set a guard to my mouth, when the sinner stood against me. I was dumb, and was humbled, and kept silence from good things: and my sorrow was renewed. My heart grew hot within me: and in my meditation a fire shall flame out. I spoke with my tongue: O Lord, make me know my end. And what is the number of my days: that I may know what is wanting to me. Behold thou hast made my days measurable, and my substance is as nothing before thee. And indeed all things are vanity: every man living. Surely man passeth as an image: yea, and he is disquieted in vain .... Hear my prayer, O Lord, and my supplication: give ear to my tears. Be not silent: for I am a stranger with thee, and a sojourner as all my fathers were. O forgive me, that I may be refreshed, before I go hence, and be no more.

CHAPTER 55

TOWARD CIRCLE

Steese Highway, north of Fairbanks
Friday, June 21, 1991
5:30 p.m.

It had been a leisurely drive; Moses had kept his speed around thirty-five miles per hour, even on the first seventy miles of paved road outside of Fairbanks. When they hit the gravel section thirty miles back, he had slowed down another ten miles an hour. They had taken a roadside break to stretch their legs almost two hours ago, but Lute's old bones needed increasingly frequent shifting in the car.

"We'll be at Eagle Summit in a few minutes," Moses said. "There's a Roadhouse there. Want to stop for something to eat?"

"Sure," answered Lute, "my treat." He dug his wallet out to check his cash. "Oh, gosh. You know, I need to take care of something while I think of it. I owe my sister some money and after tomorrow, I may be in a whirlwind of activities. I think I still have...." He fished back into a flap-covered section and pulled out a folded blank check. Pulling his briefcase up to his knees for a writing board, he made it out to Christiana for five thousand dollars, and noted "overdraft protection/savings" on the memo line. He placed it behind the cash in his wallet, knowing that would remind him to mail it after the teleconference.

Moses returned to the subject of dinner. "One of my cousins runs the place. She'll overcharge us less than she overcharges most. All the cheechakos take pictures of her counter sign. It says 'Pickles—10¢ each or 2 for a quarter.'"

Lute chuckled. "Cheechakos?"

"People like you. From 'Outside.' The Lower 48."

Lute suddenly realized that would be a bad idea. "We can't stop there if someone might know you, Moses. For the next eighteen hours, we have to be invisible."

The Eskimo pastor nodded his understanding. "Well, I'm taking us up to Circle, on the banks of the Yukon River. We pass by her place because it's right on the road. There's almost nobody else between here and the river. You want to duck down when we pass?"

"I'm sure it looks paranoid to you, but I probably will. We just can't risk anything, now that we're so close. If we can avoid all human contact until we show up at the studio tomorrow, we're safe. Otherwise...you know?"

Moses looked thoughtful. "Well, I do have to call my wife. I didn't even leave her a note when we left, and if I don't check in soon, she'll be using the tele-systems to find me."

"The what?" Lute knew he was being suckered into a joke.

"The main communications systems. Tele-phone, tele-graph, tele-woman."

Lute groaned good-naturedly. "Is there anywhere except your cousin's roadhouse to call from?"

"There's a pay phone on the highway in Central, another twenty miles. Or in Circle, about fifty. How about we pass right by my cousin's and call from Central?"

Lute agreed and they drove on. The vast valleys filled with slender birch all around them, and the interspersed low hilltops to their left—Moses had identified them as the White Mountains—intrigued Lute. He was accustomed to the Middle East's rougher and rockier countryside, but this smoother and greener landscape reminded him of Minnesota. Moses had pointed out the spring and summer flora here, and its tentative hold on the shallow soil above permafrost.

"Can you help me, Lute?"

Jolted out of his reverie, the old scholar was curious. "How? I mean, sure, whatever I can do for you, you know I will."

"I guess I'm struggling. I still can't get over it: your scroll evidence says Jesus Christ was homosexual." He pushed the last word; the wave carrying it wasn't anger or revulsion, but it certainly wasn't delight.

Lute breathed in deeply. He knew he'd better get used to this. The world was about to learn a new thing, and was about to feel threatened by it. Moses and Harald were given to him as rehearsals for the world premiere tomorrow. Even after forty years of mulling this *kairos* over—he had learned to mentally put it aside for long periods or he'd have gone crazy—it still sometimes struck him that it was incredible news. But lately that reaction had been waning. Today he felt stronger than ever that the scrolls' messages were completely synchronized with the Jesus of history and the Christ of his faith.

"I'm sorry it's tough for you to hear," he said. Moses shook his head almost imperceptibly, so Lute continued. "Look, Jesus was fully human and fully divine."

Moses interrupted, "But you don't have to have sex with guys to be fully human."

"He didn't have sex with guys; only one guy. He was monogamous. Look, He didn't come to earth as a married

Eskimo woman in this century, but is there any question in your mind that He loves your wife?"

Moses shook his head no.

"So for almost two thousand years humans have known His incarnation was as a Jewish male at what we now call the beginning of the first century. And people have known that this Jesus loved them individually, regardless of whether we were Jew, Samaritan, Gentile, male or female, in any century. He was different from us in many ways, so why is it difficult when we find out He had a different sexual orientation than most of us?"

"Because we've been raised to believe that God Himself said men should not lie with men. And because we've never given any thought to the possibility Jesus *had* a sex drive, let alone acted on it."

Lute turned toward his driver, fully engaged. "Point one, we have been mistaught for a thousand years about the holiness code in Leviticus, the Sodom story in Genesis, and several New Testament references. Remember that Jesus never mentioned this subject; what he *did* preach against was sexual immorality, which can be practiced by either gay or straight. It's immoral when it's promiscuous, orgiastic, selfish, loveless. Making sex an idol—*that's* the immorality; holding it as more important than fidelity to one partner, and certainly more important than God."

"So my biblical namesake was kidding when he said 'man shall not lie with man as with a woman, that is an abomination to the Lord'?"

"Moses! I thought you lectured on this subject last night!"

Moses grinned. "Busted. Hey, I *did* tell them what you're going to tell me, I'm sure. But then it was theoretical and politically correct. Now, with your news, my gut is twisting."

Lute reached over and clapped the younger man on the shoulder.

"So, how *are* you going to answer me? Was the first Moses kidding? Lying? Misquoted?"

"The holiness code in Leviticus prohibits all kinds of things that we no longer observe," Lute answered, then began using his fingers to enumerate examples. "Women wearing pants; people wearing cotton-poly clothes; working on the Sabbath; eating pork, shellfish or rare meat. Despite passages in the same book, we don't keep slaves, or burn prostitutes alive, or stone rebellious children to death. There are hundreds of such laws in the Old Testament. But which one do fundamentalists choose to harp on and get all lathered up about? One that makes us all queasy inside— homosexual sex. And will they tell their congregations that its original meaning prohibited male temple prostitution? Nope. They want to extend it, make it an absolute. They're willing to feign grace and patronize gays, saying, 'You are so broken.' But do they recognize the fact that their own disapproval is what *breaks* the gays and lesbians who want—too desperately, I'm sure—to be accepted? No. It's so human to prefer playing God the Judge. Much more fun than imitating Christ the Redeemer." Lute felt like he had rested his case, but Moses reminded him he hadn't.

"Point two?"

"Oh, yeah, sorry. You said something about not even thinking about Jesus as having even a 'normal' sex drive. Same song, second verse. You might be the exception," Lute grinned wryly, "but most preachers wouldn't dream of upsetting their poor congregations with the facts. In Jesus' time, a rabbi had to be married. The Jews required it. No ifs, ands, or buts. And His father Joseph's major responsibilities were to see that the boy Jesus was (a) educated in the Torah, and (b) married to a good Jewish girl. So most

Christians worldwide *should* have been taught since childhood that our Lord was almost certainly married. This explosive *kairos* in my briefcase, however, will put a whole different light on why His wife was never mentioned."

Lute had filled the Jeep with so many words, he was grateful for a break in the conversation. He rolled down the window for air.

Moses seemed to need additional reassurance. "Are you *positive* the scroll says that He was, you know, 'intimate' with John? How could that possibly be holy? How could that activity possibly *not* be considered 'sexual immorality,' which He preached against?"

"We talked earlier about not concentrating on single frames, but watching the 'movie' to get the message. Well, from the whole flow of His life—His actions, His words, His death and resurrection—what central point gets through to us? Is it hate? Is it rigid adherence to the Law? Is it judgment?"

"No," Moses answered in a soft voice. "It was love for God and love for God's children."

"When this *kairos* breaks through to the world, you know there will be weeping and moaning and gnashing of teeth. Because people just don't get it. He tried in every way to break through to hard hearts; He was the greatest iconoclast—disrespecter of rigid religiosity—of all time. The King of Kings was born in a stable. He 'worked' on the Sabbath day. He associated with the lowlifes and sinners. He ate; he drank wine. The Jewish hierarchy of the day hated Him."

Lute had worked himself up into a very unscholarly lather, but now eased down into a gentler gear to conclude. "And I believe He's sent one more *kairos* event into this old world to shake us up again."

They drove in silence. As the Jeep approached a bend in the road, Moses nodded up ahead and motioned for his passenger to bend down. Fully aware of the irony, Lute repeated God's mantra to himself: *Fear not. Fear not. Fear not.* Here he was in all his white-haired maturity, bent double to hide himself from one or two people deep in the Alaskan wilderness who probably weren't looking anyway.

"OK. We're past."

Lute straightened up.

Moses asked, "Are you tired of these questions?"

"Not from you, Moses. I owe you so much. And I don't know what you have planned, but I have nothing on my agenda until the moment we show up at your friend's studio tomorrow."

"OK. So you're saying that even though He had an intimate relationship with someone, I shouldn't feel jealous of that?"

Lute's double-take belied his surprise. *But of course, Lord! When we thought of You as a holy eunuch, we thought we had a one-to-one connection with You, unsurpassed by any other! That's the real threat in these scrolls.*

He answered aloud. "I do indeed mean that. Do you feel jealous that God didn't let you know Jesus in person? That you didn't live back then, and get picked to be a disciple? No, of course not. How much more could Christ have done to show His love for you, pastor? Nothing, right? And we don't begrudge Him His friendships, like with Mary and Martha and Lazarus. Why would we begrudge Him an intimate companion?"

Moses coughed. "It's not so much the intimacy I have trouble with, not in the regular way. It's just … despite my liberal talk, I'm afraid my gut still can't quite accept the two-penis thing. Not as holy, anyway."

Lute's head nodded understandingly, but he said, "Fear not. Be not homo-*phobic*. I have to keep reminding myself that sex is a good gift from God, and gifts sometimes come in different packages."

Moses' smile bordered on the lascivious as he added, "So to speak."

A mile passed.

"You won't be thanked, you know." Moses' prediction was gentle, but what was unsaid was unsettling.

Lute nodded assent, but added, "It doesn't matter."

"Conservatives will revile you, damn you, call you the Antichrist. On the other hand, liberals still won't believe He's God. You're in a no-win game."

Lute set his jaw. "Then both sides will lose, won't they? Because Jesus is Lord of the Universe and unbelievers are missing something wonderful. And for the poor, uptight, stiff-necked people who will not open themselves to God's continuing revelations about *both* His humanity and divinity, then that's *their* loss. Besides, the Lord predicted that for me in Luke 6."

Moses guessed. "The Beatitudes? Blessed are you who are reviled for my sake?"

Lute nodded. "Will I burn in hell for the sin of pride, claiming I know God's heart when my intellectual superiors disagree? Maybe. But when He reveals Himself to us—in His word, in our life experiences, in the quiet insistence of our conscience—isn't the real sin hoarding such revelations? Hiding for fear of public disapproval?"

"No offense, Lute, but I think we both might be overestimating public reaction. I think it'll be even worse: few will care. Apathy's a fate worse than hate."

Lute cocked his head skeptically, but both men remained silent for the next few miles. As Moses finally began to slow the Jeep, Lute saw a rest stop with a phone booth ahead —the first he had seen since Fairbanks, and an extraordinary sight in the wilds of Alaska, despite Moses' earlier mention.

Lute looked across the car. "I think I did too much talking. You said you were struggling, so I should have listened more."

Moses shook his head. "You did OK. You almost convinced my head. I hope my gut will come around."

A chill ran through Lute as they pulled to a stop by the phone. *I hope so, too. Dear God, I do.*

* * *

Moses' call was still going on almost ten minutes after Lute returned from his leg-stretch walk up the highway and back. To afford his chauffer maximum privacy, Lute re-entered the Jeep and rolled his window up. Though he tried to avoid looking, he couldn't help but notice that a couple of times Moses' conversation had become more intense than casual, and each time the younger man in the booth had turned his back toward the car. For diversion, Lute listed those who had come to know the scrolls' new *kairos* chronologically.

Sean and I, Christiana, Harald, Moses. A handful of five, if the Devil wanted to do us in. Maybe he began with Harald. Oh, Lord, please tell me it's not so. I hate to think of him gone in any case, but if I were responsible.... Sean is surely safe. Christiana doesn't know the half of it; there's safety in ignorance. Moses and I are deep in this heart of lightness, out of harm's way. Soon the truth will out. 'Not all the darkness in the world can extinguish the flicker of one candle's light.' Lute smiled. *Regardless of how hard that darkness blows.*

Moses finally hung up. He stood frozen a moment in the booth, then walked to the car and got in.

"Everything OK?" Lute asked.

"Uh, yeah. Just some, you know, stuff about Sunday's service." Moses stared straight ahead. He turned over the ignition and pulled back onto the gravel road.

Lute sensed he shouldn't probe. He looked at his watch. "Seven-thirty. It's as bright as noon."

Moses nodded absently.

Lute continued, more filling the silence than needing to communicate. "My first Midnight Sun. Tonight. How fitting, that the *kairos* should be revealed at this time and place. In a day without night, a light-filled landscape. How very right."

"You forget that the daily increase of darkness begins again tomorrow," Moses replied in a thin voice. "There's always a December."

CHAPTER 56

OPERATION DISINFECT

La Jolla, California
Friday, June 21, 1991
11:30 a.m.

Christiana answered the front doorbell, knowing it would be a neighbor or friend. Their cliffside neighborhood wasn't a gated community but it was almost never intruded upon by strangers. She was surprised to find two men in suits waiting when she opened the door.

"Dr. Hansgaard?"

"Yes?"

"Is your husband home?"

Relieved that she could truthfully say yes as a precaution against any mischief these two men might have in mind, she quickly added, "And you are...?"

"I'm Deputy Pasqual from the San Diego County Sheriff; this is Deputy DeLott." They showed walleted badges. "You have a brother in town, ma'am?"

Christiana carefully looked at the two men on her elegant brick stoop before answering, then said, "Just a moment, please." She took a few steps toward the deck door in the back and called to her husband. He came in; she beckoned him to join her.

"This is my husband," she said simply, side-stepping their prior question.

"Do you have a brother in town, Dr. Hansgaard?" the agent repeated.

"I'm sorry, I didn't get your name," Hjalmar said, opening the screen door and stepping outside. The two repeated their self-introductions and badge flashes. Hjalmar reached out to steady and inspect each badge before nodding his acceptance. He turned back to Christiana and nodded as if to say she could answer.

"Yes."

"Is he about your age, white-haired?"

"Yes."

"I'm sorry to ask, ma'am: what is his name?"

Hjalmar broke in. "What's this about, gentlemen?"

The agent behind spoke up for the first time. "One of our cruisers found a gentleman pretty badly roughed up on a rural road about two hours ago. He had no wallet or identification, and they only got him to speak a little bit ago. All he said is, "Sister" and gave this address. We have him at a trauma center, and if you have a brother matching that description, Dr. Hansgaard, you might want to let us take you there."

Both Hansgaards were visibly shaken. "Let me lock up," Hjalmar said and quickly moved back to the deck door. Christiana slumped against the inside doorjamb.

"How bad is he?" she asked.

"I don't think they're life-threatening injuries, but he probably resisted a hooligan or two. He was lying by the side of the road. We were already in La Jolla and they radioed us to come by."

Hjalmar returned carrying jackets for each of them. As they followed the men toward the unmarked car in the driveway, Hjalmar said, "How did you know our name?"

"Reverse directory. 'Unpublished' only means 'not public,' you know."

Hjalmar nodded. As he reached for the handle on the back door of the sedan, he thought he saw the almost-imperceptible flash of a smile between the men.

"Ahh, honey, wait." He turned to face them. "I think we'll follow you, if that's all right. We may need the car, and it would save you a drive back here." He watched their faces carefully as Deputy Pasqual tried to dissuade him. Christiana began to interrupt, but Hjalmar took her arm in a decades-old nonverbal signal between them, and insisted on his own plan. His authoritarian tone prevailed—surprisingly easily, he thought—and the deputies instructed them to stay close, even though they would be short-cutting through some back roads. Hjalmar agreed, and the two-car caravan soon pulled out of the driveway.

Something made Christiana take a last look back at her beloved pacific home.

CHAPTER 57

PENULT AND PENUMBRA

Upriver from Circle, Alaska
Friday, June 21, 1991
11:40 p.m.

Off the end of the little village's last road, Moses had used the Cherokee's rugged four-wheel drive to power through the brush just far enough to get out of sight. Lute and Moses had been glad to get out, to stretch, and now to stand on the narrow bank scanning the Yukon River in silence. Moses' jeans and long-sleeved bush shirt were natural Alaskan garb that contrasted with Lute's business slacks, even as rumpled as his had become over the past few days. While the sun was low in the sky to the north, Lute realized, it was nonetheless in the sky. He stole a glance down to his watch: 11:43. *Amazing. The Midnight Sun I've heard about since boyhood.*

A lazy flow of blue-green water stretched a quarter-mile across to the low bank opposite. Skinny-trunked trees crowded down to the water's edge on the north side just as they did behind the two men on the south side.

"Time is a river," Moses said, apparently unselfconscious about the cliché.

Lute nodded pleasantly until the young pastor continued.

"We swim in it a little, then get beached and bleached. It never notices we're gone."

Lute challenged his tone. "How can you turn existentialist in the face of this display of God's creation? This haven of safety and peace?"

"Looks are deceiving, Lute. And temporary. Can you come back six months from now?"

"Ah, but we're here at this moment, this incalculably precious present ... a present from God."

Both fell quiet again, appreciating the gift wrapping: soft sounds of an unrushed river, the early light of a dusk that would not turn dark, the clean smell of the wilds a thousand miles from civilization's frenzy.

"Here's a question," Lute said. "It's Friday; if there were Jews here tonight, could they begin Shabbat? It's supposed to start at sundown."

Moses did not acknowledge his new friend's playful spirit, but instead stiffened at the water's edge.

"Is everything OK, Moses?"

The Eskimo turned a sad steely gaze at the aging scholar. "You just don't know, do you?"

A long moment passed while a hundred ambiguous messages traveled the airwaves between their eyes.

"Know *what?*" He lifted his hands and shoulders in confusion. "Am I in danger here?"

Moses turned and began to walk through the dry bank's tangle of vegetation. Lute followed.

"You scaring me on purpose or just by accident?"

Moses said "I'm thinking" over his shoulder and continued to move upriver around a small bend. They were less than a hundred yards from the Jeep when they rounded that point, and Moses grunted, "Still here." When Lute caught up, he saw a canoe that had obviously been known to his guide in the past. Moses began to remove the natural camouflaging that had covered it, but Lute grabbed his arm and pulled him up from the task.

"What's going on? What don't I understand?" There was alarm in his voice.

"Fear not. Isn't that what your scrolls say?" Moses' attitude wasn't so much cavalier as challenging.

"Well, I haven't been afraid until now. I've been on a roller coaster with you, Moses. I thought we were coasting home now. Thought you were going to help me hide until tomorrow, then deliver me to the studio to 'watch' this worldwide teleconference. If I can just interrupt it and break this story, everybody's safe. But until God's finger breaks into history again—imagine! Into June of 1991 in Fairbanks, Alaska, with those scroll fragments in the Jeep—until I can pull those scraps of goatskin out of the darkness of secrecy and force them into the bright lights of the media, I'm at risk. So is my sister, my old colleague Father O'Derry...." He stopped, puzzled why Moses had continued to uncover the canoe without acknowledging his words, and why the young pastor now began pulling it down to the water.

At water's edge, Moses turned and spoke. "In a single week you began a journey in busy cities, crowded with people—Jerusalem, San Diego, Seattle. Then you made it through some quieter small towns—in Washington State, down in the Panhandle, now today in Fairbanks. Finally, tonight, you're in one of the most remote spots on earth. We're going to watch the midnight sun from the middle of the river. Your ultimate peace."

Moses' reminders calmed the old scholar's disquieted heart, and Lute added, "Before the great storm tomorrow." He nodded at Moses' ushering gesture and stepped into the front of the slender vessel. He wondered if its current-slicked sides were sealskin. Lute sat on a wooden thwart facing forward while Moses waded out, pushing them off. He hefted himself in, took the oar, and headed the little ark out toward the heart of the Yukon. He was not smiling.

CHAPTER 58

NEWSROOM (2)

Tacoma, Washington
Friday
7:15 p.m.

"Newsroom, Rosedahl." The disheveled young reporter continued the FreeCell game on the computer screen in front of him as he answered the phone.

"Oh, hi, Melinda. You at home? ... No, nothing big. If you heard the 'cast a few minutes ago, you know about all I know. Slow news day in Tacoma—now there's a redundancy—and the national 'cast proved again that you can't spell 'stupid' without UPI in the middle of it. ... Oh, United Press had a miscue on a tape, I guess; the anchor intro'd it, dead air followed, then she came back with a lame 'we'll have that report later.'"

He listened a moment then stood up. "Lemme put you on speakerphone while I look." He pressed a button and returned the receiver to its cradle. Walking toward a bank of acoustically-insulated teletype machines, he continued the conversation with his boss.

"Can you hear me?"

"Yeah, Matt. Just see if there's anything more on the wire about that death in Port Angeles this morning. Or about Catholic cardinals, or archaeologists. They're all tied up somehow, and with that guy who called me yesterday afternoon dying mysteriously today, I just feel like another shoe's going to drop."

The reporter was scanning the teletype printers. "I don't see anything about cardinals. Or archaeologists. Hmm. Nothing from Port Angeles since you looked this afternoon."

"I feel morbid asking, but look at the obits, wouldja? Has the weekly VIP summary moved yet?"

"Yeah. I scanned it and tossed it before the last 'cast." He fished in the tall cylindrical waste can next to the rip-n-read counter by the teletypes. He retrieved the short page.

"Just two. That former senator from Iowa and an old vaudevillian. Want me to read 'em to you?"

"No, thanks, Matt. OK, I just thought...."

Matt interrupted. "There was a story on the regional-wrap about a murder-suicide in San Diego. Married couple, both doctors."

"Anything about religion or archaeology in the piece?"

"Mmmm, no. Nothing here. They were probably Scandihoovians, though. Names like 'Hjalmar and Christiana'—they're probably not Greeks, eh?"

Melinda's chuckle was barely audible. "Probably graduates of ours."

"It just says, 'Two bodies were discovered on a dirt road in northern San Diego County this afternoon. The apparent murder-suicide left two prominent San Diego physicians dead, Drs. Hjalmar and Christiana Hansgaard. Authorities say both were in a car registered to them; the female had been shot at close range, as had the male, who still had the pistol in his hand. Investigators....' yada yada."

"OK, Matt. I guess no news is good news, but ever since that guy Harald's call yesterday I've had this nagging curiosity what their big news was. Maybe somebody else got the story and it'll come out soon."

"Or never," the reporter added as he returned to his desk.

"Thanks for checking, guy. You're off pretty soon, so leave a note for the overnighter and tomorrow's early morning shift to check for 'cardinals' or 'archaeologists,' OK? Have 'em call me at home if they see something."

"Will do, Melinda. Have a good weekend."

The two signed off.

CHAPTER 59

GOD ON THE YUKON RIVER

Friday, June 21, 1991
11:58 p.m.
On the Yukon River near Circle City, Alaska

E*ven an old landlubber like me knows better than to stand up in a boat*, thought Lute Jonson, *especially this decrepit canoe*. But as exhilaration flooded his mind and drowned his good sense, he raised himself carefully in the bow, and finally stood with his legs spread as far as the canoe's ribs allowed.

"Oh, my God," he whispered.

His companion's voice cracked the stillness from the back of the small boat. "Is not Alaska in June more beautiful than anywhere else on earth?"

Lute stared north up a stretch of the quarter-mile-wide Yukon. He lifted his gaze slightly from the river's cold clear surface to a perfect Midnight Sun, just beginning to skim the flat and treeless horizon, ready to rise seamlessly into dawn within minutes. The blended blaze of orange-red sky raised gooseflesh all over his skin. His arms elevated until they were straight out, palms facing the sun in an unselfconscious embrace of the pristine landscape before him. He breathed in pure river air.

"Oh, my God," Lute prayed again, this time with a soft voice that broke the silence. "You have safely guided me into Your wilderness. You have let me taste this perfect peace, prepared me to reveal your astounding news tomorrow, steeled me for the reactions of a billion Christians who'll be shocked by this final Dead Sea Scrolls secret."

Arms open wide, eyes fixed on the horizon's extraordinary solar event, lungs full of unspoiled oxygen, Lute was startled by his companion's words, especially the unmistakable anguish in their tone: "God forgive me for this." The click of a revolver cocking completed the meaning.

Lute's arms chilled instantly. *Oh Lord God, NO! This is Your answer?! This is how it ends? This can't be Your will!* Lute twisted around and found himself looking into the barrel of Moses' handgun.

The young pastor began to speak in an even, icy tone. "You knew something was wrong ever since I phoned home. You were right. Tana had a visitor there who had been waiting for me. The guy said he knew you were with me, and he had a deal to offer. I could choose to let *you* live. Or *my wife*."

Lute's mind raced. He slowly lowered himself onto the thwart, this time his back to the sun. Four feet and a death sentence separated the two men.

"Moses, it's not either-or. It's become clearer each day this week: somebody is so afraid of the scrolls in that Jeep they're killing to keep them secret. If you pull that trigger, who's left that knows about them? Only you."

"Damn you for ever coming near me. But it's not my safety I'm concerned about. It's Tana's."

Lute shook his head. "You think it's one or the other? Her or me? How could you trust somebody who'd make that threat?" His peripheral vision was laser-trained on the pistol, but his unwavering direct look was into Moses' eyes.

"I have no choice."

"Oh, but you do. You've been in training all your life for this, Moses. Do we consent to evil? You'd say it's the lesser evil, but you don't know if your wife is alive right *now*, let alone when you get home. Do you want murder on your conscience?"

Moses stared at his passenger in silence.

Lute tried again. "How could you get my body back undetected?"

"All they want is proof. Your hand. Your heart. And the briefcase."

The chill filled Lute again. He closed his eyes.

Psalm 49:8

"The ransom for a life is costly; no payment is ever enough."

CHAPTER 60

MANUSCRIPT 1Q-CETHER-7: GETTING HOME SAFELY

"From Cave 1 at Qumran. If people only knew. LJ 4-28-55"

ELDER WARNED YESHUA AND JOHANAN PRIVATELY YESTERDAY BUT FOUND BOTH ASLEEP IN [ONE] BEDROLL BEFORE SUNRISE. ELDER DEMANDED THEY FOLLOW RULE. YESHUA ANSWERED, "TWO MEN SHALL BE IN A BED AND ONE SHALL BE TAKEN. MY FATHER REJOICES [IN] HIS CHILDREN WHO LOVE AND GRIEVES FOR THOSE WHO FEAR."

[ELDER] WALKED [THEM] TO GATE TO BANISH, BUT QUIETLY PRAYED FOR [THEIR S]AFE JOURNEY HOME. SPOKE WARNINGS OF DESERT EVILS. YESHUA HUGGED [ELDER] AND WHISPERED "FATHER'S SPIRIT CARRIES ALL HOME SAFELY."

ELDER CORRECTED YOUTH, "NOT ALL. HOLINESS WILL NOT BE BLEMISHED BY

UNFORGIVEN SIN[NERS]." YESHUA WROTE IN SAND, THEN STOOD WITH ARMS SPREAD WIDE. "I AM YOUR LAMB. THIS DAY FEAST IN PARADISE."

CHAPTER 61

GOING HOME

The Yukon River
Midnight

Lute lowered his head. "Moses, you're not a killer." His voice conveyed more confidence than he felt. Even knowing he might be mere seconds away from the end of his life, he knew that what he said was true. It was his only hope, to remind this emotionally-wracked young man who he was, and who he could not—should not—be. Luther Olav Jonson summoned the strength of his lifetime to look up, into the short barrel of the deadly weapon facing him.

Moses' breathing was shallow and noticeably tense. Lute heard each inhale and exhale even above the ironically-gentle slap of river current against the sides of the canoe. Lute feared that Moses' high state of tension, specifically in his trigger finger, might do the very thing his mind clearly was trying to delay or avoid.

"You're just *not*. You're a *gentle* soul, pastor." Lute instantly wished he had not uttered the last word; his heart sank as he searched Moses' eyes for evidence that he might have sparked a reaction opposite to his intent.

"*Shut up!*" Moses screamed. The stillness of the serene dawn-lit landscape was shattered. Lute shuddered, sensing his own words had condemned him to death. Then the young pastor repeated, more quietly, "Just shut up. There's nothing you can say. Be quiet; let me think. And turn around. I don't want to see your eyes."

With greater fear than he had ever experienced and a heart pounding with the realization that Moses probably couldn't even shoot an animal if their eyes were locked, Lute swung his legs slowly back over the brace. He faced the north shore of the river. He saw nothing except his past. He heard nothing except his fear.

Holy One, speak to his heart. Don't let him do this, God. I can't fool You: it's not about the scrolls. It's about me. I don't want to die, Lord. Not now, not this way. Please. PLEASE. Damn it, Lord. I love You and I want to be with You, but this isn't right. It's not the time. Is it? Come into this moment, Holy Spirit, come in. Now. Please, please, Lord. Let this cup pass from me ... you said it Yourself, Lord Jesus. Intercede—take a stand—break into this moment by calming him down. Please? Don't let evil win this. You know I'm far from perfect, but I am Your child. I love You. Don't You protect Your children, Your innocents, those who've worshipped You all my life? Lower his gun, Lord. Enter his heart, and let him follow Your will, not his fear!

Tears coursed down his cheeks. His intellect caught the irony of his prayer.

OK! Yes, I'm afraid! Is this what you want to convict me of? Failing to listen to Your repeated commands to 'fear not'? But who made me this way? Damn it, Lord, You created this adrenalin that's pumping madly through me right now, not me! Every animal fears for its life. Why should that convict me? Why should You abandon me because I'm feeling fear? Lord, hear my prayer!!

He stopped to listen. There wasn't a sound from behind him except the ongoing rustle of water. Even Moses' breath was now inaudible. Lute felt a sense of resignation begin to fog over the clarity of his fear.

'Nevertheless, not my will.' If this is the time, Lord, let me die in a state of grace. So I ask You now to forgive me for all I am, and all I am not. I know you already have—I know I shall see you face to face because of Your Son. But I repent of my sins, especially these last few minutes when I failed Your martyr's test. I should be ecstatic if I am about to come home to You. Instead I swore at You. I am so sorry, Lord. Please don't let him pull the trigger. Please, please...

"Lute."

Oh, God Almighty, here it is. The last words I'll ever hear. Oh, God.... Lute's tears now flowed and he shook like the coward he knew he had turned out to be. Awareness of his weakness brought no power to change it, but instead intensified the disappointment he felt in himself. If courage was grace under pressure, he felt crushed by a sense of miserable failure on all counts, at the climactic moment of his life. *Forgive me, in the powerful name of Jesus. Now lettest Thou Thy servant depart in peace.*

"Lute. Let's go."

There was an unmistakable gentleness in the voice behind him, which, had Lute not been so completely self-consumed, he would have recognized as a mix of Moses' resignation and fear for his wife. Lute wiped his eyes as he turned around.

Moses slipped the pistol into its holster again, and picked up the oar.

Lute said, "You decided...?"

Moses said, "You were right. I'm sorry I scared you. We're going home." He gestured for Lute to sit, and Lute's heaviness in doing so nearly swamped the boat.

Moses dipped the paddle in and stroked the cool midnight current. He turned the old canoe around and began paddling.

Silence reigned as they glided back toward the south bank. Lute looked up briefly from his own jumble of conflicting thoughts and feelings, and saw that Moses was similarly lost. But before Lute looked down again, his wilderness guide stopped cold.

"Shit."

Lute whipped around to follow Moses' stare toward the south shore of the Yukon. With full vantage of the spot where they had put into the river and the hundred yards' distance over to Moses' Jeep, both Lute and Moses saw them: two men, emerging from their own outback vehicle which was newly parked next to the Cherokee.

Lute turned back, relieved with what he'd seen. "Hunters, eh?"

Moses, watching the newcomers who were clad in sweatshirts and Levis, stiffened.

"They've got rifles," Lute noted. "It's legal to hunt in Alaska, isn't it?"

"Only sage grouse right now," Moses answered absently.

Lute turned back to look. "Have you seen any?"

Moses dragged his oar to slow the canoe's forward motion, then pulled it out of the water. "You bring a 22-caliber rifle like the Ruger I have at home for grouse. With a four-power scope."

Very aware of his ignorance of all hunting things, Lute still strained to check the rifles the two men were carrying down toward the bank. "Like those scopes?" he asked.

"No," said Moses. There was an edge to his voice. "See the flares on both ends of those scopes? Those are like, three- to nine-powers. Like my 300-Weatherby magnum."

"Sounds pretty big for birds."

"They're not looking for grouse. Those firearms are for early September—the season for moose, caribou, bear, large animals. They're about two months early." Moses affected nonchalance as he kept their canoe dead in the water.

Lute said, "You think they're poachers?" He waited more than a minute for Moses' answer while they watched the two men scramble down to the bank and look out over the water toward the canoe.

"I don't think so, Lute."

Suddenly it was clear. Dr. Lute Jonson, world renowned Dead Sea scrolls expert and would-be *kairos* unveiler, understood. It was God's time. He was about to go home.

The men on shore approached Moses' Cherokee and stopped a hundred feet away from it. One raised his rifle toward the vehicle and, with both Lute and Moses' attention riveted to the scene on shore, the man fired several times low into the Jeep's rear end. After the third shot, a fireball erupted, consuming the car. Massive plumes of black smoke rose from what soon emerged as a charred chassis.

The scroll fragments—God's new *kairos*—became ashes as they watched. Lute stared blankly at the conflagration in the wilderness. He felt empty, halfway between robbed of a driving purpose and relieved of a heavy responsibility. If anything, he felt shock at what little loss he felt. Instead, he had a strange sense of closure.

Absent Moses' rowing, their canoe drifted 'til they were sideways to the shore.

As Lute watched the fire, the men turned toward the river. Moses stood in their canoe, and the old scholar knew instinctively it was the wrong move. Surprisingly, the young pastor called out across the water.

"Is my wife safe?"

Lute noted the acoustic delay before the two intruders seemed to hear, then cringed as he saw them react with laughter. Apparently oblivious to the incongruity, they then raised their rifles and sighted in on the Presbyterian clergyman. The Eskimo faced them squarely. Two loud shots rang out across the water, and Lute looked up in time to see the man he owed so much to fall backward into the water. Instinctively he reached toward Moses, quickly paddling with his hands to close the distance between his friend and the boat which had been kicked the opposite direction. In bare moments, Lute realized that Moses' body was inert. And sinking. He stared, grief welling up, a profound sense of responsibility compounding as another lifeless body was added to the ledger of his quixotic compulsion for truth-telling. Moses' forehead and chest oozed blood into the clear cold Yukon river.

Lute crouched low in the canoe and turned his gaze toward the shore. One of the two men was still sighting silently along his rifle toward the canoe, and the other had already begun pulling a rubber raft from the back of their vehicle. Lute looked down at Moses to see if his pistol might be retrievable, but the young body was out of reach, and sinking rapidly. Lute was alone and defenseless.

He quickly lay forward, covered by the sides of the canoe. He began to hear shots hit the water nearby, and then one hit low in the bow. The Yukon River began to fill the old vessel, and Lute broke a lifetime's habit of silent personal prayer. He prayed aloud.

"I love you, Lord Jesus. You said that some would be blessed to be cursed for Your Name's sake." A shot pierced the side of the canoe just eighteen inches from his head. "So this is how it ends." He had to raise his head as water began to fill the bottom of the canoe, but he continued. "Please let it be known that I got home safely. I leave Your next *kairos* in Your hands. I wanted to be part of it, but that's not to be...." Another puncture jarred the little boat.

Lute inhaled deeply, said "Amen!" in his loudest, strongest voice, and struggled to his feet in the rapidly swamping little ark. The gunfire sounds paused as he faced north into the Midnight Sun, now just seconds into its ascendancy from the horizon. He embraced it as he had earlier, with arms outstretched, palms up, Christ-like, ready.

Amazingly, he heard the shot even after he felt it. It was like an anvil blow from the back, pitching him forward into the deep. He was surprised to feel no pain. And he had more time to think than he had expected.

Yah...

IloveyouLordIamcominghomeImsorryforeverywayIfailedYoubutIknowYoulovemeregardlessAsaperfectFatherYouforgivemyfailuresandalwayswantedthebestformeNowIgiveupYour*Kairos*toanothertotellThankYouJesusforinspiringmylifeThankYouforNaomiandMomandDadIfIwasresponsibleforHaraldspainorChristianasorforMosesdeathImsosorryPleaseforgivemyfailuretolistenwhenYousaidFearNotespeciallytonightwhenIwassuchacowardNowIamcominghomeLordIwillFearnotfearnotfearnotfearnotfearnotfearnotfearnotIwillfearno

...weh

ACKNOWLEDGEMENTS

The author cannot begin to adequately thank the many who have contributed to this story. This published list will include those whose influence and assistance has extended in depth and/or repeatedly, but the generous support of many additional writers and friends has not been forgotten. I am especially compelled to publicly thank…

- ❏ two loving parents who raised me in the faith;
- ❏ my favorite (and only!) brothers Peter, David, and John ("Dobe Doinat");
- ❏ teachers at Pacific Lutheran University and pastors in congregations all around the country and across the years, most specifically the Rev. Dr. John O. Larsgaard, pastor, counselor, friend, born-again-faith midwife. The middle three paragraphs on page 263 are virtually verbatim from his words to the author during my crisis of faith in 1967. In his 90s now, Pastor John read that section on video. It may be seen at http://www.youtube.com/watch?v=zXZl8McNr1M. The author's explanation of the intriguing Greek word *kairos* is at http://www.youtube.com/watch?v=LsyqkfTZ-L0;
- ❏ Ron Montana, my 1992 WD Novel Writing Workshop instructor, and agent Andrea Hurst, for insightful critiques and suggestions;
- ❏ Fred Kerner, longtime publishing executive now retired in Toronto;

☐ Dr. Adolfo Roitman and Michael Ingber from the Shrine of the Book in Jerusalem, for the time they spent with me in Jerusalem and Qumran;

☐ Ed Sergent, friend, colleague, and my aviation consultant;

☐ the Rev. Dr. Mark Gravrock, whose friendship (with Peggy's) matches his biblical scholarship in importance to me;

☐ Jay Hartman, Jean Hutchinson, Jean McCord, Jim Peterson, Judy Petersen, Kimberly Cregeur, Rex Browning, Richard Wakefield and Susan Hayes (alpha order) and numerous other writers and friends whose encouragement has been rock-solid over the years;

☐ Bill Walles, friend, colleague, writer, and marketing mastermind;

☐ Claude Carlson and all my Bible Study brothers in Buffalo, Yakima, and Tacoma;

☐ Seattle's Pacific Science Center, for allowing me as a docent in 2006 to spend close-up time with precious Dead Sea Scrolls artifacts;

☐ open and affirming churches everywhere, especially Bethany Presbyterian (Tacoma, WA), and Newport Presbyterian (Bellevue, WA);

☐ Nationally-known authors Sheldon Siegel, Kittredge Cherry, and Brian McNaught for their generous reviews.

☐ the authors of excellent works on subjects related to this story, including Mel White, Jack Rogers, the aforementioned Kittredge Cherry, William E. Phipps, John Henson, Miguel Santana, Justin R. Cannon, Rev. Jeff Miner and John Tyler Connoley, Emanuel Xavier, Theodore W. Jennings Jr., Nikos Kazantzakis, and Dan Brown;

❏ And, by far the most important, my family: Jason, Jordan, and McKenna (the Centers of My Earthly Universe), their awesome mom and their adorable spouses and kids, and finally, my amazing, talented, beloved husband Bruce Reed Carpenter. ICAY!

Finally, three notes for all readers. (1) The book *Was Jesus Married?* mentioned in chapter 42 is anachronistic; it was published fifteen years after this 1991 scene. (2) This is a work of fiction: except for the Scriptures, it's all imagined. (3) Above all else: I am a committed, progressive, sinful, forgiven Christian with a deep personal faith in a radical ("back to the roots") Christ, Whose perfect truth and loving grace inspire me. I do not believe this story dishonors God, but instead it celebrates God's obvious delight in the variety of His creation, and it lifts up God's repeated *kairos* assurance: "Fear not." Soli Deo Gloria!

56811790R00195

Made in the USA
Columbia, SC
01 May 2019